ALL THE RAGE

ALL THE RAGE

COURTNEY SUMMERS

MACMILLAN

First published in the US 2015 by St. Martin's Griffin

First published in the UK 2016 by Macmillan Children's Books
an imprint of Pan Macmillan
20 New Wharf Road, London N1 9RR
Associated companies throughout the world
www.panmacmillan.com

ISBN 978-1-5098-1759-7

3 5 7 9 8 6 4 2

A CIP catalogue record for this book is available from the British Library.

Designed by Anna Gorovoy
Printed and bound by CPI Group (UK) Ltd, Croydon CR0 4YY

to susan summers,

my favorite feminist.

i love you, mom.

thanks for everything.

NOW

the boy is beautiful.

She wants him to look at her.

Look at me, look at me, look at me.

Look at her. She's young, she's vital, she's a star in the sky. She's agonized over this night, agonized over every second of getting ready, like the perfect combination of clothes and makeup will unlock the secrets of the universe. Sometimes it feels like that much is at stake.

She has never been hungrier in her life.

You look perfect, her best friend, Penny, says, and that's all she needs to hear to feel worthy of the six-letter name she's tattooed on her heart. Penny would know about perfect. Penny's got the kind of face and body that stops traffic, turns heads, leaves people open-mouthed, in awe. The kind of pretty that makes you prettier just by being close to it and she's always close to it, because they're close. Secret-keeping close.

Thank you, she says. She's never had a best friend before, let alone been one. It's a strange feeling, to have a place. Like there was an empty spot beside another (perfect) girl, just waiting for her. She pulls at her skirt, adjusts the thin straps of her top. It feels like too much and not enough at the same time.

Do you really think he'll like it?

Yeah. Now don't do anything stupid.

Is this stupid? It's so much later now and *beautiful, beautiful,* she's saying to the boy because she can't seem to shut up. She has had one, no, two, no, three-four shots and this is what happens when that much drinking happens. She says things like, *you are so beautiful. I just really wanted to tell you that.*

The boy is beautiful.

Thank you, he says.

She reaches clumsily across the table and threads her fingers through his hair, enjoying the feel of his dark curls. Penny sees this happen somehow, sees through the wall of an entirely different room where she's been wrapped around her boyfriend because suddenly, she's there, saying, *don't let her drink anymore.*

I won't, the boy promises.

It makes her feel warm, being looked out for. She tries to articulate this with her numb tongue, but all that comes out: *is this stupid? Am I stupid?*

You're one drink away, Penny says, and laughs at the stricken expression this news inspires. Penny hugs her, tells her not to worry about it, whispers in her ear before disappearing back behind her wall, *but he's looking at you.*

Look at her.

Drink.

Six-seven-eight-nine shots later and she's thinking *oh no* because she is going to puke. He walks her through his house, guides her away from the party.

You want to get some air? You want to lie down?

No, she wants her best friend because she worries she is so many drinks past stupid now and she doesn't know what to do about that.

It's okay. I'll get her. But first you should lie down.

There's a truck, a classic pickup pride and joy. There's the truck's bed, and the cold shock of it against her back makes her shiver. The stars above move or maybe it's the earth, that slow and sure turning of the earth. No. It's the sky and it's speaking to her.

Close your eyes.

He waits. He waits because he's a nice boy. A blessed boy. He's on the football team. His father is the sheriff and his mother sits at the top of a national auto supply chain and they are both so proud.

He waits until he can't wait anymore.

She thinks he's beautiful. That's enough.

The hard ridges of the truck bed never warm under her body but her body is warm. He feels everything under her shirt before he takes it off.

Look at me, look at me, hey, look at me.

He wants her to look at him.

Her eyes open slowly. His tongue parts her lips. She's never felt so sick. He explores the terrain of her body while he pretends to negotiate the terms.

You want this, you've always wanted this* and *we're not going that far, I promise.

Really? His hands are everywhere and he's a vicious weight on top of her that she can't breathe against so she cries instead, and how do you get a girl to stop crying?

You cover her mouth.

No, I'm not there . . . I'm not there anymore. That was a long time ago, a year ago, and that girl—I'm not her again. I can't be.

I'm in the dirt. I'm on my hands and my knees and I'm crawling in it, what I came from. I don't remember standing, don't remember ever being a thing that could stand. Just this dirt, this road. I opened my mouth to it, tasted it. It's under my fingernails. A night passed from the ground. Now it's early morning and I'm thirsty.

A dry wind moves through the trees off the road beside me, stirring their leaves. I dredge up spit to wet my swollen lips and lick my bloodstained teeth. It's hot out, the kind of heat that creeps up on you and makes mirages on the road. The kind that shrivels the elderly and carries them into the waiting, open arms of death.

I roll onto my back. My skirt rides up my legs. I pull at my shirt and find it open, feel my bra unclasped. I fumble buttons through holes, covering myself even though it is so. Hot. I can't. I touch my fingertips to my throat. Breathe.

My bones ache, have aged somehow in the last twenty-four hours. I press my palms against the grit and the bitter hurt of it startles me into semiawareness. They're scraped, raw and pink, what happens when you crawl.

A distant rumbling reaches my ears. A car. It passes and then slows, backs up, comes to a halt beside me. Its door opens and slams shut. I close my eyes and listen to the soft crunch of soft soles on rough gravel.

Birds are singing.

The footsteps stop but the birds are still singing, singing about a girl who wakes up on a dirt road and doesn't know what happened to her the night before, and the person standing over her, a shadow across her body that blocks out the sun. Maybe it's someone nice. Or maybe someone come to finish whatever it is that's been started. About a girl.

Don't look at her.

TWO WEEKS EARLIER

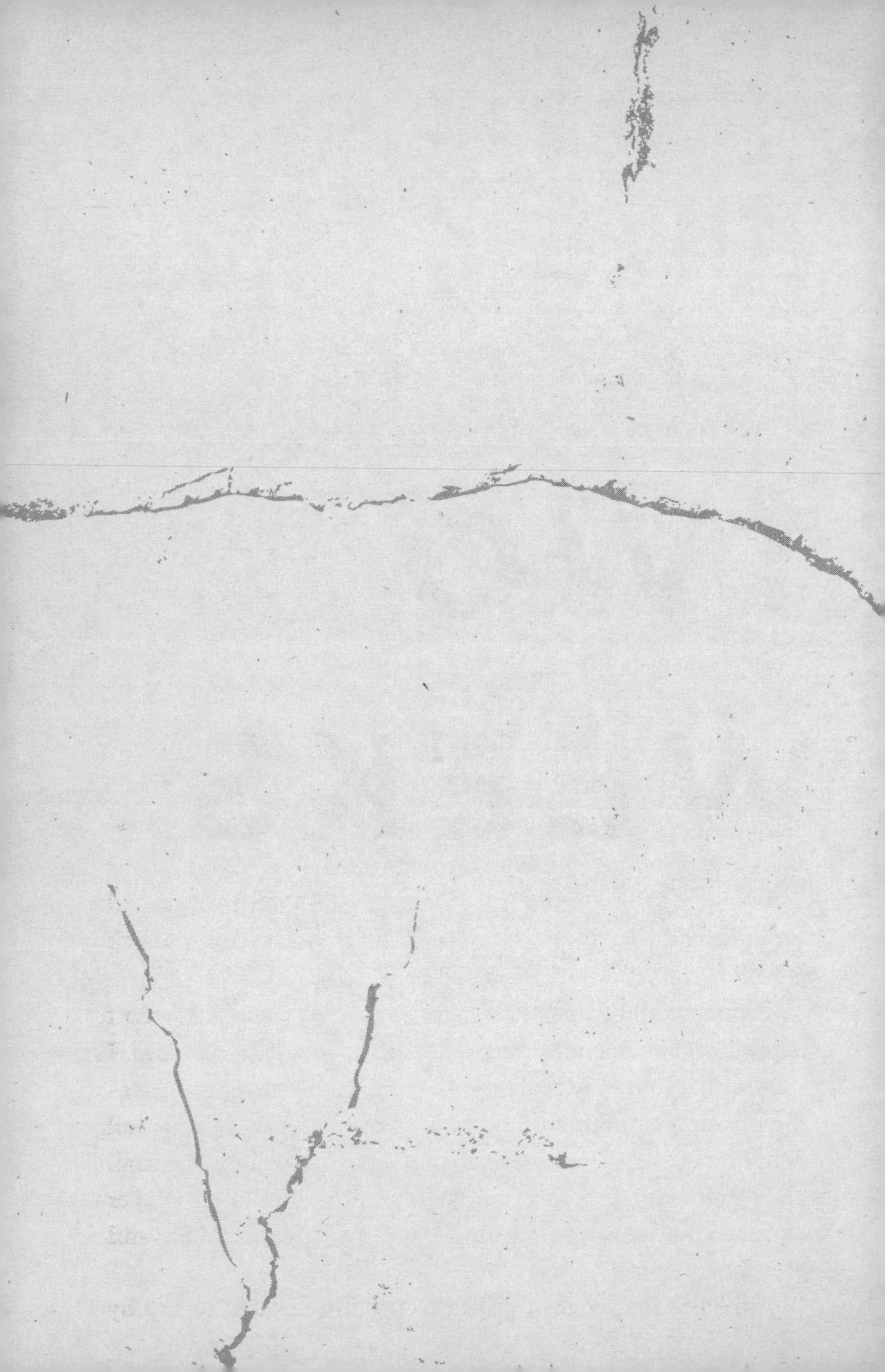

before i tore the labels off, one was called *Paradise* and the other, *Hit and Run.* It doesn't matter which is which. They're both blood red.

Proper application of nail polish is a process. You can't paint it on like it's nothing and expect it to last. First, prep. I start with a four-way buffer. It gets rid of the ridges and gives the polish a smooth surface to adhere to. Next, I use a nail dehydrator and cleanser because it's best to work with a nail plate that's dry and clean. Once it's evaporated, a thin layer of base coat goes on. The base coat protects the nails and prevents staining.

I like the first coat of polish to be thin enough to dry by

the time I've finished the last nail on the same hand. I keep my touch steady and light. I never drag the brush, I never go back into the bottle more than once per nail if I can help it. Over time and with practice, I've learned how to tell if what's on the brush will be enough.

Some people are lazy. They think if you're using a highly pigmented polish, a second coat is unnecessary, but that's not true. The second coat asserts the color and arms you against the everyday use of your hands, all the ways you can cause damage without thinking. When the second coat is dry, I take a Q-tip dipped in nail polish remover to clean up any polish that might have bled onto my skin. The final step is the top coat. The top coat is what seals in the color and protects the manicure.

The application of lipstick has similar demands. A smooth canvas is always best and dead skin must be removed. Sometimes that takes as little as a damp washcloth, but other times I scrub a toothbrush across my mouth just to be sure. When that's done, I add the tiniest amount of balm, so my lips don't dry out. It also gives the color something to hold on to.

I run the fine fibers of my lip brush across the slanted top of my lipstick until my lips are coated and work the brush from the center of my lips out. After the first layer, I blot on a tissue and add another layer, carefully following the outline of my small mouth before smudging the color out so it looks a little fuller. Like with the nail polish, layering always helps it to last.

And then I'm ready.

cat kiley is the first one down.

Today, anyway. I don't see it happen. I'm ahead, my feet kicking up track while the others pant behind me. The sun is in my throat. I woke up choking on it, my skin slimy with sweat and stuck to the sheets. It's a dry, stale summer that doesn't know it's supposed to be over. It breathes itself out slowly, wants us to forget other seasons. It's a sick heat. Makes you sick.

"Cat? *Cat!*"

I glance behind me, see her sprawled out on the track and keep moving. I focus on the steady rhythm of my pulse and by the time I've circled, she's coming around, less the girl she was before she fell. Pale and monosyllabic. Sun-jacked. That's what the boys are calling it.

Coach Prewitt is on her knees, gently pouring a bottle of water over Cat's forehead while barking out questions. *You eat, Kiley? You eat breakfast today? Drink anything? You on your period?* The boys shift uncomfortably because oh God, what if she's bleeding.

"Does it matter? We shouldn't be out in this anyway," Sarah Trainer mutters.

Prewitt looks up and squints. "This heat ain't news, Trainer. You come to my class, you come prepared. Kiley, you eat today? Breakfast?"

"No," Cat finally manages.

Prewitt stands, her has-been athlete joints crackling and popping. This small act, this kneeling and rising, blossoms beads of sweat across her forehead. Cat struggles to her feet and sways. Her face is going to meet that track again if nobody gets ahold of her.

"Garrett, carry her to the nurse's office."

The lineman steps forward. Number 63. Broad shoulders, all muscled and firm. Never trust a blond boy, that's what my mom always says, and Brock Garrett is so blond his eyebrows are nearly invisible. The light above catches the fine hairs on his arms and makes them shimmer. He lifts Cat easily. Her head lolls against his chest.

Prewitt spits. It dries before it hits the ground. "Get back to it!" And we scatter, we run. There are thirty minutes of this period left and we can't all still be standing at the end of it.

"Think she's okay?" Yumi Suzuki gasps out ahead of me. Her long hair flies behind her and she makes a frustrated noise as she tries to hold it back with one hand before quickly giving up. Her elastic band snapped earlier. Prewitt wouldn't let her go in for another because nothing short of collapsing gets you out of her class and even that gets taken out of your grade.

"She's faking," Tina Ortiz says. She's tiny, just slightly over five feet. The boys used to call her an ankle-biting bitch until puberty hit and breasts happened. Now they just call her. "She wants to be carried."

When Prewitt's whistle finally blows and we're dragging ourselves back inside, she grabs me by the arm and pulls me aside because she thinks I can run, she thinks I could get trophies or ribbons—whatever they give you for it.

"It's your last year, Grey," she says. "Make a difference for your school."

I'd burn this place to the ground before I'd ever willingly make a difference for it, but I'm smarter than saying that out loud and she should be smarter than tempting me. I shake my head, wave her off. Her thin lips twitch with disappointment before melting into all the other lines on her worn face. I don't much like Coach Prewitt, but I like her lines. No one fucks with her.

I fall in with the rest of my classmates and we stumble through the back entrance of Grebe High on spent legs, quietly moving past classes still in session. At the fork in the hall at the bottom of the stairs, Brock reappears, looking awfully satisfied with himself.

"Cat okay?" Tina asks.

"She'll live." He runs his hand over his head, flattening hair that's barely there. "Why you want to know?"

"Did you even take her to the nurse's office?"

He peers cautiously down the hall but Prewitt never follows us in, never sticks with us a second longer than she has to. We screw around in the halls, she hears about it. Makes us pay for it later.

"Eventually," he says.

"That's what I thought."

"You jealous, Tina? Fall tomorrow. I'll pick you up."

She rolls her eyes and heads for the girls' locker room, down the hall's right tine. Not being outright rejected makes Brock man of the hour, so slap him on the back and tell him, *I bet she will. I bet tomorrow she'll be riding your dick.* Do it; you're so cool.

Brock punches Trey Marcus in the arm. "See that? That's how it's done." Then he catches my eye. "What, Grey? You want to ride it?"

I follow the other girls to the locker room, where I get undressed. My fingers curl around the edge of my limp and dusty shirt. I bring it over my head and then I'm in my bra, sneaking looks at the other girls' ribs, ridges, innies, outies, A, B, C, D and—Tina—E cups. Yesterday, Norah Landers learned something new about nipples. *They're not all the same, you know.* We did, but the types apparently have different names. She ran us through them. It's not like that in here all the time. Norah just couldn't keep it to herself, I guess. So after we listened, entranced by this unexpected piece of information, and after we all glanced down and cataloged ourselves, we told her to shut the fuck up so we could go back to pretending we didn't exist in this space together while being all too aware that we do.

"So she was faking," Tina says to no one. Everyone.

I take my bra off. "If Brock Garrett said it, it must be true."

Tina faces me and the faint tan lines on her light brown skin is all she's wearing. She's always first undressed. Confrontational nudity. I don't know. Everything with Tina is a confrontation.

"What would you know about the truth?"

"Fuck you, Tina. That's what I know."

"Give it a rest," Penny Young says.

"Why would I want to do a thing like that?" Tina asks.

Penny shimmies out of her shorts.

"Because I said so and you're supposed to listen to your elders."

"Well, my birthday's next, so watch out. And how was Godwit, anyway? You didn't call me back like you promised." Tina arches her eyebrow. "Good weekend?"

Penny doesn't answer, busying herself with the buttons of her collar. Tina stalks into the showers and I hear her muttering about what a whore I am before she slips into one of the curtained stalls because Tina always gets the last word, one way or another. The rest of the girls trail in after her and then it's me and Penny, alone. She clutches a towel to herself but she doesn't look like she needs a shower. No trace of Phys Ed on her, her hair no worse for wear, her skin sun-kissed instead of sun-killed. Penny Young is the most perfect girl you know and those kinds of girls, they're put on this earth to break you. Peel back her skin and you can see her poison. Peel back mine, you can still see traces of where her poison's been.

"Moving day," she says.

She's talking to me except we don't talk. Sometimes a word or two will slip through, but only out of necessity. This is not that. I never told anyone about the move, but nothing stays secret long in Grebe. Word travels. Slurred in bars, murmured over fences between neighbors, muttered in the produce section of the grocery store and again at checkout because the cashier always has something to add. Cell phones don't run as fast as the mouths in this town.

"What did you say?" I ask.

But she's not looking at me and I wonder if I imagined it, if she said anything at all. I leave her there and find a shower stall for myself where I run the water hot as the sun. It stings my skin. I imagine it eroding lines into me, all over my pale body, my arms, my legs, and especially my face until I look like one of those women. The kind no one fucks with.

I'm last out, I make sure of it. I turn the water off and stand there a minute, my wet hair clinging to my neck, drying fast and frizzing. When I get back to the change room, my locker is open and my clothes are on the floor.

My bra and underwear are gone.

My bra, one of the two I own, is an embarrassment. That's what Tina called it, once. It's a thin strip of material with skinny straps because there's nothing on me that really needs to be supported. I wore black bikini-cut underwear, nothing special. I grab the rest of my clothes. Today was cutoffs and a flimsy black shirt that needs something underneath it, but I try not to think about that. The others silently watch me dress. They watch me take out my lipstick and press it into my lips. They watch me check my nails for chips. As soon as I'm gone, their excited voices drift from behind the door.

Was it you? Did you do it? You're so cool.

I think of myself naked in that shower, think of the water running over me while someone moved around the next room and took the things that touched the most intimate parts of my body. I make my way down the hall with my arms crossed tightly over my chest.

todd bartlett lives off the disability check the government cuts him for the car accident he was in when he was seventeen. Slammed by a semi and lucky to be alive. His back hasn't been the same since. You wouldn't know it just by looking at him.

People don't trust what they can't see, he says and that's his burden to bear. Everyone acts like it's his choice he can't work how they think he should; nine-to-fiving it in an office somewhere or behind the counter of some store or outside in the sun. I've seen him overdo it, seen him end the day flat on his back on the floor, begging for God to put him out of his misery. He's in so much pain in those moments, he tells me, he forgets how good it feels to be alive.

My mother, Alice Jane Thomson, was supposed to be in the car with him when it happened, but good ol' Paul Grey sized her up in the halls of Grebe High the day before and asked her to spend that afternoon with him instead. She marveled with Todd over the wreckage later, their luck. There was no passenger's side after the impact and if she'd been in the car with him, she would have died. And I guess I wouldn't have been born.

Todd Bartlett lives on Chandler Street in the house he inherited from his mother, Mary, who had him at sixteen years old. Mary's house is the kind that always needs a little something more but will probably never get around to having it. A cracked walkway—vines finger-stroked into the cement before it dried—leads up to a ramshackle two-story of worn white siding and red asphalt shingles with brown accents. A small, screened-in sun porch looks out at similar houses, all of them chipped and broken teeth. Todd sits inside on a lawn chair, next to a blue cooler. He gives me a lazy salute as I let myself in.

"How was school?" he asks.

"Prewitt wants me to try out for track."

"Waste of time." He opens the cooler, pulls a Heineken out of an ice bath. "You want one?" I do. I keep one arm across my chest and reach for a bottle with the other and he laughs, swatting my hand away. He shuts the lid before the delicious cold air wafting from it can so much as kiss my fingertips. "Get outta here."

"I won't tell if you don't."

He looks at me through a curtain of brown hair, long enough for a ponytail, but he likes it better in his hazel eyes. Todd is solid; gives the impression of a man with muscles despite the fact he can't really do much without doing himself in. There's a faded tattoo on his tanned right arm, an initial. *M,* for the woman who made him. He pops the cap off his beer, takes a swig.

"Where's Mom?"

"Picking up dinner."

"Kind of early."

"We've been working all day. Check this out."

He gets to his feet slowly and the melted ice pack he was resting against slides wetly down the back of the chair. I follow him in, past the kitchen with the black-and-white checkerboard floor and an old refrigerator that squeals if it's been left open too long. There are boxes in the living room, I can see them from the hall. Seems like we've got more things than space to put them. I follow Todd up the stairs to the room at the very front of his house. Our house—so my room.

Mom unpacked all my things even though I told her she didn't have to. My bed is beneath the window, looking out over the street below. The sun will rise on me. Shelves full of my books line all four walls, boxing the room in. She's even alphabetized them by author. My desk sits in the corner, laptop resting atop it. Next to the closet, something that's not mine: an antique bureau. Todd notices me notice it.

"My mother's." He moves to it and runs his hand over the top. "But we can move it, if you don't want it."

"No, it's beautiful. Thank you."

"This was her room. That okay with you?"

"It's not like she died in here."

Mary died on the main street, too many years before that kind of thing is supposed to happen to anyone, let alone someone sweet as her. A massive heart attack. It wasn't the way she was supposed to go. A lifetime of generosity and warmth was to culminate with Todd at her bedside telling her she did everything right, but I don't think he even remembers their last words to each other.

"Got time for a talk?" he asks me.

"There's nowhere else I need to be."

He digs his hands into his pocket and holds out two keys.

"One for the house, one for the New Yorker—but that one's for emergencies only. It's your place now too, kid. Short of burning it down, do what you like."

I take the keys but before I can get any kind of *thanks* out, the screen door's splintered whine and the sloppy racket of it falling back into place sounds from downstairs.

"Where are you guys? I got pizza."

The greasy smell is in the air as soon as Mom says it. Gina's Pizzeria, one of the last restaurants in Grebe still standing. There are three, altogether. Gina's, the Lakeview Diner (five miles from the lake), and the bar. Other fine dining establishments have come and within six months, they're gone. People from out of town—newlyweds, usually—end up here with the idea they can start something that gets the ball rolling on Grebe turning into one of those sweet-spot stops just before the city, Godwit—"The Big G"—but Grebe just isn't meant to be that kind of somewhere. Even being the founding home of Grebe Auto Supplies, with its countless stores and service bays across the nation, couldn't put us on the map. People think Grebe's a bird, not a destination.

"Just showing the kid her room," Todd calls.

"Oh! I'll be right there."

Mom hurries up the stairs like a six-year-old hurrying down them at Christmas and when she steps into my room, her fair skin is flushed with heat, but she's beautiful. She always looks beautiful, but it's different now she's happy. A pale blue shirt—Todd's, I think—rests over her tiny frame, hanging low over a pair of old jean shorts she's had for the seventeen years she's been my mother and I don't know how she's made them last so long. I'm more used up than they are, somehow.

"You like?" she asks me.

"You didn't have to unpack it."

"I wanted to. It wasn't a big deal."

Todd makes his way out. "I'll leave you two to it. No doubt your mom wants to walk you through her adventures in shelving. I'm telling you, kid, I've never seen anything like it."

"Hey, smart ass," Mom says, smiling. "Set the table."

She's still smiling when she sits on my bed and pats the spot next to her. "Park yourself right here," she says and I do and then she asks me again: "You like it? You think you could?"

"It's just a move across town. I'll survive."

"Just a move across town."

"Yeah."

"But it's something different."

I look away. I can hear Todd in the kitchen.

"It's a nice room," I say. "Thanks."

She gives me a hug, tells me she'll see me downstairs and heads there herself. I uncross my arms and pick through the clothes in my new bureau, lovingly folded into place.

I find my bra. I put it on.

after the plates are in the sink, I get ready for work. I change into a skirt and shirt. I got the job at Swan's Diner six months ago when I realized money was the only thing standing between me and any other town I wanted to live in. I told Todd I was looking for a job where no one would know my name. He suggested Swan's because it's right on the county line between Grebe and Ibis and *hey, there's nothing to being a waitress, right?* There wasn't, at first.

Before Leon.

It's a long, hot ride in. By the time I coast my bike into the parking lot, I think the four slices of Gina's pizza I wolfed down are going to end up all over the pavement, but it wouldn't be the worst thing someone's puked up here. I go in through the back, to the kitchen, and everyone's hustling. Holly Malhotra doesn't even have time to fill me in on the latest thing her daughter's done to piss her off and she's always got time for that.

Leon's sharing the grill with Annette tonight. He's nineteen and he started here last month, but it's not his first time. He worked here all through high school, left for a while, and then came back. I watch him for a moment. His black skin glistens with sweat, the muscles of his arms shining with it. His warm brown eyes are fixed intently on the task at hand. My stomach tightens. Leon is . . . I forgot what it was like to want before he came here.

But who said I needed to remember.

I grab my apron and catch his notice.

"You look like hell," he says.

"Hi to you too," I say. He winks at me and my tongue turns to sand because the other thing is last week, Leon told me he liked me as plainly as any person could. We were on break out back, standing next to the Dumpsters when he said it. *I like you, Romy. Whatever you want to do about that.* It was nothing like the movies but it probably never is. Did set something off inside me, though. Maybe. Enough for me to spend the rest of that shift in the bathroom trying to decide what to do about it. Leon is nice. This is what nice is: he's nice and you like him and it's nice. Until. "How is it out there tonight?"

"Busy as hell. Get ready to work your ass off."

"She's always ready for that," Tracey, our manager, says as she steps out of her office. She smiles at me. "I don't want anyone waiting to be waited on, got it? In this heat, everybody's looking for a reason to bitch."

"Got it."

"Hey," Leon says. "Break? Later?"

"Sure."

I step into the heart of the diner and Leon is right. It's busy as hell, and it's okay at first but then it starts to wear, like it always does. Three hours into my shift, I reek of grease and my ponytail is loose, strands of hair plastered to my face. I duck into the bathroom across from Tracey's office and clumsily retie my ponytail, my fingers tired from taking orders. I'll have to shower when I get home, get all this off me. If I don't, I'll wake up in the middle of the night convinced I'm still here and I've got tables waiting. When I go to the kitchen, Leon is taking off his hairnet. He scrubs his hand over his short black hair and nods toward the back exit.

"That time already?" I ask.

"Yep."

"Hey, wait for me," Holly says, untying her apron. Her long black hair is falling out of its bun, haphazardly framing her exhausted face. "If I don't have a smoke, I'll lose it."

I'm glad for her company, but a quick glance at Leon tells me he's only just tolerating it. I reach around to take my apron off, but think better of it. I like that extra layer.

The three of us head outside and shuffle into casual poses. I lean against the building and stare at the ground while Leon stands next to me and stares at the sky. The gritty flick of Holly's lighter fills the quiet, drawing my eyes up. She inhales deeply and studies the cherry, says what she always says when she smokes: "These things killed my father. Awful way to die."

"Yeah, that is," Leon agrees.

"I don't want to do that to my kids." And yet. Holly told me it's either cancer sticks or pills, that's how stressed out she is all the time. Used to be smoking was vogue. Take the edge off and look sophisticated doing it. People see you smoking in public now, she says, and they just give you this *look,* like you're not entitled. Raising four kids alone while her husband is deployed and her mother-in-law with Alzheimer's just moved in because they can't afford assisted living so all her care is getting pinned on her eighteen-year-old son when Holly's not home *but sure, look at me like I'm a piece of shit for sucking on one of these.*

She turns to Leon. "Speaking of my kids, you going to be at Melissa Wade's party this weekend?"

"Nope," he tells her. "My sister's having a get-together with all her coworkers and friends before she pops and I've got to be there."

"Damn. Annie's going to a sleepover at Bethany Slate's house and I have a feeling they're going to end up at the Wade's. You know anyone who could text me if they see her there?"

"You going to make a scene if she is?" he asks.

"Goddamn right I am. That's college kids. She's fifteen years old." She takes a drag off her cigarette. "I told her not to even think about going, so of course she will."

"I'll get Melissa to text you if she sees her."

"Thank you." She tosses the half-smoked cigarette on the ground. "Quittin' by degrees. Not even my break, but I covered Lauren's shift so I earned it."

"You've been here all day?" I ask.

"Money, money, money. Better get back to it."

She goes in and then it's me and Leon. The silence stretches between us. Words aren't so easy to come by, after his admission. It takes him a while to dig some up.

"Told you it was busy," he finally says.

"Yeah, you did."

"You know, I was joking earlier, when you came in."

"Were you?" I stare out at the back lot. The headlights of Tracey's old Sprint reflect the flickering light over the door beside us.

"You don't look like hell. In fact, you look really far from it."

His eyes are so on me. The blush travels up to my face from the tips of my toes. He slips inside before I can reply, and the compliment lingers and fades. I remind myself it's nothing I have to hold or be held to. He only said it to remind me that he's here, he likes me. That he's nice. Leon is nice. That doesn't mean he's safe.

the sun rises.

I press my palms against my eyes and listen to the sounds drifting upstairs from down. I piece together this morning's scene in my mother's laughter, in chairs scraping across the floor to be closer to each other, in coffee bubbling as it brews on the stove.

I untangle myself from my sheet, and stare at the fresh red stains next to the faded-out pink ones on my pillowcase. They come straight from my mouth, forever exasperating my mother because I picked the lipstick that doesn't wash out. I get dressed. In the bathroom across the hall, I brush my teeth and tie my hair back. I do my lips. Nail polish is still holding.

I'm ready.

In the kitchen, everything is how I pictured it. Mom smiles at me from her spot at the table. Her black curls rest limply against her shoulders, worse for the weather. She sips coffee with one hand and the other is reached across the table, her fingers twined through Todd's.

"How'd you sleep?" he asks.

"Fine."

"Glad to hear it."

"I can make you breakfast," Mom offers.

"No, thanks. I have to get to school."

She exchanges a glance with Todd. "Baby, you set your alarm wrong? You've got at least an hour before you need to be there . . ."

"I know." I step into the hall and put my shoes on. "I have to be early today."

"Why's that?" Todd asks. "I can't think of a goddamn thing you'd have to be an hour early for that doesn't qualify as cruel and unusual punishment."

Because my underwear and bra have been stolen and when things like that have been stolen, you can expect them to show up again in a very bad way. I tighten my laces and grab my book bag from the floor. "I just do. I'll see you guys later."

"Try to have a nice day."

"Yeah, have a good one, kid."

It takes a moment for that to sink in, this coupling of well wishes for the rest of my day compared to a year ago, mornings in a different house, my mother at a kitchen table alone while her husband nursed bottles hidden in places he long stopped pretending we didn't know about.

When I open the door, there's something else: the shock of the view. I look for ground I grew up on. Instead, it's unfamiliar dying grass and a cement walkway with those faded impressions of vines leading me out to the street I'll tell people is the one I live on. For a minute, I forget it *is* just a move across town, like it could be something more.

But only for a minute.

I walk to school. The parking lot is a wasteland. Old clunkers take up the faculty side and as the hour wears on, the students' side will divide itself between slightly better used or newer models of the same cars, depending on whose parents paid for them. I pull the front doors open and step inside where I'm silently greeted by two old, blank-faced mannequins in the middle of the entranceway. A boy form, John, and a girl form, Jane. John and Jane are the first things we see when we come in each morning, our daily dose of school spirit. John wears a retired football uniform and Jane wears the latest in cheerleading and when the teachers aren't looking, the boys feel her up and sometimes the girls too, a slick-quick grab of a breast because ha, ha, so funny.

Today, there's something different about Jane. Her pom-poms are at her feet, her arms are as crossed as they can be, and tucked into the crook of her elbow is a stack of neon posters. Pink, yellow, green, and orange. I know what it's for but I grab one anyway and take in the bold-faced call to action, the one I'm duty bound to answer because I have finally come of age.

WAKE UP

It's time for the annual seniors-only bash at Wake Lake, that one night of the year all the parents in town know their kids are getting trashed near the water doing what trashed kids near the water do. We came out of our mothers aware of this party. Our parents went to it and their parents went to it and their parents' parents went to it. Fuck graduation; this is It. No amount of alcohol poisoning or unprotected sex or accident or injury will get in the way of this honorable Grebe tradition, this very important rite of passage.

Every few years some concerned parent tries to shut it down. It never works. No one can make a case against it because every legendary bit of trouble that comes from the lake is committed by kids from families no one wants to make trouble for. Good families. They're the business owners, council members, friends of the Turners. And Sheriff Turner is always very good to his friends. I flip the poster over. *E-mail S L R for more info.* That's Andy Martin, the yearbook editor.

I crumple the poster because I'm not here for that. This is what I'm here for: to search the school. I look in the trophy cases, check every locker row, the girls' room and the boys', the gym and the cafeteria, the *New Books!* display in the library.

My underwear doesn't turn up.

I head for homeroom and pick my usual desk at the back, next to the sinks and not the windows, because any view of the outside world—even one as lackluster as Grebe's—makes the day drag on that much longer. After a while, Mr. McClelland comes in. He's the youngest member of the faculty and he tries too hard. I don't think I'll be here the day that finally gets crushed out of him, but it'll happen. It always does.

Students slowly trickle in, pieces of brightly colored paper clutched tightly in hands, even those who aren't members of our senior class. Some are already on their phones, e-mailing Andy for details, no doubt. It's a kind of digital vetting process, even though date and time is going to end up the worst-kept secret in this school. And you can always count on a few underclassmen sneaking past the frontlines to drink in some of the glory.

Penny Young and Alek Turner enter the room. It's Penny first, and she's still perfect. I can say it over and over because it will always be true. You can tell she's perfect by the way everyone looks at her. They stare openly or glance furtively—the point is, they want to look because the looking is good. Alek's entrance is altogether a different thing. He saunters in, a boy who claimed the world, but it's not his fault; he only took what was offered. He wears a Grebe Auto Supplies shirt, just in case we forgot he's marked for that empire.

He murmurs something in Penny's ear and they move around each other with the ease of two people who grew up together but we all did. Someone flicked a switch on them in ninth grade and called it love.

"Announcements soon," McClelland murmurs. "Everyone, be seated."

They settle in a few rows ahead of me. Even from here, I can smell Alek's cologne and it reminds me of last year, our heads bent together, scribbling about *Romeo and Juliet* for an English project and I thought it was a joke when Mrs. Carter paired us up; Paul Grey's daughter, Helen Turner's son. *Two households both alike in dignity* except there was no dignity on the Grey side, just Helen firing Paul the day he drunkenly called her a cunt in front of all the other boys in the auto shop because goddamn, it's hard to work on something with an engine when you have a vagina for a boss.

Alek senses me watching. He turns in his seat and his eyes meet mine. I rest my middle finger across my lips; red on red, the most subtle way I can tell him to fuck himself because I'm not stupid enough to say it out loud in a world that's his fan club. He turns back around, rests his arm over Penny's shoulder and brings his mouth to her ear. She gives him a playful nudge.

Sometimes I imagine taking a walk with him. I imagine leading him behind the school and into the trees. I imagine stomping on his skull until all his fine, sharp features have turned to pulp. Until all the parts of him that are too familiar disappear.

He's looking more and more like his brother these days.

"could you drive me to the Barn before I go to work?"

Mom pauses at the bottom of the stairs, Todd close behind. They're both disheveled and flushed and I don't want to think about what they were doing before I got home. I toss my book bag against the wall and decide I like the look of it there, that this is what I'll do every time I make it back from school until it's second nature. A house isn't a home until it becomes a habit.

"What do you need?" she asks. Todd slips past her and steps into the kitchen. I hear the fridge door squeak open.

"I'm down to my last bra. I'd bike but I'd be late for my shift."

"Sure. Just let me get my purse."

She ducks into the kitchen, tells Todd what's going on, and then the short, sweet sound of their mouths meeting. She reappears with the car keys clasped in her hand.

"Be nice to spend some time together, huh?"

"Yeah."

The Barn is a discount store about twenty minutes outside of Grebe, on the way to Godwit. Get everything and get it cheap, which means I can shop for clothes while she picks up groceries. We get into the sweltering New Yorker and roll the windows all the way down. The car doesn't start the first time or the second time, either. It doesn't start until Todd comes out and tells us there's a trick to it. He jiggles the keys in a way that looks less like trick and more like luck, but it works. The engine roars to life.

"You'll have to fill her up before you leave town," he tells us. He stands in the driveway and waves as we pull out. I can tell Mom likes that he does that, sees us off.

"I'll pay for the gas," I say. "It's my trip."

"Don't worry about that."

We have to get gas from Grebe Auto Supplies because it's the only station in town. It's right next to Gina's Pizzeria and there's something disturbingly appealing about the combined smell of grease and gas. Mom pulls up to the self-serve pump and hands me her credit card.

"You want to do this? I'll get us something to drink at Deckard's."

She heads into the convenience store on the other side of and just a little behind the station. I pump gas, finishing before she does, and wait in the car. The minutes eke by. When I glance back at the convenience store, I can just make her out. She's only halfway in, talking to Mr. Conway, so that should take forever. Great. Dan Conway. Biggest mouth in town. Bet he's trying to feel out our new living arrangements and whether marriage is next on Mom's list even though in his eyes, it probably should've come first.

I drum my fingers on my knees and then a Cadillac Escalade EXT pulls up to the self-serve pump next to mine, music blaring. My stomach sinks when I see Alek behind the wheel, Brock playing passenger.

It never feels fair, seeing them after school.

Brock gets out with a credit card—not his—in hand. Alek never pumps his own gas, if he can help it. Alek never does a thing he can get Brock to do for him. I watch him rest his head against the seat and stare at the world through a pair of Ray-Bans. After a second, he leans forward and presses his finger against the inside of the windshield. He pulls his hand away and studies it, frowning. He pokes his head out the window.

"Hey, clean the windshield while you're at it," he says. Brock gives him the finger. Alek scans the station before his eyes settle on Gina's. "You hungry?"

Brock raises his middle finger higher, but when he's hooked the nozzle back on the pump, he reaches for a filthy squeegee because of course he would. Brock lives one street away from me now I've moved, a street where the houses don't so much resemble chipped and broken teeth, but if you look close enough, you see their foundations are rotting. Brock is the eldest of five in a family that's no stranger to handouts. Alek got him on the sweet side of high school and that's the kind of debt you spend your whole life trying to repay, which is exactly why Alek got Brock on the sweet side of high school.

When he finishes, Brock takes the card and heads to Gina's. Stops when he realizes Alek isn't coming with him. "You gonna wait there?"

"Fucking hot outside, man."

Brock gives him a look, but he doesn't push it. He heads inside without spotting me and I exhale. I might not get so lucky on his way back.

I glance at Deckard's and Mom's *still* cornered by Conway. I get out of the car quick and go in after her. Inside, the AC is cranked and the cold air makes me shiver. My arrival brings the sound of Conway's gruff voice to an abrupt halt. Mom looks at me. She's got two unpaid bottles of Coke in her hands.

"Have I been that long?" she asks.

"I'm not going to have time, if we don't go soon."

"You're right." There's something grateful in her face that makes me think I should've broke this up sooner. Mom turns back to Conway, who is all steely-eyed now that I'm around. "Well, you take care, Dan. It was nice talking to you."

"You too, Alice." He smiles at me. His yellow teeth stretch across his pudgy face. His bald spot is barely concealed by his blond comb over. "Hope you're staying out of trouble, Romy."

Conway says that to everyone but he doesn't mean it because if they did, he wouldn't have anything to talk about. Still, the way he says it to me is different than he'd say it to anyone else. Small town nuance. Something you don't learn in the city. It's knowing when *hello* means *go away* or when *rough night* means *I know you got drunk again* or when *yeah, I'd love to see you, it's just so busy lately* means *never, never, never.* When Conway tells me he hopes I'm staying out of trouble what he means is I am the trouble.

I go back to the car while Mom pays and when I round my side, I notice a word cut through the dirt coating my door.

SLIT

Because "slut" was just too humanizing, I guess. A slit's not even a person.

Just an opening.

The sun shines off the clean lettering. I slowly face the Escalade. Alek is looking elsewhere, but there's a small smile on his lips.

I see Mom headed my way out the corner of my eye. I drag my nails through the word until it's off the car, get inside, and rub my hand on my leg, streaking it with grime.

If Mom notices the Turner boy in his luxury truck, she doesn't say so and it's not until we're on the road, heading out of Grebe that I feel like I can breathe. I watch the farmland roll past and wonder how anyone settles on this place when there's Godwit only a few hours north and Ibis, which isn't even a blink to the east, but far enough to feel like another planet.

Everything's better somewhere else.

The Barn doesn't even have the decency to look like what it's named after, it's just a boxy discount store—THE BARN, a sign in large, neon orange letters against an electric blue background over its entrance—with a parking lot that's pretty full up because more people than don't in this area get what they need to live here. We cross the parking lot and Mom puts in a quarter to unlock an orange shopping cart before we go inside.

Everything is here. Food and movies, clothes and cheap furniture that looks nice and falls apart fast. At the back of the store, there's candy, toys, decorations for whatever upcoming holiday, then all your personal hygiene needs. The grocery department belongs to itself. In Grebe, there are two kinds of people: those who shop local and those who shop here.

Mom stays close while I pick through an eight-dollar bra bin at the back of the place. They're so cheap, so unspectacular, they don't even hang them up for display. Pieces of cloth with pads, that's all. But it's all I really need.

"Okay," I say and toss them into the cart. There's something about the way she looks at them that makes my face burn. It's one thing when Tina calls my bras an embarrassment, but it's another when my mother does, even if it's not in so many words.

"Are those enough?" she asks.

"Mom."

"I mean, are they going to give you enough support? They look sort of—"

"*Yes.* They will."

She gives me a look. "You could have something nicer. I always think really nice underwear and pajamas are the best things you can get for yourself. I always feel so great when I have a good bra on or a—"

"Thanks for the nightmares, Mom."

She laughs and wanders over to a rack of pink bras with fine, black lace edging. The tag attached to them has a picture of an amazing pair of breasts. It's a push-up.

She holds it out to me. "Try it."

"No. It's okay."

"What's wrong with something like this?"

"I have what I need."

I must have this look on my face because she drops it and I let her lead me through the rest of the store and stay quiet while she loads a week's worth of groceries into the cart. At the checkout, it's just boys at the registers and I can't stand the idea of them knowing what I wear underneath my shirt. I tell Mom I have a headache, give her my wallet, and wait in the car while she pays for it all. I wish I didn't have a body, sometimes.

i'm waiting for an old man to tell me what he wants to eat because he won't let me leave his table before he decides because he knows he'll decide as soon as I leave his table and then he'll "spend the rest of the night trying to wave me down." I can't convince him otherwise, so I stand there while he adjusts his glasses and trails his finger over every menu item, waiting for something to call out to him, periodically asking my opinion on any potentials. *It's just fucking food,* I want to tell him. *It's fuel.* It doesn't have to taste good to keep you alive.

After the first few minutes, he winks at me, like it can't be helped. After the next five, I can't help but sigh and he tells me kids my age don't know shit about patience and then the air-conditioning flatlines and none of it matters anyway because he melts, he leaves without ordering. He's not the only one. Tracey tells everyone drinks are on the house and by then it's my break, thank Christ, because people are mouthing off like it's something we're doing to them on purpose.

Holly looks like she's going to kill someone. She's been in a pissy mood since she overheard Annie making plans to crash that college party this weekend, just like Holly thought she would. Now Annie's grounded, Holly's son is babysitting her on Friday and from the sound of it, no one in the house is speaking—but Annie's slamming lots of doors.

"Thank God I don't have to like her to love her," Holly told me.

I find Leon in the kitchen and he asks if I want to spend the next twenty minutes with him in his car. I say yes and we sit in the back of his old Pontiac with the AC blasting and the radio playing low, awkwardly passing time with a deck of cards. It's a vintage pack he found in the glove compartment when he bought the car and he decided it could stay because it features sexy pinups from the fifties. He's embarrassed when he tells me this, watching as I sift through the cards, admiring the girls.

"Pretty," I say.

"I've seen better," he says. I flush.

He tries to show me how to do a shuffle called the Sybil cut but it's too hard to follow, so I just watch the cards play against each other before turning back into a deck.

"Fun night, huh?" he asks.

"Real fun."

Goose bumps prickle my arms and legs. I feel him beside me, so much. Too much. I stare out the window. I see the diner from here. I see patrons inside the diner from here. The bike rack. My bike. I watch a trucker and a woman cross the lot, their arms wrapped around each other. He nuzzles her neck and she tilts her head my way and I swear our eyes meet for half a second. I wonder what she sees when she looks at me.

I wonder what Leon sees when he looks at me.

How he decided on me.

The woman and the man climb into his semi.

"So how do you feel about good food and good people?" Leon asks. It's so unexpected, I don't know how to respond. He smiles. "That bad, huh?"

"Why?"

He tosses the pack of cards into the front seat. "I'm going to a party and I'm positive I'd have more fun with you there. It's at my sister's, this Friday. She's in Ibis. How about it?"

"I have to work, Friday. You know that."

"You could get Holly to cover for you. Or one of the other girls."

"I have to, uh . . ." I forget what I have to do. He's asking me out on a date and I feel about a thousand different things at once and not all of them are bad. I stare at my nails. But. All I manage to get out of my mouth is, "I don't know."

"But that's not a no?"

"I'll have to see if . . . I'll have to see."

Because there are things I need to know but I don't know how to ask him, wouldn't begin to know how to put them to words. I don't think you can. I study Leon's profile, my gaze traveling down the ridge of his nose to the soft outline of his lips, to the sharp outline of his jaw. I wonder what it would be like to run the outside of my hand against it, to be close enough to do that. I *am* close enough to do that. I hate him a little, for the feeling between my legs.

"Do I have something on my face?" he asks.

"No," I say. And then, "How would you describe yourself, Leon?"

"I'm awesome."

"Seriously."

"Ouch." He clutches his chest. "What do you want me to say?"

"I can't tell you or it won't be true."

"I think I'm great, for whatever that's worth."

It's not worth anything. I look out the window again and I want to know what's going on inside the semi. That girl looked like she knew what she was doing, like it was easy.

She didn't look afraid.

"Look, when we go in, I'll get my phone. We can swap numbers. Just let me know sometime tomorrow if you want to come and I'll pick you up. Not a big deal if you can't."

He reaches over and squeezes my hand, startling me with his sweetness. But just because something starts out sweet doesn't mean it won't push itself so far past anything you could call sweet anymore. And if it all starts like this, how do you see what's coming?

when i run, I don't have to think about anything.

I don't have to think about Leon, or my underwear, or mom, or Todd, or Penny, or Alek, or Brock. But then that last one—he comes up beside me and matches my pace. I take a quick look behind me. Everyone else specks the distance. I want to be them. They don't have to worry about this. They can run without being chased because that's what's happening here. Brock is speaking to me with his body. It's in the way he keeps it so close to mine. In the way he breathes, so heavy and loud, I can barely hear my heart. His arms lash at the air. He's telling me the space between us is nothing, is something he's letting me have, for now. I can barely keep myself ahead of him. I'm fast, but his legs are longer.

"This too close to you, Romy?" he pants. "Gonna cry rape?"

Air burns my throat and my lungs beg for reprieve, but I can't slow. I need my body to tell his I will always be able to get away, that he should quit now and find someone weaker.

Sweat soaks the back of my T-shirt, pools underneath my breasts. I fall behind, coming shoulder to shoulder with him and as soon as I am, he snakes his foot out and hooks his ankle around mine and an explosion of words fills my head.

Tripkneesteethliphit the ground running, that's what I do.

The track bleeds into my knees and my knees bleed it back out. My face eats the dirt, drives my lips into my teeth. I taste my own metal and salt. The breath is out of me. I let the pain. I let the pain mute color, sound, mute everything but itself until rough hands turn me over and Coach Prewitt's face is inches from my own. I reel air back into my lungs while she gives me her spiel. It never changes.

"You eat, Grey? You eat today? Hydrate?"

"It's not that," I manage.

"Then what happened here?"

I wipe my mouth on my arm and leave a thin red line on my skin. Everything I say next comes out in slow bursts as I try to catch my breath around all the hurt.

"He—tripped—me." I pause to cough. "Did it—on purpose."

Prewitt turns to him. "This true, Garrett?"

"Like hell I did." But he lacks conviction, breathless as I am.

"He was *chasing me.*"

"It's *track,* Grey. Was everyone behind us chasing you too?" A few people laugh. He shakes his head, smirking. "Her legs went right out from under her. Damnedest thing."

"If you weren't running so goddamn close—"

"Enough of that," Prewitt says. I struggle to sit up, but she claps a hand hard on my shoulder, keeping me still so she can inspect the damage. "Bit your lip. Knees took the worst of it, but you'll live." She grabs my hands and turns them over. My palms are, somehow, mercifully unscathed. "Head down to the nurse's office and get yourself cleaned up."

She pulls me to my feet. Blood trickles down all my newly opened spaces. I take a few cautious steps, legs stiff and ankle protesting. Prewitt notices.

"She's faking," Tina mutters.

"Yeah, that's *fake blood*, you stupid—"

"I said *enough,*" Prewitt says sharply. "Young, walk her to the nurse's office."

Penny steps forward. I step back.

"I don't need that," I say. "Her."

"You're hurt. She'll take you in."

"No." But *no* is a dead word. "I can get there on my own."

"That's not how we do it here." Prewitt squints at me and all those lines around her eyes scrunch up. "And you know that."

I've got another *no* on the tip of my tongue, but Prewitt's just daring me to say it and I'm tired, so I part the crowd by limping through it. Penny has to jog to catch up and after that, we're evenly matched. She might even be slowing down for my benefit, which makes me angrier than I can say, but if I could speak I'd tell her I hate her. *I hate you.* I want my silence to carry that to her, somehow, because she should know it forever and ever amen.

We reach the building. Climb the stairs up. The movement pulls at my split skin and God and Christ, it hurts. I watch my blood dot the floor as we reach the fork in the hall.

Penny moves left and I go right.

"You're supposed to go to the nurse's office," she says, but I keep putting distance between us. "You should get cleaned up." A second's silence. "Brock tripped you?"

I turn and walk backward so she can see me in all my wrecked glory.

"What do you think, Penny?"

I hobble to the showers and rinse off, watching the water turn pink before swirling down the drain. I get a better view of my torn skin. It does look bad enough for the nurse's office. I finish up and get dressed, carefully edging my shorts up past my knees, trying not to stain them with blood.

I'm pulling my shirt over my head when the faint trilling of girl reaches my ear. The door swings open a minute after that. Tina leads the pack. When she sees me, she gives me the kind of look everyone else is glad they're not getting.

"Brock *tripped* you?" The other girls quiet as they begin undressing because everyone always gets quiet when they're about to witness something worth repeating later. "Jesus, what boy don't you lie about?"

The stupid thing is, I used to like Tina. Coveted her whole *who gives a fuck?* attitude more than I did her breasts, even though I wanted those too. I admired her, for the longest time, because she seemed so above it all. She's not—she was waiting for her moment to be right at the center of it. She took my place as well as she could. She's not Penny's best friend by a long shot, but she's the girl Penny calls when Penny needs a girl. Sometimes, I think Alek chose her for Penny, after the disaster that was me. Tina's father owns the Grebe Golf Club and damn, if that isn't Sheriff Turner's favorite way to spend his free time.

"Seriously, why is she still here?" Tina turns to Penny. "She lies, right? *She* lies and Kellan—" My body is an alarm gone off. My body is not my body. My skin tightens enough to suffocate, keeping me in this moment where I stop and she doesn't. "—has to leave. How is that fair? '*I want him.*'" She does the kind of vocal gymnastics that make her sound like a breathy, love-struck girl and I want to be the violence in her life. "'*I dream about him.*'"

Because teenage girls don't pray to God, they pray to each other. They clasp their hands over a keyboard and then they let it all out, a (stupid) girl's heart tucked into another girl's heart. *Penny, I want him. I dream about him.* I needed someone to hear my prayers and did Penny ever make sure of that when she forwarded my fucking e-mail to everyone in school.

"Tina," Penny says. The way she says it makes the room still. Her voice has this admonishing tinge to it, like she's defending me with inflection alone.

But that can't be right.

"What?" Tina must hear it too, for the edge it puts in her own voice.

"Stop talking and help me get my necklace untangled from my hair."

That I deflate is the only way I know I wanted it—for her to defend me. And then I'm ashamed of the part of me that still wants that.

"You're supposed to take your jewelry off *before* we run . . ."

"Yeah, well, I forgot. Help me."

I push out of the locker room on wasted legs. They're bleeding again. There's a name in my head and I want it out of my head. It's amazing what a certain combination of letters can do, how it can string itself around your heart and squeeze.

Nurse DeWitt takes one look at my knees and says to me what he says to everyone: I'm old enough to take care of myself now. So that's what I do. I sit in the corner of the room and pick at my wounds, painting my nails even redder before finally slapping a Band-Aid on every part of me that needs it.

When I'm done, I turn my phone on. A missed text from Leon, asking if I know whether I can come to his sister's yet. I debate texting him back just to tell him parts of me are covered in blood because maybe he'd forget about the part of him that likes me. But I don't. Instead, I text I DON'T WANT TO IMPOSE, which feels weirdly formal but I can't think of another way to put it. It only takes a minute for him to reply.

CAN I CALL YOU NOW?

SURE.

Why did I say that? I run my thumb lightly over the side of my phone until it buzzes. I glance at DeWitt. He doesn't care. I'm not breaking any rules, but I wish I was, so this could be stopped. I bring the phone to my ear. "Hi."

"I keep telling my sister, Caro, about this girl I like at Swan's and how I think maybe she likes me too." I twist, hunching my shoulders. If DeWitt looks, I don't want him to see what Leon's voice does to me. "Anyway, she doesn't believe it."

"Is it that hard for her to believe?" I sound steadier than I feel.

"Yeah. So even if you don't come . . . you like me too, right?" He pauses. "Because then I could at least go with that in my head."

"Maybe," I say and I can almost hear him smile.

"If you did come, I asked her before I asked you and it doesn't bother her. You wouldn't be imposing. You'd be welcome. It's a party. We'd have fun."

I close my eyes and I see a quiet house waiting at the end

of a long stretch of driveway and soft, golden lights shining through every window, a hint of music behind their glass. A pickup truck parked in the driveway and it's so clear and ugly in my head, I forget who I'm talking to and I wonder who Leon thinks he's talking to.

"What do you say?" he asks.

I open my eyes. I need Leon to tell me who he is in a different kind of language because really, if he's safe, there's only one way to find out. It's not through talking.

i find the pink-and-black lace push-up bra on my bed like it's meant to be there, a natural part of the landscape. I pick it up. Mom. She thinks she's doing a nice thing for me.

I push my fingers into the padding. Soft as it is pretty. I rip the tag off the bra and unhook the clasp. It's okay to try on here, alone. I take off my shirt and the bra I'm already wearing and toss them on the floor. I turn my back to the mirror on my bureau and start sliding my arms through the straps, but they need some adjusting. I fight with them for a minute, almost ruin my manicure trying to slide the little piece of plastic down. I adjust the cups, feel what little breasts

I have settle inside. I do the clasp up. It's a little tight.

I face the mirror.

My heart races in a weird way, like I'm doing something I'm not supposed to be doing, but I'm allowed to do this. I turn to the side and I like my profile even more, the way the bra holds me. I'm so used to being flat but the bra lifts and brings my breasts closer, forcing a kind of curve between them that resembles cleavage. It looks—good.

But I can't wear it.

If something happens—I don't want to be wearing it.

I put the pink bra away and pick up the other from the floor, slide it back on. I put on a skirt and then I make it cargo pants. I add a long-sleeve shirt and I'm sweating. I switch out the sleeves for an off-the-shoulder tee and the cargo pants for a pair of shorts. I did my nails earlier, so all that's left is to reapply my lipstick and then I'm ready.

I sit on the step and breathe the stale air while everything that's ahead of me turns my empty stomach. Mom is at her job—she cleans an office building every other night—and Todd is at the hardware store buying storage containers for leftovers from the move. They both think I'll be at Swan's because I didn't tell them otherwise. Me on a date with a boy. I didn't want to see what that looked like on their faces because however they gave it back to me would come from some place I don't want any part of.

I hear the low rumble of Leon's Pontiac before I see it. He rounds the corner and takes the street slowly, eventually easing up to the curb. He turns the car off and gets out. He's wearing dark blue jeans and a gray V-neck T-shirt that hugs his body in all the right ways. He shoves his hands in his pockets, which is okay by me because his hands are forever distracting, all the things they could do.

"Parents around?" he asks, staring at the house.

I stand. “You want to meet them?”

“I thought I’d go for a good impression.”

“They’re not around.”

“Too bad.” He looks me up and down and frowns, reminds me of how busted up my legs are because I’m letting them heal out in the open now, all scabs. “What happened?”

“I ate track in Phys Ed. Not a big deal.”

“Looks like it hurt. You a good runner?”

“When I’m not falling on my face.”

“Fair enough,” he says, and smiles. “Ready to head out?”

No. I nod and follow him to the car. The air conditioner is on but the radio is off and I sink low in my seat as we make our way out of Grebe. I don’t want anyone to see me with Leon. I don’t want him to be a question in anyone else’s mouth.

“So where are your parents?” he asks.

“My mom has this cleaning job and Todd—her boyfriend—he’s out.”

“Boyfriend? Your mom and dad divorced?”

“I guess.”

“You guess?”

“My dad kind of walked out. I don’t think he signed anything.”

“Oh. Sorry.”

“Don’t be. I’m not.”

It’s awkward for a minute and then Leon starts telling me about how his parents live in Godwit. They had Leon pretty late in life. His mother is a visiting professor at the university there, his father is a dentist. He tells me how he lives on Heron Street in a basement apartment he rents from an old woman who looks after her granddaughters every Sunday. She makes them cookies and always sets aside a dozen for him. He can’t bring himself to admit to her he hasn't really got much of a sweet tooth.

He tells me how his sister, Caroline, is twelve years older, that she's a dentist like their father. She and her husband, Adam, a pharmacist, are expecting their first child. They want Leon to move in, rent-free. All he has to do is look after the baby and the house when she goes back to work. It'd be a chance for him to save up for whatever he wants to do next instead of giving his money away to someone else. I wonder what his family would make of mine. My mother, one failed marriage behind her and a boyfriend too broken to work. And me. What am I? Dentists and pharmacists and professors . . . I pick at the thread on my shorts and stare at my knees, wondering why I didn't cover them.

"Are you going to do it?" I ask.

"Not sure. Not a big fan of babies. I can't think of anything less thrilling than looking after one all day and then heading to Swan's for the night. Might cut into my insane social life." It makes me laugh, a little. He grins. "Be nice to get ahead, though."

The path to Wake Lake flies by Leon's side. Shortly after, we pass the YOU ARE NOW LEAVING GREBE sign and I sit up and watch the houses beside the road give way to farmland.

"What are you saving up for?"

He shrugs. "I don't know. All I know is everything costs something."

Can't argue that.

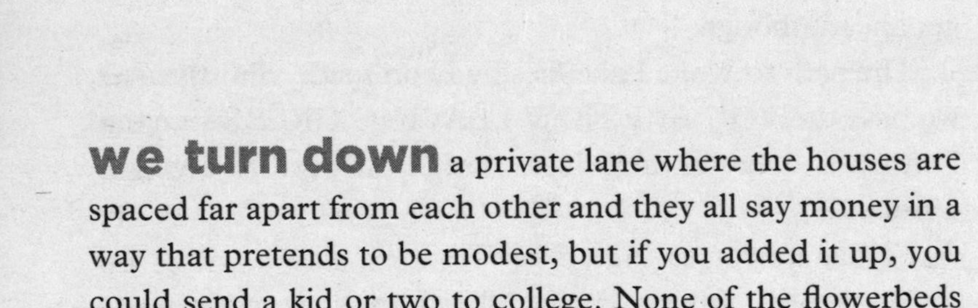

we turn down a private lane where the houses are spaced far apart from each other and they all say money in a way that pretends to be modest, but if you added it up, you could send a kid or two to college. None of the flowerbeds out here are dying and the lawns are green, but the weather hasn't changed—it's as hot as it ever is—so that says it all.

Leon drives us to the last house at the end of the street, tucked into woods just waiting to be razed for more houses. I hear music, a steady beat my heart sets itself to. Leon slows and finds a spot to park between two *much* nicer-looking cars. My palms sweat. I rub them on my thighs.

"You don't have to be nervous," Leon says.

"I'm not."

He smiles and gets out of the car. I take a deep breath and do the same. He meets me at my door and wraps his fingers around mine, and he takes me up the driveway and around the house before I can even really think about his fingers, wrapped around mine.

I can't remember being invited to anything so nice, except for maybe Grebe Auto Supply's employees-plus-family-only picnics and parties. There's a fancy spread of food to pick from and pretty little tables set up close by. I'm acutely aware of my lack of age in this small, classy crowd who seem way more socially adept than me.

Leon leads me to the beautifully decorated gazebo at the back of the yard, where a tall, painfully pregnant-looking woman holds court. Caroline. *Caro for short,* Leon tells me. She's in a burgundy maternity dress and matching lipstick that perfectly complements her black skin. Her brown hair is cropped close to her head and her hands rest on her stomach in an almost absently protective way. She's smiling, but I can tell by the way she shifts from foot to foot that she probably wants to sit down. I see the girls at Swan's do that all the time when their feet are hurting. I've done it myself. When she sees Leon, her eyes light up and it makes my heart stutter. I can't remember the last time a girl lit up when she saw me. Or maybe I can. I just didn't know I missed it until now.

"Hey," Caro says.

"Hey," he says and he gives her a hug, or at least tries to. "Christ, Caro. I can barely fit my arms around you."

"You really know how to make a girl feel great about herself," she says. When they part, she turns to me and I disappear in that second's worth of scrutiny, worried she'll see more than I want her to. She smiles, though, so she must not. "Romy. Leon's told me about you."

My name sounds so . . . welcome out of her mouth, it makes the next thought in my head: *I want you to be my friend* and the thought after that: *that's pathetic.*

"You have a beautiful place out here," I say.

"Thank you." She crosses the gazebo and grabs two beers from a small table of drinks behind her, one for Leon and one—for me, which makes me feel as adult as everyone else here, which makes me like her even more. A tiny look of longing crosses her face as she watches me twist the cap off my bottle. "Enjoy, because I can't." Then she nods at my legs. God, she's like her brother. Doesn't miss anything. "What happened?"

"Tripped over my own feet."

"In track at school. She's a runner," Leon explains. "Fast one, apparently."

"That's awesome." She points at her belly. "I can't even remember what walking is like, let alone running. All I do is waddle now."

I take a swig of the beer. "Congratulations on . . ." I nod at her stomach because it feels weird to congratulate someone just because they're going to have a kid. People have been doing that for as long as there have been people. "Congratulations."

"Thanks. Hey, do you babysit? Because Leon doesn't."

He rolls his eyes. "Don't get on me about that tonight."

"Boy or girl?" I ask.

"Parasite." She grins at the look on my face. "It's the truth! It's sucking me dry. I've never been more tired or sick in my life. I've hated every minute of this pregnancy."

"All you do is complain about it now, but you're going to love that kid when it's out of you and you're all blissed out on hormones," Leon tells her.

"Absolutely, and I'll still have hated being pregnant."

She asks Leon how it's going at the diner and my attention drifts; I'm distracted by everything, overwhelmed by this: people look at me and then—they don't. Their eyes skim over me and move on to something else. There's an unquestioned acceptance of my being here, being part of this. It's a warm feeling and I'm so hungry for it, but I close myself off to it before I get my fill. I'm not going home to that. Best stay starved.

"So are you two together?" Caro asks and I don't know who looks more embarrassed for it—Leon or me—but that's only because I can't see my face. I finish my beer in three swallows. She says, "But you're *here* together."

"Thought I'd show Romy a typical Friday night for me."

"Then why aren't you at your apartment ordering takeout and playing video games?"

He slings his arm around my shoulder. I feel the question after he does it. *Is this okay?* I don't think it is. I don't know how to fold myself into him in any way that feels right.

"That's for second dates, Caro. Everyone knows that."

"Feeling confident?" she asks which seems like something I should be teasing him about but I'm still struggling to fit. And then I realize they're waiting for me to say something anyway. The silence is so awkward. You'd think I'd never spent time with people before or that I didn't know how to talk. A million and one thoughts are firing across my brain because I want what I say to be perfect. I want it to be as effortless as them.

"He must be," I finally offer.

Leon smiles. He pulls me closer and it makes me shiver, and I feel him feel it, but I can't tell if it pleases him.

"Hey, Leon! Leon!" And like that, Leon's arm is off me just when I'm starting to understand its weight. He straightens, eyes searching out whoever's yelling for him. It turns out to be a man as tall as Leon, but not quite as lean, with dark brown skin and curly brown hair. His tie is the exact same color as Caro's lipstick. "That junk heap you drove here in—"

"Insult my car, Adam, and it'll be the last thing you do." Leon turns to me. "My brother-in-law. He's a real . . ."

"Be nice," Caro warns.

"He knows how I feel about my car."

"The headlights look great," Adam says and even though he can't possibly hear what Caro and Leon are saying from where he's standing, the glee on his face says he knows. "That why you left them on?"

Leon closes his eyes briefly.

"It's a shitty car, Leon," Caro tells him.

"Et tu, Brute?" He gives me a sheepish smile and hands me his beer. "I'll be right back."

"I'll be right here," I say and then he's gone, leaving me with his sister. A few people wander through, grabbing drinks and wishing Caro well on their way.

"They get along, Adam and Leon, in case you were wondering," Caro says after a minute. "Sometimes better than me and Leon do."

"How did you meet him?"

"Over a cavity," she says and I smile with my mouth closed, suddenly self-conscious about my teeth which are more crooked than they should be. "His. *My* teeth are fantastic. Anyway, we were friends and then we were best friends and then he fell in love with me. After a while, I caught up."

"That's sweet."

"I think so too." She takes the empty bottle from my hand, so all I'm holding is Leon's. "So you're at Swan's. Do you like it?"

"It's okay."

"Do you work there to save up for college or . . ."

"No. That's not . . ." It's probably a little too much to lay on someone you've just met that college is not a destination or a dream. "I don't think college is really my thing."

"Leon felt that way too. It used to drive me crazy but he's kind of opened my mind about it," she says. "And he's happy."

"That's all that matters, right?"

She raises her chin and studies me. Her eyes are still warm, but she's looking for something that's not there, I think. More. I take another long drink of the beer and then I remember it's not mine. Leon should be back by now. I pick at the label and try to think of something to say. "So you never said if you're having a boy or girl."

"We won't know until it's born."

I hope it's not a girl.

The thought shocks me, comes so quick it has to be honest.

So I think it again, careful and slow to be sure.

I hope it's not a girl.

I feel it even more the second time.

A woman walks up then, says *Caro, you're glowing!* and I move aside, disconnecting while I wait for Leon. He's taking an awful long time to turn off his headlights and the longer he takes, the stranger I feel. Light-headed. Familiar . . . I stare at the near empty bottle in my hands and—oh.

Oh . . . no.

That's not what I meant to do.

There's a warmth all through me. I don't drink—haven't in . . . a while. Not that I had the most amazing tolerance then, but now it must be nothing.

Because I feel it.

I swallow and scan the yard for Leon because now he's the last person I want to see. I can't be around him like this. My stomach twists, disagrees with itself. I turn to the rail of the gazebo, white-knuckling it. I can't be sick here, in front of everyone. I press my hand against my mouth.

"Hey, are you okay?" Caro's hand is on my back and then it's off again, like she's not sure she's allowed. I shake my head. "What's wrong?"

"I drank too fast."

She has to lean close to hear me, makes me repeat myself.

"Are you going to be sick?" She's surprised.

I nod and she says *it's okay, follow me,* like this is nothing, like she's been doing this her whole life: leading girls away from the party to the quiet place. I walk slowly after her, scared that any second now, I'll puke all over the neat lines of her house, where everything looks so perfect and matches. We go up some stairs, down a hallway of doors. She opens one at the very end and ushers me in, turns on the light. It's too bright. I wince and she pushes a switch until it dims.

"Guest bedroom." She points across it. "Bathroom."

"I'm so sorry," I say, because I want to leave some semblance of a good impression almost as badly as my stomach wants this beer out of me. "I was so nervous . . ."

"First time I met Adam's family, it was New Year's. I got pretty over-served," she says. "I get it. Take your time. I'm going to find Leon for you, okay?"

Caro's barely closed the door behind her before I'm in the bathroom on my knees, in front of the toilet. As soon as I hear her leave, my stomach gives one final warning lurch and most of what I drank comes back up. Stringy strands of spit dangle into the bowl from my lips and my eyes burn at the sour sting of it all. When I'm sure there's nothing left, I flush the toilet, wipe my mouth, and crawl across the floor. I rest against the cupboards under the sink.

Idiot.

"Shut up," I say.

The ragged sound of my voice steadies me, makes me feel like I'm in the room. I swallow, my mouth dry and sore, vomit-spent, and then I get to my feet. I splash cold water on my face and search the mirrored cabinet in front of me. I find a travel-sized bottle of mouthwash, toothpaste, and a glass full of individually packaged toothbrushes, which is just so . . .

I brush my teeth and rinse my mouth and then I leave the bathroom for the empty bedroom. I half expect Leon to be waiting when I come out, but he's not there. I walk over to the window and peer out at the party. I like it better from this distance, away from everyone. Safe.

After a while, the door opens behind me.

A silhouette of a boy in the hall divides me between the girl who knows it has to be Leon and the one who whispers *it might not be Leon,* but I don't know if it matters. I don't know what would make one boy more or less dangerous than the other.

"What took so long?" I ask.

"One of Caro's friends has a hard time getting around. Asked to swap parking places with me because I was closer to the house and then my car stalled halfway out. Adam had a field day with that." He steps into the room, closing the door behind him. I turn back to the window. "How are you feeling? Caro said you got a little ahead of yourself."

"I really like her," I say. He steps closer and just the sound of him moving is as easy and assured as the way he works in the kitchen at Swan's, like there's not one part of him that doesn't know what it's doing, what he's capable of. He moves behind me.

"I'm really glad you came," he murmurs and there's only one reason someone gets this close, I think, and talks so low, and says a sweet thing.

"Why do you like me, Leon?"

What do you want from me, Leon.

He laughs a little. "What?"

"You heard me."

"Just . . . soon as I saw you, I liked you."

"I didn't ask you when. I asked you why."

He's quiet for so long, I wonder how bad his answer is going to be even though this doesn't feel like any time to be honest—or maybe his silence says everything I need to know, that there is no real why. I could be any body.

"The red," he says. "I don't know. Just something about it made you . . ." He trails off when I want him to finish. Made me what? "I just thought, *God, introduce me to that girl.*"

He brings his hands lightly to my hips, asking me to face him and if I do, I know he'll kiss me. I swallow, my mouth desert dry. This is it, isn't it? This moment won't pass. It has to happen. I turn and when I see him, he's beautiful and I want that and it scares me and I kiss him and he kisses me back and I get so lost in it, I have to open my eyes to remind myself whose mouth is against mine.

The pressure of his lips is intense, gentle. I press against him and we take awkward, shuffling steps back. I put my hands against his cheeks. His skin is warm against my palms. He takes a breath and pulls me closer even though there's no space between us as it is, and his touch is hungry, searching, like however much of me he has isn't enough. We reach the bed. He sits and I put myself between his legs and he puts his arms around me and we fall onto the mattress. I'm dizzy with how he guides my body to it, like he doesn't have to think about it at all, he just understands. And then I'm underneath him. Leon.

He brings his mouth close to my neck, and then runs his tongue against it and my skin tingles, everywhere. He's hard. Against me.

Leon.

This is Leon.

I meet his lips with my own. And then his fingers tease the edge of my shirt, tugging at it, his hands trying to find a way under it and that's when I still. His hand, my shirt. Close my eyes.

"Stop," I whisper.

He—stops.

I open my eyes. He moves off me slowly, carefully, and blinks, dazed, like he was gone from his body or too far in it. He runs his hand over his face.

"Why'd you stop?" I ask.

He stares at me funny. "You want to . . ." His voice cracks. He exhales and tries again. "How about we get you something to eat."

He stands and holds his hand out. I stare at it.

He doesn't think I'm sober.

He doesn't think I'm sober and he's taking me out of the room with the bed in it.

We go back outside to the table full of food. He secures a paper plate in my hand and asks me what I like, tells me what he thinks I should try. Caro is there and she looks at Leon and then she looks at me and she smiles like she knows exactly what we were up to.

Later, after he drops me off at home, it feels like the world has shifted a little. It's just different enough that when I look at the girl reflected in the mirror in my room, it's like meeting someone new.

todd stands at the screen door and frowns at the layer of dust that's been coating the New Yorker since we went to the Barn and has only gotten worse after he took the back roads out to Andrew Ryan's house to see about the engine. Ryan is a prematurely retired mechanic who got pushed out of his seventy-year-old family business by Grebe Auto Supplies. *Only trustworthy mechanic in town,* Todd says, but he could be a crook, really—only thing that matters is he's not a Turner. The engine's good now, but the car's black finish is mottled with dirt. It fits more with its surroundings than it doesn't, but it's driving Todd crazy.

"No rain," he murmurs. "Wind's not blowing it off."

"You're going to have to do something about it then," Mom says.

"I know. I'm trying to decide if a wash and polish is worth the hurt."

Todd ends the night and starts his morning with pills so his pain never really catches up to him, but he's still got to pick and choose what he does carefully. He's only good for about an hour in the car, behind the wheel. When it's someone else driving, maybe an hour more, and that's pushing it. Any heavy lifting is always someone else's job. Todd knows what people say about him, that he's lazy, good for nothing. But he does what he can when he can, whether or not they see, and fuck them for not seeing it. I offer to help him wash it.

The smile Mom gives me when I do goes all the way to her eyes because our being together in this house, air not thick with drama or tension—she's wanted something this easy for so long and this is what having it looks like on her face. I think I'd kill the person who tried to take it away from her.

"That'd be great," Todd says.

He heads upstairs and Mom goes to the sink and fills an old bucket with soapy water. When he comes back down, he's shirtless and he's got a ratty old undershirt in his hands. He pulls it over his head and Mom watches. I notice the way her eyes linger on his chest, his arms. She blushes. I swear I can see the skip of her heart.

I can't remember her looking at my dad like that but she must have.

"This'll go twice as fast with you," Todd says. He goes into the hall for his shoes, reappears with them on a minute later. He never wears shoes with laces. Too hard to bend down and tie. "I appreciate it. I'm sure you've got better things to do on a Sunday afternoon."

"Not really."

Mom hands him some rags and a bucket. "A late lunch awaits you both."

I follow Todd to the New Yorker, a mess. He makes me go around the house for the hose, and we start there, giving it a rinse. We could probably stop there if we wanted—looks good enough to anyone passing by—but Todd wants to prove he can make it gleam, so we keep going, working up a sweat.

"Wake Lake this Friday, huh?" he asks after a while and now I know Wake Lake is this Friday. "Andrew was talking about it. Figured it'd be soon."

"You ever go?" I ask. "When it was your turn?"

"I did." He squeezes some soapy water over the windshield. "You going?"

"Not really my scene."

"Mine, either. I was fucked up on painkillers before I got there. The only thing I remember is watching your mom and dad make out through the bonfire."

"That's sad, Todd."

"Yep. But I was no good to anyone back then." He wipes his forehead with the back of his arm. "Paul—it was better it was him, then."

"Better it's you now," I say.

Todd smiles crookedly. "Thanks, kid."

He rubs his cloth along the driver's side window and I dip mine into the bucket of lukewarm water. I'm running it over the hood when my phone vibrates in my pocket. I slop the rag down and wipe my hand on my shorts before checking who it is.

Text from Leon.

HI.

And then he adds, JUST WANTED TO SAY THAT TO YOU.

I chew on my lip, my phone cradled in my damp palm like a secret. I can't stop thinking about last Friday night. I laid in bed after and ran that word over and over in my head.

Stop.

How he did.

It's hard to explain how that lack of feeling him on me . . . felt.

I glance at Todd, who watches me tap out a text.

HI.

"That—" he pauses. "That the boy who picked you up for work the other night?"

My face gets hot in a way that's got nothing to do with the weather. I don't know how Todd knows. I don't know if I want to know how Todd knows.

"What are you talking about?" I ask.

"Saw you leave with him when I was just rounding the corner on my way home." His voice is innocent as anything. He keeps his attention on the car.

"What makes you think it's him?"

"Your face." He shrugs. "Or maybe I'm mistaken."

"Maybe you are," I say. But I wonder if I gave something away like my mother does, something I had no control over—if I blushed. If anyone looking could see my heart skip.

i wake up with blood on my sheets.

I was eleven when I got my first period. A dull ache in my abdomen had me in the bathroom five minutes before I was supposed to leave for school. Five minutes after that, I was staring at my underwear, that weak streak of red. I wasn't ready, but I didn't have a choice. I remember searching the bathroom for pads, anything, and coming up empty. Dad was at work and Mom was at a dentist appointment for two impacted wisdom teeth. I stayed in the bathroom until a neighbor brought her home and she was too swollen and dopey to talk me through it, to say anything that meant something.

I was on my period the time I was thirteen and gross Clark Jenkins gave me a shy first kiss at Grebe Auto's annual employees-only holiday party. I got it the day my aunt Jean died and there was no one left on my mother's side. I got it the Saturday my father came home from the bar drunker than he could've paid for and cried at the kitchen table about how none of it was good anymore, just none of it.

Every time it happens, I can't help but wonder what's coming next.

I get dressed and sit at the kitchen table, resting my head against it, too nauseous to eat. Mom mutters something about how it must be Wednesday because she thinks they're worse than Mondays—so close to and far from the weekend—but it's not that. It's when my body decides to remind me it can do more than I'll ever want it to, it is so painful.

In Phys Ed, I tell Prewitt I'm not feeling well enough to run. She reluctantly lets me sit out because I never sit out. I'm not the only one with a sense of self-preservation. Trey Marcus nurses a pulled muscle and Lana Smith tells Prewitt she woke up too late for breakfast, so she'll just skip running and spare us all her eventual collapse. She gets a detention for that.

The sun bears down on us, holds tight my skin to my body. I lace my fingers together, turning my hands into one giant fist, and press it hard against my abdomen, pushing my outsides against my cramping insides. Lana and Trey talk quietly about Wake Lake. Two more days.

I watch everyone circle the track. All dogs, no rabbit.

Eventually, Prewitt blows her whistle, signals the showers. The best part about not working up a sweat is not having to wash it off, so when we head inside, I break from the class and find a spot for myself wedged between the wall and a broken vending machine, like a sick animal crawling off to the woods to die.

I fall into a hazy sleep that feels like a second by the time I jerk awake, drool all down my chin, but I know it must have been longer than that. I wipe my mouth and check the time on my phone. Five minutes before the bell and it's too quiet. That's the first thing I notice. It's too quiet. This should be the mad rush before third period, halls congested with students trying not to get to their next class too early or too late. But it's not.

I get to my feet and walk until a murmured frenzy reaches my ears and guides me toward the front of the school. Two girls hurry past and when they see me, they explode into giggles that tell me they know. They know what it is.

Two giggling girls.

A dull, warning ache.

This is what comes next:

Jane. It's so funny, what's been done to her. It's funny that her cheerleading outfit is in a crumpled heap at her feet, exposing her body, all those years of wear and tear to anyone who wants to look, except for this small allowance of modesty—

She's wearing my bra.

My vision tunnels. I step back until the dark edges fade, allowing me to see more of this thing I don't want to see.

The red.

They've painted her nails and her lips red.

Her mouth is a perfect, startled O.

John's hands are raised triumphantly over his head.

My underwear is draped over his fingers.

i hide behind a nearby locker row and watch Coach Prewitt chase away the crowd until the bell rings. Stragglers amble by after that, braving her wrath, hoping for a glimpse of the show even though nothing they see will be as good as the retelling.

When the hall is completely empty, Prewitt redresses Jane carefully, shaking her head and muttering to herself. *Stupid goddamn kids.* My bra and underwear are clutched in her hands. She contemplates them a moment, then, disgusted, shoves them into a nearby garbage can and leaves. I wait until I'm sure I'm alone and then I go to her. Jane.

I hold my hands out next to hers and exhale. This close, I

can see a subtle difference in shade. Off by degrees. That's not my red. It's some other girl's. Problem is, far enough away, it's easy to mistake for mine. I have to make sure no one else does. I bring my fingers to Jane's mouth. Marker. Permanent. The nails too.

But I can get rid of this.

I pick at the surface of her "skin" until it starts to flake. The circle around Jane's lips goes slow. The outer layer is weirdly stubborn. I want to talk to her, ask her how she's doing because it feels like she's real and I'm not. *You okay, Jane? No, nobody saw. But if they did, it doesn't matter. Whatever, you know? Fuck them.*

It takes a bit of elbow grease until the red O is gone except it makes it worse somehow—what's left behind is a white stain. I work on her right hand, chipping the polish off her fingernails carefully, to preserve my own. Pieces of her get under my thumbnail, make me hiss and wince, but I keep going until there's no red on her anymore and then—I'm done. I step back and stare at her and I know who she's not.

I go to the garbage and my hand is almost in it before I realize what I'm doing and it's that exact moment I feel eyes on me.

Penny's at the end of the hall. Her face is blank, but there can't be a single part of her not enjoying this and I wonder how long she's been there, if she saw it all. I try to think back, try to pick her out of a crowd of blurred faces, but I can't. It doesn't matter. She knew it would happen. She let it happen.

I'm not allowed to leave, but they can't expect me to stay. I walk out of school, scratching at my arms until angry finger marks flare on my skin and slowly disappear. By the time the house is in sight, I remember my bike but I'm not going back to get it.

The front door is locked, even though the New Yorker is

in the driveway. I knock, just to test it, and no one's home but I have a key for the house because it's my house now.

I have a key for the car too. Emergencies only.

This feels like it could be one.

I stand in the sun porch and the quiet pulls at me, and different parts of me want different things. There's the part of me that wants to go inside and sleep. There's the part of me that wants space, distance, because it all feels too close.

The part of me that wants to go is louder.

And then I'm in Todd's car, I'm in it and it's on and then I'm outside of Grebe, twisting along back roads so deserted it doesn't even matter which side I drive on. I forgot how it felt to push foot to pedal, to go fast, fast, faster and break, watching the tires kick up dust in the rearview. I learned to drive when I was fourteen. My mom took me to an abandoned lot out of town and showed me in case there was an emergency and my father was too drunk to get behind the wheel, like we lived in a world where help could never come to us. It wasn't long after when I discovered my father was the emergency. Mom saw it coming, what I didn't. She finally got a steady cleaning job and started working nights and he'd get so wasted, just drink the house dry and still be thirsty after and what do you do when you're thirsty? Get more to drink. Couldn't walk straight but *sure* he could drive and *hell, no* he wouldn't call a taxi and you can't call the cops on your dad because—you can't. So you beg him to wait until it's dark out and the streets are empty and you take him yourself and you never get caught.

He was so glad when I finally got my license because everything didn't have to be such a production anymore. I could pick him up from the bar, or the houses of any of his friends who would still have him, and it didn't matter who saw me. My father loved my mother's work nights. He could fall down guilt-free because the only person he had to answer to was me and as far as my father was concerned, no parent was ever meant to answer to their kid.

I circle the outskirts of Grebe over and over, pretend I'm actually going somewhere but I never really manage to convince myself.

I don't know how long it's like that, just driving, before the lights flash behind me.

I don't even understand what they mean until the short shrill burst of a siren follows.

Oh, Jesus.

I pull onto the shoulder while the unmarked Ford Explorer behind me does the same. I squeeze the steering wheel as I mentally catalogue all the things that are wrong, like my license isn't on me. Oh, and this isn't my car. Was I speeding? I think I was. Shit. *Shit.* I turn the car off and roll the window down, listening to the footsteps crunch across the ground until they reach my door.

"Romy Grey. Shouldn't you be in school right now?"

The voice is familiar in the terrible way most recurring nightmares are.

"What do you think you're doing?" he asks.

"Why don't you tell me?"

He's good at that, telling me.

"Step out of the car, please."

All the Turner boys look the same. I guess that means they all look like their father but when I see the father, I see the sons. Sheriff Turner exhales impatiently through his nose because it takes me too long to step out, but I couldn't do it before my legs felt sure enough to stand.

"This your car?" he asks.

I hate you.

Such an easy thought, I'm lucky it doesn't come out of my mouth.

"What?"

"I asked you if this"—he points to the New Yorker—"is your car."

"It's Todd's." He knows it's Todd's.

"He know you're driving it?"

"Yes."

Turner squints at the farmhouse in the distance. "So he reported it stolen for kicks?" I turn to ice. I can't even swallow, I'm so frozen. Turner nods to the house. "We got a call from Mr. Conway. Told us a suspicious-looking car come tearing down this road almost a dozen times." Conway. Christ. He's probably watching this from his window, binoculars pressed against his eyes to better the view. "Been drinking?"

It's as good as a slap in the face. "No, sir."

"So if we did a roadside sobriety test, you'd pass, that what you're telling me?"

"Yeah, that's what I'm telling you."

"But you've already lied to me once. Today." He runs his hand over his mouth, like he's considering it, letting me go, because he's trying to make a fool out of me, thinks he can put hope in me that I'll walk away from this with no trouble at all. I'm not a fool. He lowers his hand and points to the space of road in front of him. "Okay, Romy. I need you to stand right there. Feet together, hands at your sides."

"What?"

"Feet together, hands at your sides."

My eyes drift to his holster, that's how much I hate him. I'm boiling with it. I press my lips together and at first I want to fight this but I know I can't win because that's not what I was put on this earth to do. I drop my hands to my sides, feet together. He holds his hand up, raises his index finger, tells me to focus on the tip of it and then leads my eyes side to side, up and down and that is not even the end of it. He makes me walk a straight line, heel to toe, turn and walk it back. He makes me stand on one leg and count and when I pass all these tests with flying colors, he tells me he's calling my mother. I can't get any more dead while I listen to him say he's recovered the car and oh, guess who was driving it. His voice is getting to me, turns this open space into a coffin. I start scratching at my arms again.

He hangs up and shoves his phone in his pocket.

"There's a lot of ways I could make this go," he tells me. "You were speeding, driving erratically. That's not your car and I'm guessing your license isn't on you. So that little sobriety test would be the least of your worries. But know what? I'm going to give you a break and hope you learn something from it. Now get in Todd's car. I'm following you in."

I take the drive in to Grebe at a crawl, wasting his time and delaying the inevitable. When we finally get back to the house, Mom and Todd are waiting on the porch. She's upset, that's plain across her face and in the way she's holding herself, arms wrapped tight around her middle. Todd looks too serious, doesn't look right too serious. He grimaces when he sees the dirt on the car and I wish that I could take this whole thing back. The screen door whines as she pushes it open. They meet us halfway up the walkway.

"You all right?" she asks. I nod. She holds out her hands. "Good. Keys. Now." I hand them over, my eyes everywhere but hers. "Are you kidding me with this? What were you *thinking,* Romy?"

Todd clears his throat. "AJ, I think we can figure this out inside." Mom flushes when she finally realizes who she's embarrassing me in front of. Todd reaches out, shakes hands with the sheriff. "Levi, we appreciate your help today."

"It's my job. I've got to do it for everybody." He turns to me. "And you. You learn something?"

"Every single time," I tell him.

After I've been banned from driving the New Yorker until we all forget about the time I took it without asking and the sheriff brought me home, I have to ask my mother to drive me to Swan's. It's a quiet ride out. She keeps clenching her jaw. It's not until we reach the town sign, she asks, "What happened today?"

"Nothing."

"You don't just get in a car and go for nothing." She pauses. "If something happened and I can do something about it, you should tell me."

"Nothing happened."

She sighs and turns the radio on. Cattle graze in fields off the road and they look sleepy with the heat. When I was nine, my mom got hired to clean a hall out in the country after it got rented for a wedding. Dad had been at the bottle all day and she didn't want me to stay with him, so I went with her. I filled my pockets with diamond confetti that got all over the floors while she swept, vacuumed, scrubbed, and wiped down surfaces.

Behind the building was a field and when the potpourri scent of her cleaner made me sneeze, I went outside. There were calves there, these sweet things that watched me with less interest than I watched them. There was this raggedy one, sitting in the middle of the field, its mother nearby. I didn't realize it was sick until it tried to get up and it couldn't. It kept trying and it couldn't and then, eventually—it didn't. After a while, a truck drove in. A man and a boy got out, looked it over while its mother stood close. It was dead, the calf. Dead and too heavy to load into the truck bed, so they tied a rope around its neck, tied the other end to the truck and dragged it off the field like that. Its mother watched until it disappeared and when it was out of view, she called for it. Just kept calling for it so long after it was gone. Sometimes I feel something like that, between my mom and me. That I'm the daughter she keeps calling for so long after she's been gone.

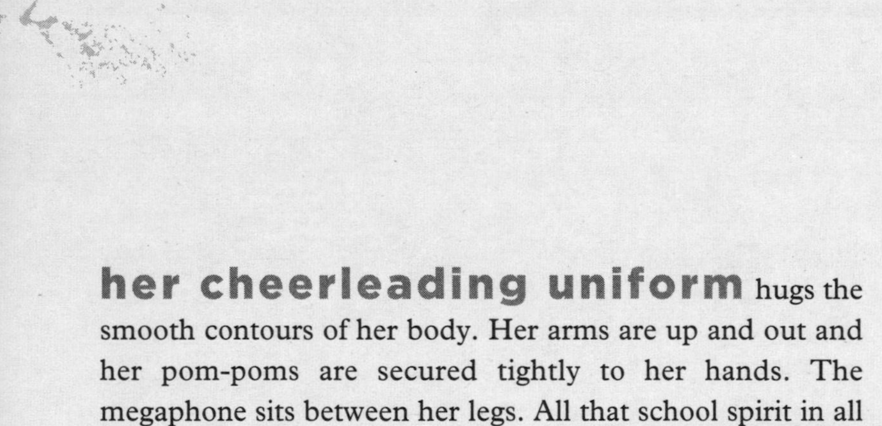

her cheerleading uniform hugs the smooth contours of her body. Her arms are up and out and her pom-poms are secured tightly to her hands. The megaphone sits between her legs. All that school spirit in all that girl and in a single day, they wasted her. She inspires nothing now.

I'm making my way to homeroom when Brock's shoulder clips mine and sends me staggering back. The sharp hurt of it radiates out, promising a bruise. He whirls around and I've got so many variations of *fuck you* to throw in his face but I swallow them all when he smiles at me with every single one of his teeth. He glances at Alek beside him. Alek holds his hand out, signaling Brock to stop, so Brock does. Brock shoves both his hands in his pockets and makes himself look almost conversational.

"Hey, Brock," Alek says loudly, as a group of students pass. They slow. "You hear about how my dad pulled Grey over yesterday night? She was drunk."

Another few students come down the opposite side of the hall and they stop for this. Brock raises his voice. "No, Alek. I *didn't* hear about how your dad pulled Grey over yesterday night. You say she was drunk?"

"Yeah." Alek steps toward me. "Feet together, hands at your sides, right, Grey? That what he told you to do because you were so smashed?"

"I wasn't—"

"Swerving all over the road? That's what Dan Conway says, and he's the one who called your sorry ass in." Alek's eyes gleam. "Like father, like daughter, right? Meanwhile *my* dad had to waste his time seeing you home, make sure you didn't kill anyone."

It's amazing how bad you can make the truth sound. As long as you keep it partially recognizable when you spit it out, a crowd will eat it up without even thinking about how hard you chewed on it first. They're all rabid for Wake Lake, all of them, and I'm the bone that's going to keep their mouths wet while they wait. I let them have it because some things you can't do anything about. So it's bell to bell, class to class. They look at me, whispering those words that came straight from Alek's mouth. *Like father, like daughter*. At lunch, I pass a guy who calls me *Jane* and then immediately apologizes with a shrug of his shoulders.

"Sorry," he says. "All you bitches look the same."

By the time the last bell rings, three of my nails are chipping.

When I first started with the nail polish, I didn't know anything about it. The red would flake off before the day was half out, my nails would split and, over time, they turned yellow. And then I learned. Removing polish is a process too.

It's less of one than the manicure itself, but still. I open my bedroom window and lay everything I need on my desk before I begin. Scrub brush, remover, a bowl and cotton balls, Q-tips, nail strengthener, and a piece of cardboard to protect the finish of my desk.

I wash my hands in the bathroom and start with the scrub brush, working it back and forth under my nails until they feel clean. Next, I unroll a cotton ball and tear it into fingernail-sized pieces. I pour the remover into the bowl and dip the bits of cotton—one at a time—into it and then set them onto the nails of my left hand. I give a few minutes to let the remover do its job, to eat away at the color. When those minutes have passed, I press into the cotton and swipe the polish off. I take a Q-tip dipped in remover for the edges because I never get it all. Repeat with the right hand. I apply the strengthener and wait for it to set. After enough time has passed, I clear off my desk and get everything else I need to finish the job. Cleanser and dehydrator, base coat, polish, top coat.

A ceramic file this time too, to round out edges.

My dad used to say makeup was a shallow girl's sport, but it's not. It's armor. Leon wasn't at Swan's last night. Had to trade shifts with someone and the day before that, the diner was too busy and we were two girls short. I didn't even get my break. The most he and I got to exchange were orders. Every now and then, though, he'd give me this smile I didn't see him giving anyone else. I brush a thin layer of red onto my last nail, and wait for it to dry before I reach for the top coat. I apply the top coat and then I'm ready.

before the last bell, Principal Diaz comes over the PA and tells us to *be safe, be good, be sober.* The impossible dream. Everyone's humming with the excitement of the lake ahead but if they took a minute to think about it, they'd realize they could get drunk and fuck things up anywhere. Everywhere. But I guess it's not the same. Not as epic.

It's good for me, though. In a few hours, there will be stolen kisses and fights and after the weekend, everybody will be talking about someone else—at least for a little while. It makes me feel some kind of lightness and that's nice. I hold on to it until I get to Swan's and then I let Leon take its place.

"Break later?"

He asks it as soon as I come in and in that moment before I put my apron on, I swear he can tell what's different underneath my shirt. It makes me feel warm and weird and maybe not as ready for this as I thought—but I'm wearing the pink bra tonight, either way.

I reach behind me, knot my apron strings, and nod.

"Oh, to be young again," Holly says, watching us.

"You're not old," Leon tells her.

"You're my favorite, you keep that up."

It's the kind of night that's slow and impatient. No one's got anywhere they need to be but they all want to be somewhere else, so they're not happy. If my dad taught me anything, it's that you can't make people like that happy. You just have to survive them as best you can. I deal with a woman determined not to tip me no matter how fast I bring out her food and how wide I smile. A man who asks for another waitress when he sees the healing scabs on my legs. An elderly woman who requests Holly, but who refuses to move to her station to be served by her. A boy who sends his burger back four times just because he feels like it.

By then, my break with Leon is staring me down. I glance back at the kitchen. The door swings open and I glimpse him at the grill. His hands. I go to the women's bathroom and touch up my lipstick and then I think I could be ready for whatever is going to happen with him next. I wash my hands and step back into the diner.

What I thought was the diner.

This is the place where truckers stop to fill their bellies before they hit the road again, where Ibis College kids come to soak up the alcohol after drinking at Aker's farm; this is the place where the booths are green and the floor is a grimy gray linoleum and the walls are covered in nostalgia pieces and the radio only plays country music. This place, where I work five nights a week and no one knows my name—is not that place anymore.

Across from the wall with the vintage Coke sign, sitting small in a booth, is a girl. Her long blond hair reflects the golden light above, making it look lusher, and the rest of the diner duller. She's so different from everyone here, so immaculate, she's impossible to miss.

Penny.

She turns her head my way. I stay perfectly still, like she couldn't see me if I was still. What if she's not alone? I look to the window, my gaze sweeping the parking lot for Alek's Escalade or Brock's busted-up Camaro but I only find her white Vespa. A gift from her parents to make the divorce easier, like that made any sense.

Out of the corner of my eye, I catch Holly making her way over and if I know anything, it's that I *don't* want Holly at Penny's booth. It's her station, but she can't have it. I rip my order pad out of my pocket and pull the pencil from behind my ear. I know I'll get hell for it later, but it's the better hell. I cut Holly out. I go to Penny, plant my feet in front of her. She stares at me calmly. I smooth my apron with my trembling hand, trying to figure out how I'm going to do this. How do I do this? *It's your job.*

So I do it like it's my job.

"Can I take your order?"

My voice wavers. I hate myself for it. And there are all these questions in my head, demanding answers. How did she find me out? Her mom? She spends her weekends in Ibis with her mom, but this isn't the kind of place a Young would eat.

Penny picks up the single page, laminated menu and pretends to look it over.

She says, "I'll start with a drink."

I'm supposed to ask her what kind she wants because that's my job and I need to do this like it's my job, but seeing her here, in my space—all I know is I want to hurt her until she's out of it. She asks for a Coke. That's all. I write it down like an idiot.

When I head back to get it, Holly corners me and she's pissed.

"What the hell are you doing, Romy?"

"I'm sorry," I say quickly. "You can take the next two of mine. I just—I thought it was someone I knew. I'm *really* sorry, Holly."

"Even if it was, you could've asked—"

"I know. I'll never do that to you again. I wasn't thinking."

"You better not."

"I know. I'm sorry."

Holly steps into the kitchen, shaking her head and muttering to herself. I disrespected her and it's not okay but it is so small compared to what I'm up against right now. I grab the Coke and head back. The country song playing in the background is blurring into one long, sad note and when I reach Penny's booth, I'm shaking with anger I can do nothing about. I set the glass down, spilling some of the drink onto the table. I watch a little of it waterfall onto the floor. I take a rag from my pocket and sop it up quickly.

"What do you want to eat?"

"Nothing. I want to talk to you."

"What?"

"I want to talk to you and then I'll leave."

"Yeah, well, that's not going to happen, Penny, so I guess I'll get the check—" She grabs my arm. I try to jerk away but she holds fast. Touching me without permission. There should be a death penalty for that. I watch her pink nails dig into my skin but I don't feel it. "Let go."

She says, "Please."

I can't remember Penny ever saying *please* to me, not even when we were friends. Why waste time on a word like *please* when you're going to get what you want anyway? It's not right coming out of her mouth. It's so wrong, some part of me thinks she shouldn't have to say it, ever.

"How did you know I work here?"

"Grey, we've always known."

She says this and I feel some small part of me leaving.

She lets go of my arm.

"Sit down," she says and I do, but not because she asked me to—because I need to.

I ease into the booth and the back of my thighs instantly stick to the vinyl. The diner sounds swell, people eating, talking, dishes clattering in the kitchen, the sizzle of the grill. I don't look at her. Don't say anything.

"So is it true?" she asks. "About the DUI?"

It forces eye contact. Maybe this close she's not as perfect as I've said. Maybe she's got flaws or maybe I need to see them so badly right now, I'm pretending. Maybe that's a sunburn across her nose. Maybe her lips are dry and maybe her skin is flaking a little, just under her chin. She chews her bottom lip.

"I know it's not true," she admits. "And I didn't know about the underwear." I give her a look that doesn't believe it. She concedes: "I knew Brock got Tina to take it for Alek, but I didn't know what they were planning."

"What do you want, Penny?"

She smiles but it's not really a smile, just a twitch that briefly takes both corners of her mouth up. She brings her hand to her forehead like a thought wants out but she's not sure of it enough to say. A memory skips across my mind, lays itself over this moment. Her, excited, about to change lives.

The Turners' house. It's going to be you, me, Alek, and . . .

Not here.

"Shouldn't you be at the lake?"

You, me, Alek and . . .

"Kellan," she says, like she can see inside me. I flinch. His name is hard enough to think, but spoken aloud it's a weapon. That hard *Kel*—a knife going in sharp and easy the less resistance it has to meet—*lan*.

"No," I say.

"I—"

"No." I say it louder because she must not have heard it if she's still talking.

"Alek took me to Godwit for my birthday. We stayed with Kellan," she says, and I stare at the little beads of condensation slowly dripping down the outside of her glass while her voice—her voice. "We went to a club he likes, Sparrow. He and Alek went to get drinks. There was this girl—she came up to me." She pauses. "She saw me with Kellan. She told me it wasn't safe to be alone with him. She wouldn't say why, but the look on her face . . ."

Less real, I think. I need this to be less real.

"The look on yours."

It's not—my face. I shake my head, my eyes still on the glass. No—no. Fuck her. Fuck her for saying that. You can't just see something like that on someone's face.

You can't.

"You didn't report it. You can still report it," she says and I reach under the table, dig my nails into one of the scabs on my knees until the wet tells me it's open. "I looked it up. You still have time. If you do it—something would have to happen."

I almost laugh, but my voice has left me. The chance of that happening is as dead as the girl Penny's talking about and that's what I really want to say to her. *She died, Penny, you know that? You know all the ways you can kill a girl?*

God, there are so many.

"I wasn't even going to tell you. But then I saw you in the hall picking at that mannequin and I—" She looks away. "I can't make it right. I can't make it right with you, Romy. I know that. But what happens if another girl—"

"Then get *her* to report it," I say.

I have to get out of this booth. I need to get out of this booth and do my job but I can't move. Penny waits. She waits and I don't move and I don't say anything and then she goes into her pocket and tosses a few bills on the table. More than enough to cover the order. She slides out of the booth and I sit there stupidly, staring at the crumpled money.

"What are you doing, Romy?"

I look up and Holly is looking down at me, like I've done so much that's wrong tonight. I open my mouth but nothing comes out and she says, *you can't stay in this booth* like I didn't know that. I stare at my hands, at my nails until they blur red.

"Romy," Holly says. She sounds different now. "Are you all right?"

I move out of the booth so fast, she has to step back. I push through the door and I run into the parking lot. The thin roar of Penny's Vespa engine reaches my ear.

I watch her leave.

NOW

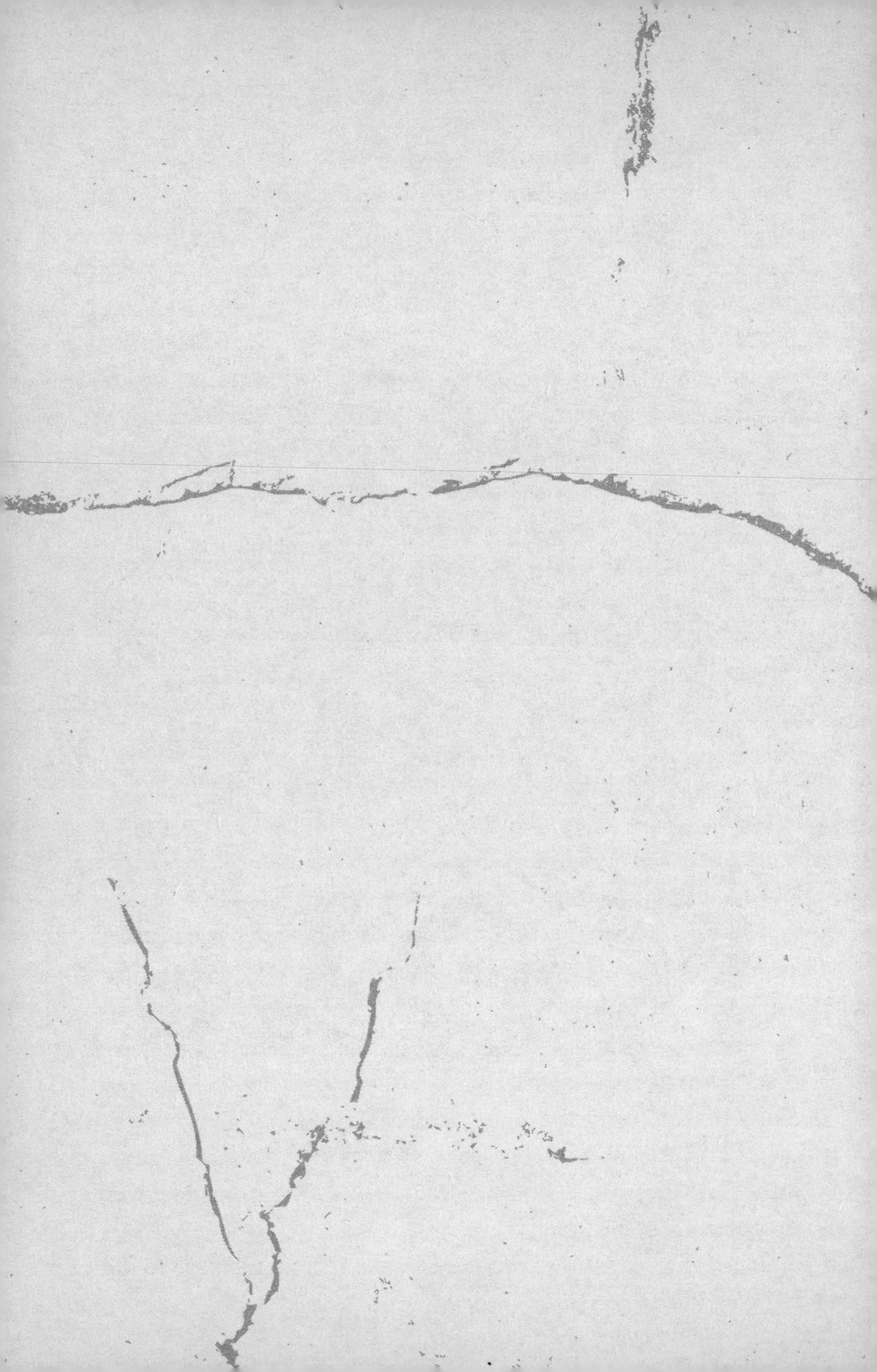

a wolf is at the door.

He's not wearing his uniform. It's strange, seeing the sheriff not in his uniform but *this doesn't have to be anything official, yet. I'm just here today, parent to parent.*

Her mother. Doesn't know what to do, hasn't known what to do since she found her daughter in the shower, under the running water, still drunk and crying, babbling the truth to the tiles. That next morning, her mother, in tears, asked about it.

Romy, you said something last night. I need to be sure of what you told me.

A truck bed and a boy.

A text, later, from her best friend: YOU DIDN'T DO ANYTHING STUPID, DID YOU?

Devastation roots her family if denial is not moving them forward. Her father disappeared, couldn't handle it, and she stayed inside with her mother, trying to figure out what they needed to do and how they needed to do it. She's any girl and they're any family, but this boy. He's special and his family is special.

And now, a wolf at the door.

So let him in.

Paul was at the bar the other night and laid out some pretty serious accusations. You know how word travels around here. He said my son raped your daughter. And then, as they process this one thing, her father (sleeping last night off upstairs) taking it to the world before she knew if that was what she wanted, the sheriff says, *of course, no one believes it but that still doesn't mean he can go around saying it. I want to know why he's saying it.*

God, they are so flustered, so sick, so looking for direction, any direction, they invite him in, they sit him at the kitchen table, they let the conversation start out with coffee, with *one sugar or two* and do nothing when it moves to the crush she'd been nursing on his son these months and *you can't deny you were attracted to him.*

No, she can't, is what her silence says back to him. She can't deny that for months she imagined his son's hands on her body, in that truck, in a bed, anywhere. She pictured it over and over except in her head, she wanted it and her eyes were open.

She hates her heart, that misguided organ in her chest.

Why didn't it warn her?

You were drunk at my house, Friday night. I've talked to my sons and I have talked to Penny. No one else was drinking. You're underage. I could pursue it, if I wanted. But I won't.

Because he's just here today, parent to parent.

Thank you, her mother says, without thinking.

He says, *they say you chase after him. That you wore an outfit, hoping that you would catch his attention. Short skirt, skimpy shirt.* They? And, reaching into his pocket, unfolding a piece of paper, *tell me about what you wrote in this e-mail here:*

Penny, I want him. I dream about him.

This cuts a thousand times, her e-mail in his hands. There's only one place he could have gotten it. The betrayal is more than she thinks she can bear; the one girl who believed in her, doesn't believe her.

You know what they're saying? They're saying Paul's telling people my son raped your daughter to get back at Helen for firing him. Now maybe they fooled around and maybe she was a little too drunk at the time, but rape? You can't just call it something like that.

Then what do you call it?

He says, *nobody believes it. They think it's ugly. I think it's ugly.*

He says, *I hope we can get this sorted out before you make it worse for yourselves.*

He says, *but I want to understand, Romy, so you tell me what you think happened.*

And it's not that she tells him it didn't happen, it's

that by the time he asks, she no longer has a language of her own. But that's enough. It always is.

Every time I close my eyes, there's a memory. Every time I open them, I'm still on the road. I'll never get off this road, not alone. But I'm not alone, I remember. The footsteps stopped. A shadow across my body. Maybe someone nice—but I'm too afraid to look.

"You with me?"

Dirt against my hands. I'm so heavy with heat, my head struggles against it, tries to tell me important things like *this is not a safe place* and *leave*.

But I can't leave if I don't know how to stand.

"You with me?"

I don't know what that means. I don't know anything except this, the air—too dry—the small movements I'm making—hurt—the sun—hot—the sky—it makes me dizzy. I finally squint up at the face above and am relieved to find, not a wolf, but a woman, just like me.

Until I see the uniform.

"romy grey, you hearing me?"

The deputy crouches, setting a bottle of water in front of me. It teeters on the ground, the water sloshing against its plastic sides before settling still as anything, as still as the—lake.

"Oh," I whisper. My first word in this after.

I try to make sense of her, the deputy. It's hard to focus at first but when I do, I see brown eyes, curly red hair, a smattering of freckles across a pointed nose. Leanne Howard. Morris Howard's daughter—he teaches at the elementary school. She's just shy of thirty.

"You okay?" she asks, but I don't think she'd ask if I was.

I stare at her. "You got a lot of people worried about you, you know that? How'd you get all the way out here?"

Too many questions.

I want—Mom. I reach into my pocket for my phone and only find my lipstick. My phone is gone but I had it last night. I know I did. I look down at myself, at the uneven alignment of my buttons and my heart seizes but—wait. I did that. I did that before Leanne's car pulled up, remember . . . I did that because—my shirt was open. And something's wrong underneath . . . I remember that too. My bra. I feel it now, undone.

Oh.

"Hey," Leanne says and she looks past me, over my shoulder. "You alone? How'd you get out here? Can you tell me how you got out here?" My gaze travels from my buttons to my bare, scraped legs, worse than they were from track. "*Romy.* How'd you get out here?"

"The lake," I mumble. It comes to me sickly fast, in flashes. Penny. Leaving the diner, biking the highway. The path to the lake—the path. And my feet on it. And the music, music thrumming, bass thumping, *thump, thump, thump,* I squeeze my eyes shut but that thumping, the pulse pounding in my head, it goes on. The lake. There. I was there. And lights and eyes were on me, and just after the path opened to the water, it cuts to—nothing.

I reach for more but there's nothing.

I was at the lake.

I'm not anymore.

"Are you hurt?"

I need to be standing. No more . . . no more questions before I'm standing.

I bring my arm to my mouth and cough into the crook of my elbow before I press my hands to the ground. I get to my knees and bite back the urge to hiss at my raw palms meeting earth. I *am* hurt. But that has to be where the hurt stops.

"Your mother called us, said you were missing."

Leanne offers her hand but I ignore it. I find my feet on my own and then I'm standing but I don't feel like I'm standing.

"My mom—"

"You alone? Penny with you?" she asks. I shake my head and this is a mistake. The world tries to throw me off. Leanne reaches for me. I step back. My body isn't working the way I need it to, to get out of this. "Come sit in the car. I'll get the cold air going. I have to call this in and then we'll get you to a hospital, get you checked out—"

"*No.*" I'm not letting anyone look at me before I look at myself. "No—" Leanne tries to insist, *you need it, Romy, you need to be checked out,* and all I can say is, *no, no, no* and the word gets louder the more she makes me say it, and for once someone finally hears it coming out of my mouth. She says, "Okay, *okay*—Romy, just—I said *okay*—"

She grabs my arm. I stare at her hand on my skin. She lets go. I put my hand where hers was, aware of the parts of me that are covered and the parts that aren't.

I need the places that aren't covered to be—covered.

"Do you know where you are?" She grabs the bottle of water off the ground, holds it out to me. "Drink that. You need it."

I look around, wait for the *here* of this place to reach me, this place I ended up, but the road says nothing. The trees on either side of it say more of the same.

"It's Taraldson Road. You're about thirty miles from Godwit—"

"Grebe—" No. Godwit? "But—"

"You know how you got out here?"

Godwit. Grebe. Wake Lake—did I . . . how—

I'm thirsty, I'm too thirsty to think. I take the water from her and she looks relieved I'm doing that much. I unscrew the cap and drink slowly, small sips. It's lukewarm but it brings me back a little, just enough to tell her again I'm not going to the hospital in a voice I almost believe.

She crosses her arms. "So what I'm getting from you is you blacked out, you don't know how you got like this, and you don't think you should go to a hospital?"

The question goes bone deep. *Got like this.* This. My thoughts turn into vultures and those vultures circle, one ugly possibility after the other. What happened to me? I can't—

I can't think about that right now.

"You know how it is at the lake. What—" I force a laugh and it sounds so wrong. "Take me to the hospital for a hangover? Turner would love that."

She hesitates, just enough for me to know I have her. Rookie.

"You guys don't have anything better to do today, really?" I ask. "I'm telling you, Leanne. He's going to hate it if you waste any time on me, you know that."

"Well, how about I ask him, huh? I have to call this in."

She walks to the Explorer and I feel like I'm slowly coming online, all the things she's said to me so far hitting me a second time.

"What about Penny?"

She doesn't answer, so I stay where I am while she calls Sheriff Turner, calls me in. My bra shifts in a way it shouldn't, itching at my skin, and the steady parts of me, what little reserve I have left, disappear. My eyes burn. I blink. After a minute, Leanne comes back, uncertain.

"I'm taking you home. The sheriff's going to meet us there—"

"Why is he going to meet us there?"

"Come on," she says. I stare at the water in my hand and I can't find it in me to move until she says, "Your mom's sick about this, so let's not keep her waiting."

Oh, that's a magic word. *Mom.* Okay, let's not keep Mom waiting. Leanne lets me sit in the front. Hauls herself in. The engine rumbles on and the car rolls forward. She tells me to buckle up and I do. The seat belt feels too tight and I can't breathe against it. I close my eyes.

"Still with me?" She sounds nervous. I open my eyes. "Say something and let me know it or I *will* take you to the hospital. I don't care what my orders are." She pauses, mutters, "I should be taking you there, anyway."

But she won't. Everyone bows to the Turners.

Thank God, just this once.

"It's hot."

My eyes drift to the clock on the dash. Eleven. Eleven in the morning. I've lost—too many hours. Leanne reaches over and turns the air-conditioning on. I lean into it and wait for it to turn me to ice, but I don't feel anything but hot and caught between the road I ended up on and Grebe, somewhere still ahead of us. I pull at my seat belt, trying to figure out what it is my body wants. It wants out of this car, but it's too late for that. I push my legs out, press my feet against the floor. I need home. I have to go home. I need to see myself.

My teeth sink into a cut on my lip that I don't know how it got there. This feels like . . . hungover, but—worse. Because I don't remember drinking, but . . . I rest my hands in my lap, my palms up. The scrapes remind me of when I was small, running down the street, tripping on my shoelaces, skidding across the sidewalk and my dad—was there.

I stare at my legs. The space between them.

i can't see myself.

My head rests against the window, the side-view mirror of the SUV so grimy, there's not a hint of me through it. I need to see myself.

The sheriff's Explorer is parked in front of the house.

Todd and Mom wait on the steps. Turner is close, but not, and didn't we just do this? No, not really. What I thought was bad then is nothing compared to now. Mom brings her hand to her mouth when she sees me. She's in yesterday's clothes and they've gotten too big for her overnight. Todd too, still in the same shirt and jeans he was wearing when I said good-bye to him, before I left for Swan's.

They'll see it before I do, whatever's on me. I'll be the last to know.

I open the door and get out slowly. My legs are rubbery, like they haven't walked enough or they've walked too much. I count steps forward, trying to assure myself the ground is there, crossing over from sidewalk to walkway, my feet on vines.

Home.

Mom hurries to me, taking in everything I can't hide. She reaches for my face, lightly brushing her fingers over my cheek before pulling me to her, the weight of this reunion half-lost on me because I didn't even know I was gone. Turner's eyes drift over me, whatever he's seeing, and he frowns. He turns his attention beyond us.

"You say you found her where?" he asks.

"Taraldson Road," Leanne answers.

"Okay, Howard. Thank you. I've got it from here."

The sound of his voice is so awful, more awful than it's ever been. It makes me want to be sick. Mom whispers in my ear. *Let's get you inside, baby, come on,* and I must look bad. I must not look right. My legs itch to run, to find a place I can deal with this on my own. On the way up the steps, Todd reaches for me. Puts his hand to my arm and squeezes it. Their relief is more than I can take right now. I need to see myself.

Leanne is gone by the time we're inside. I head for the stairs, reach the banister and grip it tight, pull myself up that first step when Mom says, "Romy, where are you going?"

"I have to . . ." I can see the bathroom door from here. I just need to be behind one closed door, so I can see myself. "I have to . . ." I look back at them and the three of them look at me like they don't know what I am. I can't tell them what I need. "I don't feel well."

"Okay." Mom steps forward and rests her hand over mine, her touch warm on my warm skin. "You have to talk to the sheriff first." I shake my head. "Romy, you have to. I'm sure it won't take long and then you can go to bed—isn't that right, Levi?"

"We'll see."

"Please," I whisper. She flinches. It hurts her. It hurts her because she can't give it to me and I never ask her for anything. "Can't it wait until tomorrow or—"

"No," Sheriff Turner says. "This is important."

"I'm sorry," Mom whispers, guiding me from the stairs. No choice. I have no choice. She leads me to the kitchen and sits me at the table and I rest my head in my hands while they talk coffee, coffee and *no, thank you, Alice.* The perfunctory politeness of it makes me want to break—everything. I don't want this. I want to see myself.

"What's he doing here?" I ask and I'm met with silence and the silence makes me too aware of my body, and I can feel my head trying to assess hurts I can't see, of whether or not certain places—if they—if.

"I need to ask you some questions, Romy, and then I'll be on my way."

He pulls out the chair across the table from mine. He sits. I don't look at him.

"You hurt?" he asks and I shake my head because he's the last person I'd take anything like that to now. And it works out because he doesn't want me hurt in a way he's got to worry about. Sure enough: "So just a little roughed up and a lot hungover. How'd you end up on Taraldson Road?" I don't say anything, can't think of anything to say. The impulse is to lie, but I'm working with so much nothing, I can't. And I don't know what the truth is. He clears his throat. "Alice."

"Romy," Mom says.

I stare at the table. "I don't remember."

"You remember being with anyone?"

"No."

"What's the last thing you do remember?"

"Being at the lake."

The path, the lights, in my head again. Bodies at the lake. The memory dissolves slowly, can't hold itself to an entire night . . .

"You left work, middle of your shift without telling anyone, to go to Wake Lake?"

"Holly said you ran out," Mom says. "She said you seemed upset."

They're going to know this at Swan's. Of course they will. Mom would've called them first, asking where I was. I have to make this something I can take back to Swan's.

I have to make this something that's not as terrible as it is.

"I had a bad customer. I went outside to cool off and then I kept going."

"You kept going."

"Biggest party of the year," I say. It's weak.

"So you stayed at the party and decided to get drunk," he says and I recoil because I don't know how he'd know that, if I don't. Mom and Todd, they don't look shocked, so . . . they knew it too. "We have quite a few accounts of you at Wake Lake, that you were extremely intoxicated—"

"What is this about?" I ask because I don't want to hear that. I don't care if they know, but I don't want to be in the room with them, hearing that. "I don't understand—"

"Penny didn't come home last night, either," Mom says.

I lean back in my seat, letting it sink in but I don't know how news like this is supposed to sink in. I don't know how to receive it. I swallow, bring my hand just to my mouth. "She didn't?"

"Morning after the biggest party of the year is always the biggest mess. Kids, they get wasted, they wander, they come back and I've got to sort out the real emergencies from the rest of it." Turner doesn't bother hiding his contempt. "Sorry to break it to you, but Jack Phelps holds the record. He made it all the way to Godwit blackout drunk, his turn at the lake."

"Jesus, Levi," Todd says. "I'm sure she was going for the record. Should we talk about what *you* did when it was your turn?"

"Bartlett, there's no need—"

"No, there *wouldn't* be if you'd do your goddamn job. You didn't even *start* looking for her until the Youngs called you this morning about Penny, and then you had to. I was out there *all* night doing your fucking work—"

"And it was *still* one of *my* people brought her home," Turner snaps, his face cycling through every shade of red there is. Todd huffs out a breath and for a second, it looks like he'll leave, but he stays. The sheriff turns to me. "It's like this. Two girls were reported missing on the same night. One still is. I'm going to want to find out whether there's a connection there so we can start narrowing down where to look, you understand? Is there any possibility Penny was with you at any point or is there anything you might be able to tell us that would help?"

I think of her in the booth, at the diner.

What she said to me.

You speak against a Turner, you best pray you never need help in this town.

"Where was she last seen? Was it with me?"

"At the lake," Turner says. "But not with you, not that we know, so far."

After she saw me.

"At the lake," I say.

After.

So I don't have to tell them what she was doing before.

"I don't remember anything, but I doubt I was with her. We're not friends."

"If you do remember, you need to tell me," Turner says. "But, right now, it's looking like you got drunk, scared the shit out of your mom, and tied up a good part of my department for the morning."

"Yeah, that's what it looks like," I say. My stomach turns. I swallow hard. "Can I please go?"

"I'll do you a favor, Romy, because I can tell you need to sleep it off. I'll let this be enough for now, but I'll still need you to come down to the station tomorrow and go over this with us, if she's still missing." The chair screeches as he pushes out from the table. He stands slowly, like his holster is too heavy. He's known Penny since she was a little girl. "And it's damned foolish, getting as drunk as people say you were. I ever catch you at it, I *will* write you up."

"See yourself out, Levi," Todd says.

It goes quiet while we wait for him to walk the length of the hall, for the slam of the screen door to signal his exit. I pull at my skirt, under the table.

I need to see.

"Romy," Mom says and I stop.

remember.

I keep my head down, let my gaze wander, let it skim over the floor tiles and walls, to my hands, to my white knuckles gripping the edge of the sink counter, to the sink itself, to the water slowly dripping from the leaky tap. I press my finger against its opening, stem the flow. I hear every breath pass through my lips and vaguely, beyond that, Mom in my room.

My body speaks to my missing hours, but I don't understand what it's saying. I just need the night to come back, that's all. Just one single night. *Remember.* Just let me remember. It's there, inside me, and I only have to remember it. I tap my teeth together and close my eyes.

I raise my head and I open them.

My bottom lip is swollen, puffy and cut, a sour pain. My right cheek, there's a bruise. No, the road. It has to be the road. The road is on my face. I turn the faucet on, hold my hands underneath the cold stream of water, soothe the sore skin. I wet my cheek and rub. It aches, but it doesn't come off.

A bruise.

My hand drifts slowly from my face to the collar of my shirt. I pull at it and it's so heavy, this is all too heavy, that I close my eyes again. Feel the awkward hold of my bra around me, but loose. Drunk. Said I was drunk. I want that memory, I want the memory of that stupid—*stupid*—girl. Me, drinking. How little did it take this time?

Stupid.

I'm missing two buttons.

The last two.

No. No, no . . .

My fingers fiddle with their absence until I have to believe they're gone. Two of the buttons on my shirt are gone and my bra is undone.

I lower my hands and then I unbutton the rest of my shirt slowly. When it's halfway open, I see a deep red stain on my stomach—blood? Is it—my fingers turn frantic, make quick work of the buttons left and I pull off my shirt and my bra curtains apart.

My trembling hand moves toward my abdomen, hovering above the red on me, the red words on me. Not in blood, not dried blood. Not that kind of red. I press my finger to one of the letters and my hand jerks back, like I've been stung. I fumble in my pockets until I find the black tube. I rip the cap off and twist the bottom until the lipstick appears, its tip flattened and ruined. I let it clatter into the sink and stumble, the back of my legs hitting the edge of the tub. My reflection still in the mirror. The red on my body—letters. Letters on my skin, reversed in the glass, turning themselves into this—

RAPE ME

I bring my fingers to my stomach, digging into the skin until I feel red under my red nails, red, my red, me, until what I feel is something outside of me, until it's something I've done to myself. I move away from the sink, my hands in my hair, room tilting, trying to get a sense of myself. I lift my skirt, clutching at the thin material and I bite my lip until I taste blood but my throat is too tight to swallow, so it sits on my tongue, heavy and coppery. My cheeks are damp. I drop my skirt and wipe at my face. I don't want to do this. I don't want to do it.

Knock on the door. "Romy?"

I take a shuddering breath and pull my skirt up until I see my pink underwear. I don't want do this. I pull it down. Slowly. Clean.

I swallow the blood in my mouth.

"Romy?"

I slip my hands between my legs and my fingers find my tampon string easily and my legs are weak with it still being there—it's still there. I stare at the light overhead until it's all I see and then I look away until the world burns itself back.

"I'm going to take a shower," I say.

"If you need anything, let me know?"

"Okay."

I take the old tampon out and get rid of it. I slip out of my bra numbly, let it fall to the ground next to my underwear.

All that's left are the words on my stomach.

I turn to the tub, my hands struggling with the faucet, trying to get the water hot enough, then pull the diverter out. I step in and lower myself slowly until I'm sitting. I reach for the soap and I scrub it across my stomach hard until the lather turns pink, until the pink turns white, until it disappears.

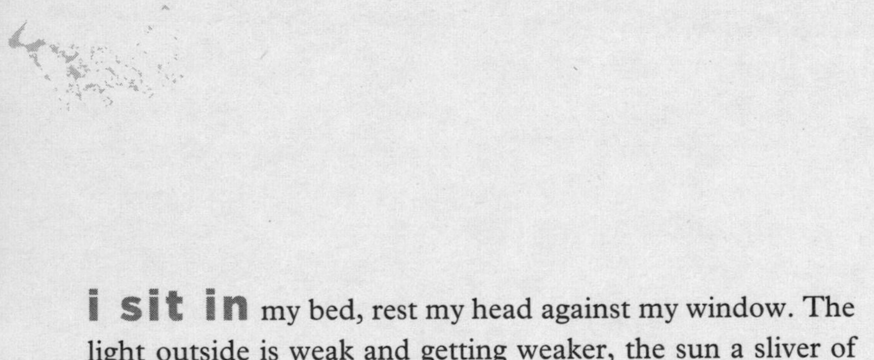

i sit in my bed, rest my head against my window. The light outside is weak and getting weaker, the sun a sliver of pink on the horizon. Still the same day. It's not done with me yet.

On my nightstand, a half-empty bottle of water. Mom wanted to take me to our family doctor, at the very least, and I got vicious about it, told her we've seen worse hangovers or had she forgotten. After that, she pulled the blanket over my legs, told me to sleep. I slept and I woke up and when I did, all I could think was *wake up.* But this is it now.

My bedroom door opens.

Mom slips in, hesitates when she sees I'm awake.

"Did Penny come home yet?" I ask.

"Haven't heard," she says and it's in my gut, this strange mix of shock and longing. My head tells me I still hate Penny but my body must've wanted a different answer.

Mom sits on my bed, moves back until she can put her arm around me and pull me close. She rests her head against the top of mine. I listen to her heartbeat and I think of Penny, if she's still out there or if she ended up like me, if she's on a road somewhere, waiting for her turn to be found. It doesn't make sense. Penny is not a lost girl.

"You know what the hardest part of being a parent is?" Mom asks after a minute. "It's not being able to . . ."

She doesn't finish. She doesn't have to. She's said this to me before. It's this: it's not being able to protect your kid from The Bad Stuff. To stand by, helpless, while they're suffering and not being able to do a damn thing about it. But that's life and life happens. Only one thing's going to stop it.

"If I were the Youngs, I don't know what I'd do. You were gone, Romy. I lost my mind. I can't even tell you how it felt to sit here and not know where you were or if you were okay . . ."

"I'm sorry."

"I thought you just . . . had enough of everything. And then I thought—of course she would. Of course she would. Why wouldn't she? I could've done so much better."

"Don't start that again," I whisper.

But once she starts, she can't stop. "I kept trying to justify it. It's better to have two parents, even if one . . . isn't much of one. And I'd see you shouldering it all. You just accepted it. That's so unfair."

"It's not that simple."

It couldn't have been. It was complicated. We were all so much more complicated than that because if we weren't—

Then it should have been so much easier.

"Maybe," she says. "But it shouldn't have been like that. And now you just take everything on and you don't ask me to take it from you, even when you can barely stand it. You scare me, Romy. You take the car and you just go. You get drunk at Wake Lake and picked up off a road and you don't remember anything about it."

For her, I should paint a party, a crowd, music, stars in the sky, a girl dancing in the middle of it all, wanted. Maybe she's drunk but maybe in this version—people looked after her. Except even my mother wouldn't fall for that. Not me, not in this town.

"Romy." The way she says it, I know what question is coming next and I want to be gone from here before she asks it. "If anything happened to you, please tell me."

"I don't know what you mean."

"You were in the bathroom for a long time."

"Don't—" I force it out. "Don't make it into something it wasn't."

"But you'd tell me? You would tell me if . . . something happened to you. If you woke up on that road, and something wasn't right? Because I'd help you . . . I'd . . ."

No. I nod and twist away from her, because I can feel it, the guilt she's carrying and I don't want to feel it anymore. I don't want to feel anything.

"You really don't know how you got on that road? Penny wasn't with you?"

"Don't make me say it again," I say.

"We have to take you down to the sheriff's tomorrow," she says. "You're going to have to say it again then . . . unless something comes to you. Maybe something will come to you."

"Maybe," I say.

leanne howard calls while I'm asleep, tells Mom they received new information ruling out a connection between me and Penny but she wasn't at liberty to say what it was. I want to know what it was. I want to know why one girl came back and one didn't. Todd says Grebe is leveled by Penny's disappearance and when I look out the window, our street is quieter than usual. Everyone stayed inside their houses, kept there, silent by the shock of it.

"They're doing a hell of a search," Todd tells us. "I saw Dan Conway at the drug store this morning and he said they're covering ground and air—getting a helicopter. There were a few reporters and news cameras trolling around the lake too. Penny was supposed to end up in Ibis at her mother's house and she never got there."

I pick at some loose threads on the couch and try to picture it. Penny on her way to her mother's in the dark, and me, headed in the opposite direction under that same sky.

I hope she's still missing by Monday.

Another one of those thoughts in my head, so easy it has to have come directly from my heart like *I hate you* and *I hope it's not a girl.* I hope she's missing. What kind of thought is that to have? It's not that I don't want her to be found, but I want my moment to expire first. I want everyone so distracted at the start of the week no one's thinking about me, how I was at the lake, however I was at the lake, because I don't want to find it out from them. At all.

But if it's bad, I'll find it out from them no matter what.

"How Dan finds this stuff out, I'll never know," Mom says from the kitchen. I wonder if Dan Conway's heard anything about me.

"Didn't I tell you? His son, Joe, works at the sheriff's department now," he says. "Just makes coffee by the sound of it, but they're paying him well to do it."

"Joe Conway? They're letting him work there?"

"Well, come on. The Turners always look after their sycophants," Todd says. "No matter how goddamn stupid they are."

Todd eases himself into the recliner across from me, wincing. His back is hurting him bad and he won't say it's because of all the time he spent in the car, searching for a girl who isn't even his daughter. I should apologize to him, but I can't bring myself to do it. I ask him if he needs anything instead.

"Nope. You feel okay?"

"I'm fine."

He looks at me skeptically. "You two were best friends."

"Were," I say.

But I keep my eyes off him when I say it. My hand dips into my pocket for my phone out of habit, just so I can push buttons, maybe get Todd to stop looking at me, but then I remember it's gone. Missing. Anger washes over me, more anger than a lost phone deserves, considering everything else that's happened this weekend. Still. It makes me want to go somewhere and wreck something with my bare hands.

"Romy, get the door?" Mom asks.

"What?"

"Someone's here."

I glance at Todd and he's eyeing me still. I get off the couch and make my way down the hall, past the kitchen, and when I see the Pontiac through the screen door, my chest tightens.

I turn and Mom's there, guilty.

"We called Swan's first when you didn't come home. Todd met Leon. Leon went out looking for you too. He was still looking when I called him to tell him we found you. I invited him to lunch today. I hope that's okay with you."

"Why didn't you tell me?"

"Because if there's a boy," she says, her eyes flickering away, "I want to meet him."

I open my mouth and then I close it and I feel an all-over sick, inside and out.

I face the door. Leon's out of the Pontiac, leaning against it and staring uncertainly at the house. No—me. He can see me through the screen and I wonder what that looks like from here. The shaded-out figure of a girl in a sloppy shirt that's longer than her shorts.

I run my hands through my hair and then I push through the doors. I meet him on the walk and take him in taking me in. The way his eyes go over my torn-up legs and past my abdomen. I cross my arms, like he could see through my shirt, see a hint of what was written there. He frowns. He brings his hand to my cheek and the way he's looking at me feels wrong, goes all the way to his touch. It's like when you're a kid and you start testing the taps, turning the water on as hot or as cold as you can get it and holding your hands underneath for as long as you can stand it. I don't know which one of us is outlasting the other.

He lowers his hand.

"Holly said you had a bad customer and you got upset. Thought you went to the parking lot to cool off," he says. "It was break, but I figured maybe you'd want some space. It wasn't until after we realized you'd left. I called you and you didn't pick up."

"I lost my phone," I say.

"And then your mom called and then Todd came—"

"You want to go inside?" I ask quickly, as a car rounds the corner. It could be anyone, but odds are it's someone who knows me. Welcome to Grebe, Leon. No. They can't ever know you here. "We should go in."

"But—"

"Let's go in." I grab his hand. "My mom wants to see you."

"Romy—"

"Leon, I know." I lead him in, sensing his confusion, but I offer him nothing more for it. Todd is up and about now, setting the table. Mom moves away from a cutting board of veggies and gives Leon a warm if restrained smile, like she's meeting someone likable at a funeral.

"Leon." She wipes her hands on a cloth and then grasps him by the arm. "Not just a voice on the phone. It's so good to meet you."

"It's good to meet you too, Mrs.—"

"Alice Jane, please. Or just Alice. No need to be so formal."

He smiles and I stand there awkwardly, introductions taken right out from under me. Todd reaches out his hand for Leon's and they shake. I built this and I wasn't even there when I did it. It's like I'm living in two different spaces at once, that I'm here, but I'm not here. I bring my hand to my mouth and—I'm not wearing my lipstick.

No wonder Leon wasn't looking at me right.

"I'll be right back." I gesture over my shoulder. "I just have to . . ."

"Sure," Mom says. "You want something to do, Leon?"

"Absolutely. How can I help?"

She sets him to work chopping vegetables for the salad she's making. I head upstairs to the bathroom where I open the drawer Todd set aside just for me and find my lipstick. I take the cap off and bring it to my mouth and then stop. The tip, all smashed into nothing. I tighten my grip on the tube, but I can't get myself to put the color on. I stare at it and I see words, vivid on skin even in the dark. A girl on the road with her shirt open and her bra undone, waiting to be read. If I put this on and open my mouth, what will come out?

The red makes me, though.

That's what Leon said.

And he stopped for that girl.

"Romy," Mom calls. "You coming down?"

I toss the lipstick into the garbage and then I go into the drawer for another unopened tube. I rip the plastic off the cap and twist the bottom until that burst of color appears and it's different. Same color, but not the same lipstick and that matters. It matters that there's only one place this lipstick will have touched. I put it to my bottom lip. *From the center out,* I think. From the center of the lip out. My hand shakes. I tighten my grip. Pressure. Just give it some pressure. I push in, make my lips red, and it doesn't feel there. I don't feel ready.

But maybe it's like the nail polish now.

Maybe I need something to seal it in.

"Romy?" Mom.

I tell her *yes, I'm coming,* and I run the water, rinse my hands. I hurry down the stairs and find food on the table. When Leon looks my way, he sees the red—he smiles. We sit and eat a salad that tastes like summer, even though it's not.

"So," Mom says to Leon. "How long have you worked at Swan's?"

"I've worked there for a while. I worked there through high school and stopped for college—briefly—and then came back."

"You're not in school now?"

He shakes his head. "Wasn't my thing."

"Wasn't mine, either," Todd says.

"What is your thing?" Mom asks Leon.

"Uh." He gives a nervous sort of smile, like he's not selling himself so well here, but he looked for me last night. They're already sold. He says, "I kind of run this Web site design and development business, actually. That's my thing."

"What?" I stare at him stupidly. "I didn't know."

"Really?" Mom asks.

"Yeah. I have a knack for coding and design, I guess. I started out making themes for blogging platforms and selling them and one of my themes got really popular about a year and a half ago and now I've extended my business into designing and developing personal and professional Web sites."

"Nice," Todd says. "So it's doing well?"

"Yeah. I'm doing some author and up-and-coming band sites, some local businesses in Ibis. My sister sends all her friends my way," he says. "I've got a few in the works right now. It looks like I'm on an upswing and I'd like to keep it going and turn it into my primary source of income. Scale back on hours at Swan's."

I'm stuck between the surprise of this and the guilt of finding it out, like I should've known or asked. I don't know what to say.

"Well, that's fantastic," Mom says. "Holding two jobs like that. You like Swan's?"

"It's all right. I like the pace. Very fast. I like the people."

"Like my daughter."

Leon's fork hovers over his plate.

"Mom," I say.

He smiles. "Yeah, like your daughter."

"You *like* my daughter," she says. I kick her lightly under the table, which doesn't feel like the natural order of things. She doesn't even blink. "I can't tell you how much I appreciate you going out there and looking for her."

"Of course."

Silence. Awful, awful silence. What am I supposed to say? Sorry? Again? Except I didn't even say it to Leon once. I stab my fork through some cucumber and tomatoes and shove them in my mouth because I can't say it at all if my mouth is full.

"That other girl," Leon says. "Penny Young."

I swallow. "You know about that?"

"Yeah. Her mom lives in Ibis. She's there on the weekends—"

"Did you know her?"

"No. But everyone's talking about it in town. I guess Grebe's Sheriff's Department is working with Ibis's. What are we coming up on? Forty-eight hours? That's never good."

I set my fork down, appetite gone. I don't know if it's

because it's such a bad thing for him to say or because part of me still wants her to be missing on Monday in spite of it.

"Romy knows her," Todd says.

"What?" Leon asks. "You do?"

"We go to school together. She's in my grade."

"They were very close at one time," Mom says.

"Oh," Leon says. I keep my eyes on my plate. "I'm so sorry."

Mom and Todd wash up, leave Leon and me to our own devices. He suggests I show him Grebe but I tell him I'm feeling tired and show him our backyard instead. We sit on the dried-up lawn and stare at the neighbor's fence.

"Why didn't you ever tell me about the Web site stuff?"

He shrugs. "I thought I'd show you at some point."

I run my palm over the grass. When I look up, he's watching me in a way that tells me we're going to talk about things best left alone. I'm an expert when it comes to that look on people's faces.

"I'm sorry for sticking my foot in it about Penny Young. I should've thought—"

"It's okay," I say. "We're not close. Her and me. Not anymore."

"I was going to say, inside . . . waking up and hearing about that—about Penny, after driving around all night looking for you. I mean, it was something else, looking for you, but hearing about this girl that didn't make it home. I don't know. Got me thinking. I called your mom and asked if I could come see you." He pauses. "I had to see you."

"Here I am."

"What happened, Romy?"

I rip up a tuft of grass. I want to say nothing, but I guess I have to give him more than that, even if it's all going to amount to nothing anyway. At least—it better. "You know about Wake Lake? About the party? We have it every year . . ."

"I know about it," he says. "Ibis has dumbass traditions too. Stupid."

"Well, stupid me."

"You walked out on your shift to go to a party?"

"Yep."

"Seriously?" He sounds so unimpressed. I just nod. He shakes his head. "I feel like I'm missing something here, Romy, because—"

"You ever do anything stupid before?"

"Well, yeah, but—" His forehead crinkles. He stares at the ground like he's angry at it and it makes me angry with him because I can tell he's not just going to leave it which means I need to be lies ahead of any of his questions and I'm not sure I can think that fast today. "When your mom called, she said they found you on a road thirty miles out from Godwit. She said you were . . ."

"Drunk?"

That quiets him a second. "No. Just wrung out."

I stare at the fence, try to fill the blank space with the right kind of lie; the right kind of lie for Leon. *Jack Phelps.* It comes to me, in Turner's voice.

"This guy, Jack Phelps—he's kind of a legend around here. Be my mom's age now. When it was his turn at the lake, he got drunk and ended up in Godwit. Seemed like a neat idea to see if I could get that far." God, it sounds just stupid enough to my ears, it could be true. "I bet you're sorry you looked for me now."

"Why would you say that?"

"Because a real girl is missing."

"What?"

"Because a girl is really missing and I was okay."

"You're telling me you were so wasted you thought

heading to Godwit on your own was a good idea? Doesn't really sound to me like you were all that okay."

"I'm okay now."

"Well, good." He looks at me and I make myself look back. I need the girl he was looking for to be the one he's seeing now. He says, "I'm not sorry I looked for you."

You. You. Me.

Her.

He leans over and gives me a small kiss. Seals it in.

i get up quietly. I get myself ready.

I brush my teeth and then my hair, pulling it into a ponytail that makes the bruise on my cheek more pronounced because they'll tear me apart if they think I'm trying to hide anything. Downstairs, Todd's making coffee. He glances at me. Grabs two mugs and holds one out. I shake my head and he puts it back.

"Thought I'd let your mom sleep in. She didn't get much shut-eye this weekend."

"Sorry," I mumble and I sense an apology coming because Todd isn't the kind of guy who makes digs and he thinks I took it that way. He was just saying how it is. Mom didn't get much sleep this weekend and it was because of me. "Any word about Penny?"

"Only if word is she's still missing." He crosses his arms and leans against the counter. "Be front of the *Grebe News,* I bet. Definitely talk of the school."

"Yeah."

"Bet plenty of people'll be relieved about that, after the lake."

Sometimes I want to ask Todd how he's so good at that. Knowing more than he lets on. But I have a feeling it's from all those years he spent on the outside after his accident. When all you can do is watch, you see.

"Maybe. Anyway. I better go."

"Straight to school." He says it so firmly, it startles me, seems to startle him a little too. "You go straight to school."

"I will."

I walk slowly. I'm in no hurry to get there. When the building finally comes into view, my body starts to rebel, one part of me right after the other. My chest tingles, my pulse doubles, my throat constricts. A girl is missing.

Let that girl be the one they talk about.

It's quiet when I reach the parking lot, a point in the morning between arrivals. I spot something out of place on the student side, sinister as a black dog; Turner's Explorer. There's life past the front doors—bodies moving on their way to wherever. John and Jane holding up the background. Jane. That was less than a week ago.

I take a deep breath and step inside. There are eyes on me, eyes giving me good, long looks that make me want to disappear but what they're talking about is Penny.

While they look at me.

I pass the main office, and I see Turner, the grim center of a group of faculty members pressing him with questions.

His mouth is moving but his gaze flicks my way and lingers. A cold sweat breaks out on the back of my neck. I don't want people to see me near Turner, for the thoughts that would make them think. I slip past some lockers, turn a blind corner, and then I'm standing in an alcove and Brock is nearby, at his locker. He spots me before I can find somewhere else and at first, it seems like he's not sure what he wants to do about this. Alek isn't with him. Penny gone. Me, here. He closes his locker, takes me in from the bruise on my cheek down.

"Wow," he says softly. "You sure got fucked on Friday."

My heart in a fist. Is a fist.

"Say that again, Brock."

"Up," he amends. "I mean fucked up. You need someone to tell you about it?"

"What makes you think I need telling?"

"Well, the good sheriff says you don't remember a goddamn thing. But I could let you in on it. You want to hear?"

"Where's Alek?"

"That's nothing you need to know."

"Why are you here if he's not?" I ask and his cheeks turn just pink enough to stand out. "Oh. He told you to be here, didn't he? You're here. Because he told you."

"Just being a friend," he says. "But I guess you wouldn't know what that's like, on account of you not having any."

"That's the best you can do?"

"I could do a lot worse."

I look down the hall. It's just the two of us here, alone together, and I'm the one that has to bear the burden of it. He steps forward—I walk away.

"So did you enjoy it?" he calls at my back. "Getting fucked?"

In homeroom, everyone is quiet, even McClelland. His

hands are clasped, brows drawn together. I sit at the back of the room and watch people come in, faces so sad. I stare at Alek's and Penny's empty seats. The bell rings, but the cue for video announcements doesn't sound.

"There will be a special assembly," McClelland says. "There's a special assembly—" He glances at the clock. "Now. In the auditorium. Line up single file and follow me there."

We do as we're told. It reminds me of elementary school, of being escorted from one class to the next because we were too young to be trusted to do anything on our own.

But now we're supposed to be old enough to look after ourselves.

Mr. McClelland opens the door. Mrs. Leven's class is lined up across the hall and we all march together, side by side, to the auditorium. We're directed into rows, don't even get to pick where we'll sit.

I keep my eyes on the stage. There are three empty chairs behind the podium and when everyone is seated and the lights are dimmed, Principal Diaz, Vice Principal Emerson, and Sheriff Turner walk out. Emerson and Turner take the first two chairs but Diaz takes the mic.

"I wish I'd gathered you here under better circumstances," she says. "I'm sure most, if not all, of you know about the unfortunate news regarding a beloved member of our senior class. In the interest of making sure you have the *correct* information, we thought it best if you heard it from us and the local authorities directly. Penny Young is missing."

And even though I already know this, the news goes over me like ice, like I never really believed it at all. Frantic whispers fill the room. The teachers allow us a brief conference about what we've just been told.

I scan the rows and find Tina next to Yumi and Brock. Yumi is crying, but Tina's face is angry, set. I can't remember ever seeing Tina cry. When something hurts Tina, she hurts it right back. She doesn't give herself over to it.

"We're not exactly sure what happened yet, so there's no point in jumping to any bad conclusions," Diaz continues and I think of what Leon said. Coming up on forty-eight hours, but we're past that now. "But if you need someone to talk to, the guidance counselor is here to listen, as are all members of the faculty. Our hearts go out to the Youngs at this difficult time. We'll be praying for Penny's safe return. Sheriff Turner will speak now and I expect you to listen quietly and respectfully to what he has to say."

Diaz sits and Turner moves to the microphone, his expression so perfectly grave. Penny, the daughter he never had, the daughter-in-law he expected to have. I try to imagine Alek, desperately searching for the girl he thought he'd marry while the rest of us are here being told about how she's gone. I am so hungry for the Turners' pain, I will take it in any context.

"Morning."

Turner surveys us, makes us shrink in our seats. It's always uncomfortable around a cop, like they somehow know every terrible thing we've done or thought about doing.

"This is what we know," he says. "We know Penny was last seen on Friday night at the Wake Lake party. She left between ten-thirty and eleven on her white Vespa scooter. She was supposed to arrive at her mother's house in Ibis, where she was spending the weekend, but never arrived. At this point, we don't know if Penny left Grebe or made it to Ibis, but searches of the surrounding area have been and are currently underway. We're working with the Ibis Sheriff's Department and have their full cooperation.

"If any of you have any information—if you saw something

suspicious in person, if you saw or heard something online, on social media the night of the party or since then, if you spoke to Penny and she said something you think might be of any significance, a deputy will be in the school's administration office until noon and, of course, you can call the station anytime. We have a number for anonymous tips. If you *do* know something, we encourage you to come forward as soon as possible. Time is of the essence in these matters."

"Does that mean you think she was kidnapped?"

A boy asks it, some boy sitting somewhere up front.

Diaz gets to her feet and her voice booms across the room without the aid of the microphone.

"Lex Sanders? This is not a Q and A. See me in my office when this is over."

"We've told you what we can," Turner says. "Penny hasn't been seen or heard from since Friday night. Once again, I must emphasize the importance of you sharing any information you think might be useful in helping us to find her. Thank you."

Sheriff Turner returns to his seat and Diaz goes back to the podium. "This is a time to respect your fellow classmates and the people who know and love Penny Young. When we have more information, you will have it. In lieu of your first-period classes, we are going to take this opportunity to process the news as a school community, together."

No one makes a sound until Diaz returns to her seat and Emerson and Turner lean in, murmuring quietly to each other and then the whole room comes alive and I can't take it all in as fast as it's happening. Our beautiful blonde. They cry for her and twist their hands in a way they never would for me. This is what happens when a girl befalls a fate no one thinks she deserves.

prewitt stands before us on the dusty track, her clipboard tucked under her arm.

"I know it's hard, but you have to keep your head in it. It's about focus. That's how people get found." She clears her throat. "Today, I want you to be *faster.* Better than you've *ever* been. Beat your personal best and tell Penny all about it when she comes back."

I think that's pretty stupid, but maybe it would be worse if she hadn't said it at all. We get in position and the short, sharp sound of her whistle starts us off. We run in silence, no one even attempting to pant out a conversation. I can't keep my head quiet, though. My thoughts are a snake eating its own tail. Penny, the lake. Penny. I'm so mad at her. I'm mad at her for being at Swan's, for making me go to the lake and I swear—it makes me faster. It makes me fastest.

Come back, Penny. Let me tell you all about it.

In the locker room, I peel out of my shirt and my shorts, I feel watched and when I turn, Tina's leaning against her locker, staring. She's half-undressed, her face shiny with sweat.

"You plan it like this?" she asks.

"What?"

"Penny going missing same night you get fucking sloppy at the lake," she says. "Because if she was here, that's what we'd be talking about right now."

"Never known anything to keep you from running your goddamn mouth before."

"You know how wasted you were?" she asks. "It was the best impersonation of your dad I've ever seen." Her gaze wanders to my chest. "Nice bra, by the way."

I cross my arms but I don't say anything. I don't know if she's talking about the bra I'm wearing now—or the one I was wearing then.

"What's that supposed to mean?"

She pushes off the locker. The other girls undress around us carefully. Don't want so much as a rustle of clothes to get in the way of what they're hearing.

"Know what Brock told me?"

"I can only guess."

"Grey leaves the party." Tina says this to Yumi, to everyone. "You saw how fucked up she was. She leaves and she wanders almost all the way to Godwit. Her mom reports her missing. Leanne Howard picked her up off the road next morning. Had half the department out looking for her. Half."

I glance in the direction of the showers and realize only after I've done it that I expect Penny to break this up, to wander out—*I was here the whole time!*—and tell us to shut up or something because as rarely as she defended me, it's not like she was always in the mood for Tina's bullshit, either. I ache and I can't even pretend I don't know why.

I miss the unwelcome feeling of Penny in my life.

"She gets drunk, she goes driving. She gets drunk, can't drive, she walks. Don't forget—she lies too. All the time. The girl who cries rape and half the department was out looking for her on Saturday morning. They brought Grey home. Not Penny."

I turn back to my locker and grab my clothes. I'm not staying here for this. I step through my shorts and button them up.

Tina's not done, though, no.

"Better hope that wasn't the half that would've made the difference," she says.

And it's in their heads now, that I took something from the search for Penny. I feel the beginnings of a whole new level of hate stirring in them. I pull my shirt on and try to make my mind blank while the room turns to vicious whispers.

"Why," I hear a girl say, "her?"

when i get home, I go to my room, sit at my desk, and open my laptop.

Sheriff Turner's words followed me all day, made me feel stupid. *If you saw or heard something online, on social media the night of the party or since . . .* I deleted all my accounts a year ago, but I should've thought of this, that if it was bad—if I was as bad as Tina says I was—there's going to be something of myself, of my night, in the last place I want to see it.

I open a browser and stall for the longest time, chewing on my lip.

I need this part over with.

So get it over with.

I know which sites to go to, where everyone in my high school is, because I used to be in all those places with them. I could start out by searching for a girl with my name, but I'm not ready to be that specific. I type in a hashtag, **#WakeLake,** instead. I get nothing. Of course they wouldn't be that obvious, but they needed something, something that would have tied them together online, so none of them missed a single moment of the party they were all at.

I find it.

#WakeUp

I click it and a story unfolds via status updates.

I move past a week's worth of anticipation **(can't wait for #WL #yes #WakeUp)** until I'm at the party itself. It opens with Andy Martin, who posted a photo of a table full of plastic shot glasses, half of them filled to their brims with amber liquid. It's a jolt, seeing the rows of shots and I'm afraid that means it's a memory. Did I drink one?

He captions it **work in progress. #WakeUp**

Next, a photo of the lake's placid surface, from Andy again.

#WAKEUP

Everyone does.

I scroll past everything that means nothing to me. Outfit selfies, On the Way selfies, At the Lake selfies. It's all so endless and once upon a time, it would have been mine. I would have been adding to the pool, so ready for it, feeling every possibility of what lay ahead like none of it could be bad, and maybe, once—it wouldn't have been.

I stare at lights strung up on trees, the place where all the cars were parked, blurry trails of people in motion, too fast for a camera. I can almost hear the music . . .

Pictures of Penny and Alek show up, one after the other. Their faces manage to startle me because I'm looking so hard for myself. There are hasty snapshots of them, some filtered into something more intentional looking. It's like everyone wants a piece of them, desperate to take a photo of the golden couple, hoping it'll get a like or a favorite from either of them later, just so they can feel a little golden themselves.

I scroll and scroll, until the shock of my name moves up the screen.

who invited grey #WakeUp

There's a shaky photo—me? I recognize the shirt, the skirt. Oh, God. It's me. Here. Here, here, here. I am at the party now. My heart beats fast, faster than it does after a run. I'm here, I'm at the lake. Now. Then. I swallow and scroll down, past other people living their own nights. It's about an hour after my arrival when a status update lands in front of my eyes and bites.

how does a girl get that wasted in an hour #damn #talent #WakeUp

Doesn't mean it was me. It doesn't mean it was me, but the indictment is all over me because why couldn't it have been me? Why couldn't it have been about me? My hands start to shake. I scroll until another familiar name shows up. It's not my own, but it's as painful as a kick in the teeth.

Paul Grey WELL represented tonight #WakeUp

Tina posted that. So many people have favorited it.

There's nothing for a little while. Everyone else, the star of their own movies, reaching out to each other in @ replies, so they can know what's happening where and make themselves there. I'm looking for moments I'm the walk-on, and then—

wow sloppy drunk mess by the bonfire #WakeUp

And all the people who aren't by the bonfire want to know **who??**

I open the conversation.

RG.

Everything disappears but those initials—my initials—starred and starred again by my classmates. This is what Tina promised me I was, a sloppy drunk mess at the lake. I stare at the exchange, trying to will it into nonexistence, either it or myself, because I don't want to be in a world where I'm those words, where I was those words. And what's behind them? What does that mean? What was I doing? My head, infuriatingly blank. It won't let me have my night. I scroll through the rest of the **#WakeUp** hashtag for more, worse. There are photos, lots. I go through them fast, forcing myself to look but there are none of me, just updates that might be about me.

that was pathetic #WakeUp and **dumb drunk bitches #WakeUp**

A memory of Penny's voice comes to me, soft and teasing. *You didn't do anything stupid, did you?*

Did I?

I keep going and all I see is **#WakeUp #WakeUp #WakeUp #WakeUp** and then, hours after me, hours after I think I must've been gone, Alek asks the question on everyone's lips now:

Where's @PennyYoung?

I click to her stream and I find the last update she posted. It's time-stamped when the night began, after she talked to me at the diner.

I'm here

at swan's, tracey calls me into her office.

She sits behind her desk, looking as stern as I've ever seen her, and my stomach somersaults at the thought of her asking me about Penny, what Penny was doing here the same night we both disappeared because Holly doesn't miss a trick. She has to have figured it out by now and told it to everyone.

But it never comes up.

"I've fired people for less than what you did," Tracey says. "But I'm glad you're okay. Consider this a warning. Now get out there and get back to work."

"Thank you," I tell her. I step into the kitchen, my skin crawling from the reprimand. I hate being scolded like a little kid. When Holly comes in, I ready myself for more of the same but she passes me, grabs her apron, and puts it on without a word.

I say, "Hi, Holly."

She heads into the diner. She's not speaking to me and that makes me think Penny must've faded from her mind, turned into some faceless blonde just passing through, like so many before.

Holly's cold shoulder is contagious. Some of the other girls keep their eyes pointedly off me. Even the ones that don't really talk to me—there's an edge in how they're not doing it now. I glance at Leon, who's missing exactly none of it.

"Break later?" I ask, because I want Leon to take the feel of this off me but I don't mean it in a way that wants his hands everywhere—even though I think I want that too.

"Better not," he says. He tells Annette to watch the grill for a second and then he comes over. He lowers his voice. "Work through your break."

"What?"

"Work through your break, Romy," he tells me. "Now you're back, everyone's got time to be mad about it. Let them cool off and show them you're not going to mess around."

"But I wasn't—I didn't."

He gives me a look that stings, but—in his version of Friday night, I guess I did.

"I know it sucks, but look at it this way—they're mad because they care."

"Okay," I say.

"I mean it. Holly was a mess. She'd go out, do her tables, and come back in and lose it. You got to let them be mad and you've got to try to make good."

"Then I'll work through my break."

"That'll help, especially with Tracey. Holly might be

tougher to crack, but she'll come around and once she does, everyone else will calm down," he says. "And then you just never have to do anything that stupid again."

There's a roughness to his voice when he says it, and I guess maybe he's still a little pissed about all of it too. "Thanks for the advice."

"I'm not going to be here tomorrow," he says. "I've got to take Caro to see her doula."

"What's a doula?"

"They support the mother, like throughout the pregnancy and the labor. Emotionally, more than medically. Caro says it helps a lot."

"How close is she?"

Annette gestures for him to come back to the grill. He nods in acknowledgment. "She's about overdue. That kid doesn't seem in any rush to get out."

"Can you blame it?"

He laughs a little, like I just told a joke.

i trudge through the heat, my skin and eyes dry with it. It's unending. We're going to turn to dust wishing we'd worried about the weather sooner and maybe that wouldn't be the worst thing. Grebe High looms ugly ahead and it's not until I'm halfway across the parking lot I notice Jane and John have been dismantled. An unsettling blank space where school spirit used to be. Penny's gone and she took it with her. Inside, there's a notice board by the stairs; now the party is over, a new call to action.

FIND PENNY

VISIT THE LIBRARY
BEFORE 1st PERIOD OR LUNCH
TO FIND OUT HOW YOU CAN HELP

Wake up.

There's a photograph of Penny underneath. It makes her seem less real somehow. Her eyes and smile flat, her hair so pixelated from being so blown out, it's lost its sheen. I close my eyes and try to picture it another way. Instead of her face, I see a sign that says FIND ROMY. I wonder what it's like to be missed. Wherever Penny is now, she has to know what she's inspired, that she's being searched for because people want her back. What would happen if it was me? Maybe they'd forget. Maybe they'd like me better. Would that even be possible? I think I'd trade places with her to find out. Either way, I'd get to disappear.

The door swings open behind me and then a shoulder meets my back, shoving me forward. I'm too far out of the way for that to have been an accident, and when I turn—Tina.

"There's going to be a volunteer search party," she says. "Next week."

"So?"

"You going?"

"Why would I?"

"It's the least you could do."

"Is that right?"

"I don't care who's out there looking for Penny, just so long as they're looking."

"Maybe you should see if Alek feels the same way," I say. She goes shamefaced, didn't think that one totally through. "He back?"

She doesn't answer, so he's back. I'm surprised he hasn't

dressed the school in his grief, painted it black. Tina stares at the notice.

"Should've been you," she says.

I bite my tongue but I want to hurt her so bad. A few other people come in and start crowding the board. It's as good a time as any to rid myself of the moment, so I walk away.

"Did you see her last tweet?" I hear a girl ask.

"Whose?" Tina asks.

"Penny's. It was creepy."

I'm at my locker when "Time-wasting bitch," gets hissed at my back. I turn and there's Trey Marcus, his eyes fixed steadily ahead, like he didn't say it. It's another cut and if I know anything, I have to cut back where I can, even if that puts me in places I don't want to be. I head for the library. I'll make myself part of their effort, see who calls me a *time-wasting bitch* to my face then.

They can't have it both ways.

The Required Reading display is gone and three tables have been pushed together in its place. A small crowd has gathered in front of it, and standing behind the tables are Alek and Brock. Brock is so close to Alek, he could be his puppeteer. He mutters something in Alek's ear. Alek nods grimly. He's trying to hold himself tall, trying to look like a man commanding a crisis, but he's so see-through. He's The Stricken Boyfriend. His usual pressed-to-perfection self is rumpled and there's a staleness about him, like he spent the night in his clothes, awake. There are dark circles under his bloodshot eyes and the red makes the green of them more vivid. His lips are as pale as his face. He'll fester soon. If he's already this bad, and it's just the start—if she doesn't come back, he'll let it eat at him until he's nothing. He straightens a little, tries to put on a braver face and I wonder who it would be, if it was me? Who would stand at this table, looking even a little broken about it?

Her.

There's a basket of white ribbons in front of Alek, for us to pin to ourselves. (What color would mine be?) A stack of MISSING posters and a sign-up sheet. Andy Martin hovers close by, his camera hanging heavily around his neck. His fingers tease the button, like he's not sure if this is something he should be taking pictures of, for the yearbook.

I edge up to the table and everyone looks at me. Everyone. Alek's breath gets caught in his throat. I hear it, the catch. Brock reaches across him and moves the ribbons away. I grab the basket before he can get it entirely out of my reach. I take a ribbon and pin it to my shirt.

"Take it off now," Alek says. I move to the posters, grab a handful of them. He goes to snatch them back but stops himself when I clutch them to my chest. He takes a deep breath. "You take the ribbon off and give those back."

"No. Tina told me I should help."

Alek looks at Brock and I know Tina's in for it later, so my work here is done. Cat Kiley steps forward, nudging me out of the way. Her doe eyes zero in on Alek.

She says, "I am so sorry about Penny."

"Thank you," Alek says faintly. He's still staring at me.

"She'll come back, though. I know she will." She nods at the sign-up sheet next to the posters. "What happens when I put my name down?"

This is all becoming too much for Alek, so Brock takes over.

"You leave your e-mail and phone number and we'll send you any and all updates relating to Penny, calls for action—like putting posters up in surrounding areas—and we'll be in touch about the volunteer search party at the lake next

Monday. Big stuff like the search party will also go out to the GHS student announcement listserv, but Diaz told us not to overwhelm it, so . . ."

"Wait, I thought the police already searched? You think they missed something?"

"I'm sure Sheriff Turner didn't miss anything," Brock says. "But a second look can't hurt."

Cat turns red. "I didn't mean it like that." She scribbles her name and then hurries away. I pick up the pen. It's warm from her grasp. I stare at the paper. I think I did this wrong. I shouldn't have come here but it's too late to take back.

I put my name down.

"i went to the lake, now it's settled down over there."

It's how Mom greets me when I come home from school. She's at the door, like she's been there for hours. I imagine her peering down the street, waiting for a glimpse of me, unwilling to believe I'll be home until I *am* home, right in front of her. I take the missing posters out of my book bag before tossing it on the floor, so they don't get wrecked.

"I looked everywhere," she says. "But I didn't find your phone."

"You didn't have to do that. Thank you."

She squeezes my shoulder. "Could still turn up. It's red,

it's got your name engraved on it. It'd be hard to miss, if it didn't end up in the water."

"I wasn't by the water."

But I don't know if that's true. I want to believe it is. I want to believe that whatever happened at the lake, no matter what anyone says to my face or said online, there were moments I could count on myself, even for something stupid like staying away from the water wasted.

She's surprised. "You weren't?"

I hesitate. "No."

But it gives me away and all the sympathy I don't want is in her eyes. The posters in my hand become a perfect distraction. I give her one and she holds it as carefully as a newborn, running her thumb over the side of Penny's grainy face.

"You should take these to Swan's, if there aren't some already there."

"Yeah," I say.

But I don't take the posters to Swan's with me, not at first.

They stay on my desk and it's worse, having them there, because I keep thinking about what else Tina said to me, half the sheriff's department looking for me. *Better hope that wasn't the half that would've made the difference.* Maybe there's some trucker who's seen Penny, and they'll come through Swan's and the only thing in the way of his saying so is whether or not the posters are up. I don't know. I just want them both—Penny and Tina—taking up less of my thoughts, so I give in and bring the posters to work and Tracey gives me the go-ahead to tape them to the notice board out front. She looks at the awful black-and-white photo of Penny and sees Penny alive in it in all the ways I don't. She murmurs, *beautiful, she's so beautiful* and it makes me feel like the level of tragedy here is directly proportionate to Penny's looks. I ask for

Monday off, for the search party, even though I haven't decided if I'll go. She says, *of course* and on my way out of her office, adds, "It makes you think, doesn't it? You're lucky, Romy."

I wonder if that means she thinks I'm beautiful enough to be as tragic.

But I say, "Yeah," because it's what she wants me to say.

Leon has time before his shift starts, so he helps me put the posters up, manning the tape while I clear away out-of-date flyers to make room.

"How is it in Grebe?" he asks, taping Penny's corners down.

"How you'd expect." I place another poster right beside the one I just put up. People will overlook one, but maybe not two or three. "Sad. There's a volunteer search party next Monday. How was the doula appointment?"

He grimaces. "Gross. I mean, it was good. But now I know about something called a mucus plug? So . . ."

"Oh. Ew."

"Yeah. I could've gone a little longer being ignorant of that."

"How's Caro doing?"

"She's getting quiet," he says. He tapes the last corner of the third poster down, smiling a little. "Never known my sister to be quiet." He nods toward the kitchen. "I have to get ready. You coming back?"

I tell him I'll be there in a minute and take the tape from him. I stare at the posters for a long moment. Three lined up, side by side, almost kind of like modern art. But that's good, that's eye catching, I think. I wonder how it looks just coming in, so I step outside, walking backward until I can't see the posters through the door and then I move forward like I'm anyone stopping in for a bite. I want to know the exact moment my eyes register MISSING and Penny's face—but then Holly comes out and blocks my view.

"You walking out on us again?" she asks. It's the first she's spoken to me since Friday night. I point to the posters behind her.

"I just wanted to see how they looked."

"You said you didn't know her," Holly says.

"What?"

She crosses her arms. "Penny Young. She was in here, that Friday. As soon as I saw her in the paper, I recognized her. You sat right across from her in that booth and then you both got upset about something and you both left, one after the other. Now she's gone. I keep waiting for you to say something about it, but you were never going to, were you?"

My heart stops. I thought Penny got past Holly, but nothing gets past Holly. I was stupid to believe it could.

"No," I finally say. "I wasn't going to."

She's not expecting an honest answer. It catches her off guard enough that I can slip by her. She reaches for me. "Romy, just a minute—"

"Leave it, Holly."

But another thing about Holly is she doesn't know how to leave anything. She follows me to the kitchen, right at my heels. When we're behind the door, she starts in on me.

"Did you at least tell the police she was here?"

This gets everyone looking. Leon's head turns my way. Girls on their way out—order pads and pencils in hand—stop to hear what Holly's got to say.

"Did you tell the police Penny Young was here?" she demands again.

I go from zero to a hundred, in a second flat. "Holly, would you *shut up*?"

"*Hey,*" Leon says sharply and Holly's mouth hangs open

because I've never mouthed off at her before. He sets his spatula down, wipes his hands on his apron. "What's going on?"

"Penny Young was in this diner the night she disappeared," Holly tells him, pointing at me. "She's the customer Romy looked after, before she walked out and she told me she didn't know her. Now I'm wondering if she's been as honest with the police." She looks at me. "You don't mess around with this kind of stuff, Romy. It's serious."

"It's also none of your business," I say. "*Yes,* I told the police about it, but this wasn't the last place she was seen so it didn't matter and I'm not your fucking daughter and I don't work for you, so back. Off."

I storm out of the kitchen, through the back door. It swings shut behind me. I kick the Dumpster. My foot meets the metal hard, the impact recoiling up my legs. That felt too close, like my mom almost getting in the car with Todd the day of his accident. I shouldn't have hung those posters up. Try to do good for a girl who never did me any favors and it turns out worse than it ever needed to be. Fuck you, Penny. Just—fuck you.

I rub my palm over my mouth and then the panic hits, so ingrained after a year of hypervigilance—*you wrecked your lips, fix it*—that my other hand finds my pocket, then my lipstick, and I trace my mouth with it because after a year of hypervigilance, I know its shape enough to know how to make do without mirrors.

Leon comes out just as I'm ready. I pocket my lipstick and move away from the Dumpster. I try to look sorry, but I know it won't be enough.

"What the hell was that?"

"She was in my face—"

"No, she was asking you a question. A good one," he

interrupts. "You don't talk to Holly like that. You know the kind of shit she's going through at home, Romy. Come on. She doesn't need this."

"I don't need it, either. She was getting in my face," I repeat, because I don't know what else to say, but I have to put something out there so the last thing isn't his chastising me, because if it is, I'll get mad enough to do something dumb. I don't need any boy telling me how to talk to other people, but I don't want to be dumb around Leon, either.

"That's not what I saw," he says.

"That's what it felt like."

He exhales and looks up, like he's plucking all the words he wants to say next from the sky. I hope they're the right ones. "I don't think you get what you put us through here. You walked out on your shift to get *drunk*. Just think about that for a second—"

"Leon—"

"No, just *think* about it," he says and I shut my mouth, but I can't make myself think about it. Maybe I got drunk, but I didn't leave my shift to get that way, Leon. And everything that happened after—I didn't leave for that, either. "You've got people in there who want to give you the benefit of the doubt because they can't believe you'd do something like that in the first place. You're not making it easy tonight, Romy."

"Neither is she," I say.

"She doesn't owe you that. And she's not the only one you're making it hard for."

He's angry with me. No. Is this where I lose Leon? I don't want to lose Leon. He's the boy who stopped and I'm the girl he stopped for and what happens to her, if he goes away?

"Oh," I say.

I press my hands against my face and split myself in two.

Push away the side that's the truth because that's the side that wants to be angry at him for how wrong he is because of all the things he doesn't know. I focus on the side I've shown to him. There's so much missing, but it's better that it's missing. And as long as it's missing, that makes everything he's saying to me now—right. I take a breath.

"You're right." I lower my hands. "You're right. I'm sorry."

My apology turns him so relieved, like he was worried I'd make this a bigger fight, worried this was going to be the part where I'd lose him too.

"I'm not the one you need to apologize to."

"You're right again."

He moves a little closer. "You going to be okay?"

"Sure." We stare at each other and there's something about the concern in his eyes that makes me want to shake myself off. Just because he's not angry anymore doesn't mean I've fixed this yet, the way it needs to be fixed. "Just ask about Penny if you want to know."

"But you don't want to tell me," he says. "Because you didn't tell me."

"And what if I don't?"

"Well, I can't force you, and if you don't—you don't. But you should know it'd be a weird thing between us. And I wouldn't like it."

No, he wouldn't. I don't have to tell him, but my not telling him would leave this uncomfortably open, wanting us to return to it, whether or not we ever did. And probably ending us, if we don't. So I definitely need to lie now.

"I told you we were close, me and Penny."

"But you didn't tell me she was here that night."

"Because she's not my friend anymore. I mean, we hate each other." I cross my arms. "In junior year, we had a falling out over a . . . boy."

Boy. Tastes like blood to say it.

"She came to the diner on Friday to make sure I—"

The unfinished lie falls from my tongue. To make sure—what? To make sure I . . . I see Penny at the diner there, her mouth moving, and those things she said to me. I can't, won't, give them voice. I force the memory away. I reach for the pettiest thing I can think of because no one has a hard time believing how petty a girl can be.

"To make sure I wasn't going to the lake later. That's how bad it is between us. I could bring down an entire party for her just by being there. It made me so mad she came in to *my* work, got in *my* space and ruined *my* night, I thought I'd return the favor. I went to the lake to do that. It's not a nice story. Especially now. And that's why I didn't tell you."

Leon's face falls a little as he thinks about it, and maybe I'm not so in the clear after all. Who wants to be with a petty girl? It strikes a fear in me I try not to show.

"I didn't know she'd go missing," I say.

"Well—no," he says. "You couldn't have."

"I hate thinking about it because now she's gone, I see—" I have to redeem myself, but these words taste like blood to say too: "I see . . . how awful I was."

His expression softens. "Well, Penny doesn't seem all that nice in this story, either." He pauses. "I could talk to Holly, if you want."

I'm capable of having my own conversations, but this whole night is wearing on me. It's barely started and I'm tired and I don't know that I could tell the same lie half as well, especially to Holly. Leon might.

"Would you?" I ask.

"Yeah. Just give me a minute and I'll lay it out for her," he says.

He turns to the door and I say, "Leon," and he turns back and looking at him—

I need to tell him something that's true.

I want something between us that's true.

"I like you," I say. "I didn't mean to make it hard for you to like me back."

He hesitates, and then—he moves to me and kisses the side of my mouth before disappearing back inside. It happens so fast, my heart barely realizes it at first, but when it does, it's like some small part of my world has righted itself.

I'm still her.

When I'm about to go in, the door opens and Holly comes out, an unlit cigarette dangling between her lips. I stand there awkwardly while she lights up. She doesn't speak to or look at me until after that first, long drag. She savors it.

"I didn't know you and Penny Young had a history," she says. "I might have done things a little differently if I had."

"I shouldn't have run my mouth at you like that. I'm sorry, Holly."

She nods. She pats the space of wall next to her. I lean against it.

"You're right," she says after a minute. "You're not my daughter, but I'll be damned if I don't worry about you girls. I worry about my daughter and the shit she seems determined to get herself into, lately. I worry about Annette and that loser she's decided to move in with. I worry about you when you wander off and now I'm worried about this Penny Young, who I don't even know, because I have a daughter. Anytime something bad happens to a woman close to me, it's how I think. *I have a daughter.*"

"You have a son."

She shakes her head. "It's not the same."

"They're going to find her," I say. "Alive."

She tosses the cigarette and grinds it out.

When it's time for me to clock out, I leave through the front door, try to get a good look at those posters again. My eyes are on Penny and her eyes are on me, until I round the building. I'm unlocking my bike from the bike rack when a truck pulls up beside me. There's a parking spot so close, I don't realize the man inside the truck is talking to me until he's repeating himself.

"I said, where you headed on that bike, this late?" I turn. His arm hangs lazily over his open window. He looks young—early thirties, maybe—but the kind of young that's been in the sun too long. He sniffs. "Not safe to be out this late around here. A girl's missing."

I imagine her getting into a truck like this. Getting into this truck.

"What would you know about that?" I ask him.

He smiles, taps his fingers against the outside of the door for a long minute, and then he shakes his head and drives away.

todd is on the front porch when I get home.

He sits on the lawn chair, his feet propped up on the blue cooler, a half-drunk bottle of beer resting between his thighs. His head is tilted back and his eyes are closed. It looks like a life worth having and it's strange, appreciating his repose. Whenever I'd see a glass or bottle in my father's hands, my whole body would steel itself for the inevitable drama of a man who didn't know when to say when. Todd—I know he'll stop here, at this one drink, and if he doesn't, he won't go past two. I push through the screen door and he cracks his eyes open.

"Your mom's running errands. How was school?"

"It was school."

But it wasn't, not really. Penny's absence is changing the landscape and it feels less and less like a place we go to learn and more a place we exist just to soak in the shock of it.

This morning, I watched Alek watch himself on the video announcements. His chin rested in his clasped hands as he mouthed along to his lines about the search party next week as he spoke them on-screen. It was like he was dying in two realities—on TV and in the flesh.

Brock, who always waits for Alek between classes they don't share, who always plays errand boy for Alek for whatever Alek might need, who always provides a barrier between his best friend and the rest of the world like a personal bodyguard, now filters this routine through her disappearance. Brock waits by doors dutifully, so Alek won't walk alone, Brock stands in the lunch line and gets two lunches so Alek won't have to receive sickly sweet condolences from the cafeteria workers who slop food onto his tray, and Brock stands in front of any questions about Penny Alek might not want to answer himself.

"You doing okay?" Todd asks.

"Sure."

He picks at the label on his bottle. I can tell he doesn't buy it, but I don't know what Todd's definition of *okay* is. Maybe it's some impossible standard we're all going to fail to meet. Besides, I don't see how I'm not okay, all things considered.

Before he can reply, the phone rings from the kitchen and a half second later, the ring echoes upstairs. The landline is a holdover from Mary's time. Mom tried to convince Todd to get rid of it because we all have cell phones now—well, most of us—and it's just one extra bill to pay, but Todd refuses. He says the day one of us needs an ambulance or something will be the day every cell phone in our place dies. The way our luck runs, I think he might be right.

He gets up slowly and follows me in. I toss my bag on the floor while he goes into the kitchen to answer the call.

"Bartlett here," he says and it makes me smile. I don't even really know why. I slip out of my shoes. "Uh, just a—hey. Romy?"

I turn and he stands in the hall, the phone cord stretched all the way from the far kitchen wall, the receiver pressed against his chest. He looks at me weird. It makes my skin prickle.

"It's for you," he says. "It's the sheriff's department."

the grebe sheriff's Department is hidden behind the main street, across the road from the post office. I coast up to the small building on my bike, hop off and rest it flat on the sidewalk, blocking the entrance. I hesitate at the front door, my palm flush against it. It's not that I expect everything to stop when I walk in. It will go on like however it always does, but whoever sees me—

When I'm gone, they'll open their mouths.

I exhale and step into the frigid cold of the place, cold enough to make me shiver and rub my hands together. I step through another set of doors and a metal detector and head to the front desk where Joe Conway—the Conways' youngest son—sits. Todd told me he's been working here about a month, I guess, and *everything gets back to Dan,* so be careful what I say. I can't think of anyone worse for the job. He gives me a toothy smile, eyes flickering over my body. *Paul Grey's kid.* That's what he's thinking. *She—*

Whatever thought he has after that, he can't make me take.

"Leanne Howard said you had my phone. Found it at the lake."

He blinks. I took the *hello* right out of him. He looks around, like he doesn't know what to do about it and he probably doesn't.

"I'll just look into that for you," he says.

He gets up and slips through a frosted-glass door. I lean against the counter. The quiet is unexpected. For some reason, I thought this place would look like in the movies, maybe, Penny's disappearance being the life in the room, making it frantic, but it's not. That's just what I want to see, I think. How can they find her if it isn't?

When the frosted-glass door Joe Conway left through opens again, Leanne steps out. She's in full uniform. Her hair is knotted back into a bun and she's thick on the eyeliner today. She's got my phone and it's a relief to have this one thing from that night back where it belongs.

"Do you need my ID?"

"I think you're who you say you are."

She sets the phone down on the desk, back facing up, etching in clear view.

Romy Grey.

"Where did you find it?" I pick it up.

"Just off the path, in some bushes, some of the boys did," she says. "We've had it since Sunday night and I told them to call you about it, but—" Big surprise, they didn't. "When I saw it still sitting there today, I just thought I'd get the job done myself."

"Thank you."

"Glad you look better than the last time I saw you. You feeling it?"

I can't tell if it's a jab at me or not. I glance at her and she looks soft, not vicious, but a lot of people in this town are a soft kind of vicious. I say *sure* but instead of leaving, something keeps me where I am, something I need to know.

"Can I ask you about Penny?"

The door behind her opens again and Joe comes out. Before Leanne says anything to me, she turns to him. "Joe, you want to go upstairs and get me those reports I asked you for over an hour ago?"

He turns red. "I was going to do that after I—"

"Don't give me excuses. Just get them now."

She watches Joe shuffle off and doesn't face me until she's sure he's gone and I swear she rolls her eyes before she does it. "What did you want to ask me about Penny?"

"You called that weekend, said you didn't need me to come in."

"That's right. I talked to your mom."

"So what did you find that ruled out a connection between me and her?"

She grimaces. "Romy, I'm sorry but I'm not at liberty to—"

"I need to know," I say and I can tell she's readying to refuse me again. "Because a lot of people were looking for me."

"We were looking for you both."

"But maybe if they hadn't been looking for me, they would've found her and maybe that's the differencc." I swallow. "Or maybe it's not . . . but I need to know."

"Oh . . . Romy, honey—" No. I hate that. *Honey.* I didn't ask her for that. I step away from her kindness, clutching my phone. "If I could tell you, I would. I'm sorry, but I—"

"Forget it, I get it," I mutter because if she won't give me what I need, she doesn't get to look at me like she's sorry for me. "Thanks—for my phone."

Leanne seems like she wants to say something more, but Joe comes trundling in with a folder full of papers. He eyes us suspiciously. Leanne looks away.

"You have a good day, Romy," she tells me.

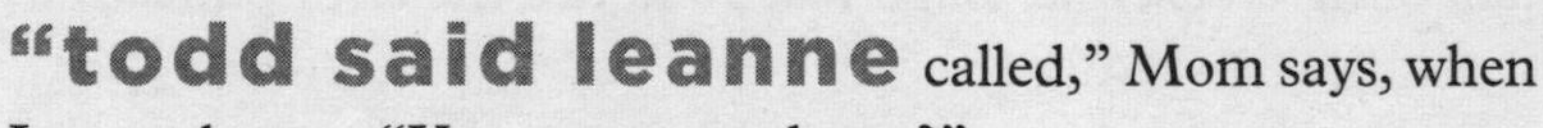

"**todd said leanne** called," Mom says, when I come home. "You get your phone?"

"Yeah."

"I told you it'd turn up."

I go to my room, find my phone's charger, and plug it in. I lay on my bed and fade out for the time it takes to get enough power to run and then I inspect it. The screen is okay, but its back and sides are a little worse for wear, scratched up. It's strange looking at it, knowing they found it while they were searching for Penny, anything about her.

I turn it on and the notifications chime, one after the other.

Voice mails first.

Five frantic messages from my mom.

Romy, where are you?

We're getting worried . . .

By the last, she's in pieces and she's pleading, *come home, please,* and promising, *I'm not mad at you.*

Todd calls too. *We'd really like to hear from you, kid.*

It doesn't go down easy, this proof of being loved.

The last message is from Leon.

Hey, Romy. I hope you get this. Pause and static. There's a hum in the background, like he's driving and he probably was. *Please get this and call when you do. Please. Um.* Pause. *I don't want to hang up.* He laughs, awkwardly. *So call when you get this. Or maybe I'll see you first . . . that'd be okay too. I really hope you're all right.*

This is what it would've been like for Penny's family.

This is what it's still like for them, for her mom and her dad, for Alek. Their love, desperate messages sent out to the universe, waiting to be returned and her silence—

Her silence.

I stare at my phone until it starts to blur. The first tears fall, bring focus, and that's when I notice the last notification. 1 UNSENT E-MAIL.

An e-mail, waiting for me to send it.

But I haven't sent an e-mail from my phone in a very long time.

Did I leave a note for myself, and I was so drunk I put it there? It seems stupid, reaching, but who else would—I fall through the thought before it's complete, hit the ground hard.

Who else would, if not me?

I find the e-mail and open it.

In the TO field, the address of GHS's student announcement listserv. Any time a student has an announcement—club meetings or volunteer work opportunities or tutoring offers and now, searches for missing girls—they're invited to put it on the listserv and it goes out to the entire school: the faculty, the student body. After students started sneaking trash talk about teachers and each other in their messages, a code of conduct was written up and Principal Diaz got tough. Every time someone fucks around on the listserv, the entire school loses some kind of privilege. To further prevent any misuse, signing up has also been open to parents. It's our choice whether we want to show them the kind of monsters they're raising.

There is no message in the body of the e-mail. What's the point in sending a blank e-mail to everyone in school? But then I see the attachments at the bottom—

Photos. From my phone.

Only the file names are visible. All the possibilities of what they could reveal become a vise around my heart, makes the question of whether I did this . . . or someone else that much worse. I check the sent folder to make sure nothing got out—that this wasn't the last e-mail in a long line of e-mails, but it's empty. Nothing was sent.

I go to my photos and as soon as I'm there, I glimpse thumbnails, tiny bursts of colors, shapes that make people, a night. I let it sink in. My phone screen dims, conserving its battery, while I try to find the will to tap the screen and pick a photo.

It brightens when I finally do.

I've hated having my photograph taken since I was eleven. There are albums full of me before that age, this smiling, happy kid, playing it up for the camera. After that, it's all hands in front of face and *Mom, don't.* She thought it was natural; a girl gets to be a certain age and she doesn't want to see herself anymore. But it wasn't that. I didn't understand who I was looking at. I could see the beginnings of a takeover, a body turning, growing, changing into something that didn't feel like it belonged to me and every moment since then I've spent trying to hold on to the pieces of myself I still understand.

The girl in the photo is a waste of a girl.

A wasted girl on the ground, folded in on herself, her head against her knees and she's surrounded by a small crowd with their backs to the camera and I don't know who I feel more betrayed by—them or her.

I make myself numb as I switch to the next photo and the camera is closer to the girl, too close, at a nauseatingly perverse angle. The girl's shirt is loose and wrinkly and dirty, her hair is half out of the ponytail it was tied in, and the parts of her face that are visible look wrong, like she's so far from where her body happens to be.

I switch to the next photo and she's staring right at me now—the camera. Her eyes are half-open and I feel it, she's dead. She's dead. I feel her deadness, feel her stuck between two places, the party and the rabbit hole beneath her.

Fall, I think. Be anywhere else.

In the next photograph, her hands are at her shirt, fumbling with its buttons. No, no. I ache at the picture after—a first button is undone, her hand snaked past her collar, resting against her skin. In the next shot, the camera is even closer. Another button is undone.

I bring my hand to my own shirt and it's hot in this room, the air weighs on me, more than normal heat, pushing on me from the outside, from the inside, something I want to separate myself from. The next photo, the girl is looking up, up, up, eyes searching for something she's not finding. Her hands rest uselessly at her sides. She looks so small and exhausted.

In the next photo, her shirt is open.

The pink-and-black lace push-up bra.

There are hands on her shoulders, keeping her upright, keeping her from slouching forward just so everyone can see.

But that skin has been shed now. That skin, all of that touched skin has been shed now, cells have regenerated. Those hands aren't on her anymore.

Whatever was on her then is gone, now—

My head throbs. The kind of headache that makes you want to vomit, but I swallow against that feeling and click forward and I imagine it how it must have been that night, all these people around this girl, trying not to laugh, but it's too hard. It's *so hard* not to enjoy this because how can you put something so golden, a girl who can barely open her eyes or her mouth—how can you put something like that in front of them and expect them to be better people?

Because in the next photo—the last photo—the girl's hands are at her bra, her red nails teasing the clasp and I think wildly that I could reach through and grab her wrist, like I could stop her and take her away, because no one else is doing it. Because no one else did it.

I put my hand to the screen, covering hers.

We're wearing the same color nail polish.

i sit at my desk with everything I need for my nails and every application of polish ends up feeling the same, ends up feeling like it's leading me back to the water. Over and over, I paint the color on and each time I finish, it's still too close. I have to take it off, try again until it's right, because I can't give up the red. It's mine. It makes me.

"Romy, you're going to be late."

I press the brush heavily against my nails, letting my hand shake the color on. Something I never do. It doesn't make for the best manicure, but the weight of the polish feels differently than it normally does and then I'm ready.

At school, I stand in the entranceway, and I think the

heat outside would be better than choking on the same breathed air of the people who crowded around me, saw me with my shirt open. My eyes skim their faces, their hands—hands on my shoulders. Whose hands? Who was holding my phone, taking photos with it to send to the school? I close my eyes and hear a muddle of voices and try to imagine which one said they should, because that's how it started, didn't it? No. First it's a thought, a thought in someone's head and then said aloud, and then me, on the ground, with my shirt open.

"Jesus, Grey. When aren't you in the way?"

Brock is behind me and Alek lags behind him. They're both carrying two hefty baskets full of bright yellow T-shirts with bold black lettering across the front. FIND PENNY YOUNG. And underneath that in tinier, but still visible letters, GREBE AUTO SUPPLIES. I move and they shuffle past before they're waylaid by some underclassmen who ask about the shirts as an excuse to get a closer look at Alek's haggard face.

"They're for anyone who wants 'em," Brock says. He nods at Alek. "Mrs. Turner had them made. They're free. If you take one, make sure you wear it for the search on Monday. The news is probably going to be there. This'll be a chance to—"

"Get Grebe Auto Supplies some free publicity?" I ask.

Alek turns awkwardly, weighed down by his basket.

"Don't you fucking dare," he says and the underclassmen look at me like I'm scum, like I disappeared her myself. But they already think that.

"Yeah, because the last goddamn thing a national brand needs is free publicity," Brock snaps. It probably doesn't hurt, though. He grabs a T-shirt off the top and whips it at my chest. It drops from there to the ground. The letters get mangled into the folds and the only word still visible is PENNY.

"Pick it up," Alek says but he's not talking to me.

Brock turns to him. "What?"

"Don't leave it on the fucking ground."

There's a hint of panic in Alek's voice, enough for one of the freshmen to snatch it from the dirty floor and put it back in Brock's pile.

"Man, I didn't—"

But Alek is already walking away.

By midday, the halls are a sea of yellow, making Penny a part of every single moment, a relentless reminder for everyone of what they think I took from her search.

I get so tired of the constant glares that at lunch, I hide in the bathroom, in the stall farthest from the door and become a tableau of a girl crouched stupidly on a toilet seat, so she won't be seen. Over the hour, girls come in and out, in and out. I can't stand every boring, worthless piece of conversation I overhear because they make me wish I could be a part of them, be some nobody girl with nothing to say.

After a while, Sarah Trainer and Norah Landers come in.

"This shirt looks awful on me. They should have different colors to pick from," Norah says. Sarah makes a sympathetic sound. I peer through the crack in the door. "You think if I asked him, Brock would get me more Georgia Home Boy?"

Norah smirks, makes air quotes when she says *Georgia Home Boy.*

"He said that was just a Wake Lake thing."

"But I'm having Trey over this weekend."

Sarah laughs. "What, you planning to wine, dine, and date-rape him?"

"Fuck off. Wake Lake was amazing and if you hadn't been

too chicken shit to try it, you'd know it. All in the dosage."

"That still didn't answer my question."

"Shut up. I'm going to ask him."

"He'll probably make you blow him for it."

Norah considers it. "There are worse things."

They inspect their reflections in the mirror and then they leave. I take my phone out of my pocket and search Georgia Home Boy.

Georgia Home Boy
Slang for Gamma Hydroxybutyrate (GHB)

leon texts while I'm getting ready for work, lets me know he swapped shifts with Brent Walker and won't be in tonight. I text BUT I'M OFF FOR THE WEEKEND like he doesn't know after all the time we've worked together, I get the weekends off. & MONDAY FOR THE SEARCH PARTY.

It upsets me in a way I'm not proud of, but I don't know why. Is it weak to want to see him? It can't be wrong to want to see someone because you like the person you are when you're around them. That's probably one of the best reasons you could have.

At Swan's, the air-conditioning plays tricks again, on and off, on and off. Every time we pass Tracey's office, wc hear her swearing about it through the door.

"You're going to the search party on Monday?" Holly asks while I put on my apron. She fans her overheated face with her hands.

"How'd you know?"

"I'm picking up your shift."

"Thanks."

"Money for me." She shrugs. "You think you're going to find anything?"

My fingers fumble with the apron strings and I have to start the bow over. I fight with the question because I've barely thought about the searching, let alone any finding. It doesn't really matter if I think we will but . . .

"We have to," I say.

The night floats by, I float through it, trying to keep my head clear, trying not to think about things like Brock and GHB because I don't want to think about it. I can't.

I can't think about it.

Leon not being here makes that hard.

I do a quick check on the pain-in-the-ass family I've been looking after for most of my shift. They're on their way to something they think I should care about but they're running late and it's my fault. Their twin boy toddlers smile at me, making grabby hands at everything they can hold. Their parents don't smile. They scowl when it takes me five minutes to bring out their drinks, even though it took them over twenty minutes to order them in the first place. The food doesn't get cooked fast enough for their liking. When I clear their table and get the bill, they write MEAL TIME SENSITIVE, SERVICE TOO SLOW – NO AC!!!!!! on the tip line.

After they leave, the air conditioner rattles on. I turn my back on the diner a minute, enjoying the cool of it, and when I face the room again there's someone familiar in one of my booths.

Caro.

"Third trimester sucks," she declares when I reach her. Her hand rests on her stomach and I wonder why pregnant women do that. If it's out of instinct. Or if it's out of awe. If it's out of some need for assurance that the baby is still there. Or maybe they do it because they think they're supposed to. She smiles at me in the same nice way she did at her place and it puts that night in my head. I feel instantly stupid about it, as if it was happening all over again right now.

"What brings you here?" I ask.

"I used to come in all the time when I was in high school. Sit in a corner booth and be by myself. I got nostalgic."

"Leon's not here today."

"I know. He's not why I came," she says. "I'm hungry."

I take her order, a burger with extra cheese and bacon and caramelized onions on a toasted bun with a side order of fries. She wants to wash it down with a glass of ice covered in a splash of Coke and asks, "Is the air-conditioning on? I'm going to boil my baby."

"It's been on and off all day," I say. "But it's on now. I can make your order to go, if it's going to be a problem for you and the . . ."

"It was a joke, Romy," she says. "Except I can't believe Tracey still hasn't gotten around to fixing it. It's been broken since I was in high school too."

"Oh." I am so awkward.

Her expression turns serious. "Leon said you knew the missing girl, Penny Young. How are you doing?"

There's so much in everything she's just said, I don't know where to start. If Leon told Caro about it—that means they were talking about me. It's so hard for me to wrap my head around that, them, together, talking about me, like I'm something worth talking about. It flusters me enough to say, "I'm fine. Are you?" Because I guess I'm destined to be stupid around Caro.

She gives me a puzzled look. "Yeah, besides starving."

"Right." I walk to the kitchen, my face burning. I put the order in and get the Coke, filling it with as much ice as the glass will hold and by the time I've walked it back out to her, she's playing with her phone and I have another table waiting on me.

"I'll be back out with your order soon," I say.

"Thanks, Romy." She glances out the window at the parched parking lot full of cars and a few semis. The heat turns the air above the pavement all wavy. "It needs to rain."

"It's never going to rain."

She smiles but there's something off about it. I don't know Caro, not really, but when someone comes at you the way she did when I first met her, you can see when the spark has dulled, even a little. I look after my other table, then I go back to the kitchen and wait for her order. When I bring it out, I tell her to let me know if she needs anything else.

"I will," she says.

She doesn't touch her food, for someone who's supposedly starving. Two girls come in from a run, panting and ravenous and I look after them. By the time they're halfway through their meal, Caro still hasn't eaten a bite of hers. She keeps picking up her phone and putting it back down. When I check on her, she sets the phone down quickly, like she's done something wrong.

"Is the meal okay? You haven't touched it . . ."

"What?" She looks at the food and it's all so unappetizingly room temperature now. She picks up the burger and ventures a bite but that's all she can manage. She pushes the plate away. "What a waste."

"I can reheat it. Or I can pack it up and you could reheat it at home."

"No, forget it. I should go."

"Okay. I'll get the check." I pick up the plate and hesitate.

Her phone vibrates. She turns it off quickly and presses her lips together and for a minute, I think she's trying not to cry. Something's definitely not right, but I don't know what, if anything, I should do. I feel like I should be like how Caro was with me at her house. I should understand just enough to say the right thing. I stand there instead, the plate of uneaten food in my hand. She saves me, like before.

"I'm sorry," she says. "I'm being weird, I know."

"Not weird. Are you okay?"

"I'm overdue." She points at her stomach. "If nothing starts happening very soon, they're going to induce me. Maybe they'll even cut this kid out of me, with my luck."

"I was a cesarean," I say unhelpfully.

"Yeah?"

"Yep. I was early, though, like four weeks. And when the doctor made the incision, he actually cut me, so I was the only baby in the maternity ward with a Band-Aid on my ass."

Caro laughs. "Cute."

"So you're okay?"

She shrugs. "I was in a car accident the other day."

"Oh my God." I set the plate down. "Leon never said—"

"Leon doesn't know."

"Were you hurt? Was it bad?" I peer out at the parking lot and my eyes immediately land on a dark gray sedan with a crumpled bumper. "Is that yours? The sedan?"

"Yep. I'm not hurt." She looks at the car. "It wasn't my fault. Some asshole behind me was texting when the light turned red. Today, I was supposed to see my doctor and set an appointment for membrane stripping, which might jump-start my labor. I didn't show and now Adam's furious."

"That's not good," I say.

"He'll get over it," she says. "I was on my way there before I came here. It just hit me, if it works . . ." She pauses. "I'm going to have this kid and I'm going to be a mother and . . . I want that so much, Romy, I can't even tell you . . .

but the accident made me—I don't know. I thought I was ready for this and now I guess I feel like it doesn't need to happen anytime soon, so—" She forces a laugh. "Why not stop in at Swan's and have a burger? So stupid."

"It's not stupid."

"Well, let's not talk about it anymore." Caro's eyes fix on something behind me, and I realize it's the MISSING posters. "That's so sad."

"There's a volunteer search party on Monday," I say. "I'm going. They did a search—the police did, the weekend it happened but . . ."

"Well, I hope something turns up this time. Something good."

"Excuse me?" a girl's voice across the aisle. "Can we get the check?"

The runners are finished. They've been finished a while, judging from their crossed arms and unimpressed faces. "With you in a minute," I say to them, and to Caro, "Is there anything else I can get you or . . . ?"

"Just the check is fine."

I toss Caro's uneaten meal and get both tables their checks. After she's paid, she yawns. "Guess I'll go deal with my ornery husband."

"Good luck."

"Don't need it. Take care, Romy."

"You too."

Before she steps back into the heat, she smiles at me like we have a secret, just us girls. The niceness of it hits me like that kind of niceness does, reminds me of a space that is always open and empty inside me, that didn't used to be. I watch Caro cross the parking lot. Her enormous belly leads her way and I can't even imagine what that's like, having a person inside you, making life. There's a miracle there, but there's something so awful about it too, bringing someone into all this now, this world where a girl can't even trust a drink that passes her lips. I can't figure out the kind of heart it takes to do something like that.

"are you sure you want to do this?"

I study my reflection in the mirror. Mom watches me from my bedroom door. I won't be wearing yellow today, but I pick up the white Penny ribbon and pin it to my shirt.

"Why wouldn't I be?"

"There's going to be a lot of people there. I don't think one more is going to make a difference." She steps into the room. "You don't need to go, Romy."

The search will extend into the woods on the opposite side of the lake, and after, depending how it goes, The Find Penny Effort will begin the process of covering the highways and back roads from Grebe to Ibis. Our footsteps pressed in every place we think hers might have been. If we find nothing, do we stop? Or do we run through those places again and again, until we finally see her in them?

"I want to," I say.

"What if somebody gives you a hard time?"

"Be like any other day, then."

She winces. "I could go with you."

"I don't need you there."

"Maybe I want to look for Penny too." But I can see in her eyes that even if she thinks Penny deserves to be found, she doesn't think Penny deserves to be looked for by us. It's moments like these I understand my mother the most. I feel like I'm her daughter. "Why do you want to put yourself through this?"

Because they'll hang me if I don't. Because they'll hang me if I do. Because I think Penny would've looked for me. Because if I found her—at least this part of it all would be over.

"I have to."

"Romy . . ." At first—just by the way Mom says my name—I think she's going to tell me I'm brave, that I'm a good person for going, but she doesn't, which is a relief because it's not the kind of thing you should pat someone on the back for. She sighs. "If you want a ride home, call and we'll pick you up. Text me when you get there. If you don't want a ride, text me before you go, so I know you're on your way back."

I tell her I will and then I make sure to tell her I love her because more and more, I'm thinking about the last things I say before I leave.

the traffic to the lake is heavy, so out of place for Grebe on a weekday evening. I keep close to the shoulder and then I make my way up the congested path to the lake, passing the cars that just passed me. I stare at the brown pine needles littering the ground.

I walked here, that night. I remember it. That moment ghosts over this one, makes my skin tight, makes my fingers tingle. Every step forward, I swear I hear the fake click of a cell phone camera's shutter and a picture flickers behind my eyes: a girl on the ground, surrounded. A girl with her hands at her shirt. A girl—some other girl.

I take the white ribbon off and clutch it in my hand.

When the water comes into view, so does the crowd. I stop at the path's opening, forcing everyone behind me to go around. There must be over a hundred people: kids from school, some with their parents and siblings, most of them decked out in FIND PENNY shirts.

I see faculty members from both the elementary and high schools: Prewitt, DeWitt, Vice Principal Emerson, deputies from the sheriff's department. Principal Diaz is talking to reporters. There's Pam Marston from the *Grebe News* and I'm pretty sure the guy next to her is from the *Ibis Daily*. It's surreal. Cars crawl past and fill up the parking spaces. At the center of it all, there's a long table under a FIND PENNY banner. Brock is manning it and people mill behind him—

Penny's parents.

Seeing them makes me forget how to think. A memory of Penny skitters across my heart. *The only way you'd get my parents in the same room for longer than thirty seconds is if I*—us, in her room, a year ago. Her bedroom—*is if I died.*

It's eerie, what Penny took from her parents. She took Mr. Young's blond hair and his perfectly straight nose, Mrs. Young's blue eyes and petite frame. There is an ocean between the two of them, a bitter divorce, and it's awkward, ugly. I wish they'd fake some kind of closeness, just for this day, but they don't.

Alek comes up, filling the space, and he looks terrible.

Just beyond him is his mother, Helen. Matriarch. Queen of Grebe, Grebe Auto Supplies. My mouth goes dry.

Her black hair is tied into a tight ponytail and she wears a sky-blue GREBE AUTO SUPPLIES shirt with FIND PENNY emblazoned across the front because she's the kind of woman who would do that. Print up one color for everyone and wear another herself. She's tall, imposing, hasn't changed in the seventeen years I've known her. At those company picnics I attended when I was so young I barely came up to her knees, she looked exactly like this.

She turns her head my way, her eyes on me. It makes me cold. She was invisible, after, but I could feel her. Sheriff Turner made it clear the second we might've wanted to talk it out with her in the room, it would've meant lawyers. Helen Turner hates me and the way Helen Turner hates me feels like the worst kind of betrayal. A woman who doesn't think about daughters she doesn't have.

There's a little bit of time for mingling, for people to express condolences to the Youngs. After that part's out of the way, Brock brings a megaphone to his mouth. The breath he takes before speaking sends an ear-piercing shriek into the air.

"Once you've arrived, make sure you've signed in."

People move to the table as slowly as a herd of overheated animals. I'm about to make myself part of them when the last car rolls up and stops me dead in my tracks. My hand opens and the ribbon drops, flutters onto dead grass. I know that car. I know its body, its color, its backseat and its driver.

Leon.

The Pontiac idles momentarily before he finds one of the

last parking spots. He waves to me and my hands stay limp at my sides.

He gets out of the car and makes his way over.

No . . .

I try to figure out where everyone's eyes are because they can't be on us. They can't connect me to Leon because if they connect me to Leon, if they put us together—

"You look not happy," he says when he's close enough and when he's close enough, I step away. I try to smile because I can't let him know how wrong he's made everything, except I can't smile because he's made everything so wrong. "But that's probably understandable."

"What are you doing here?" It comes out harsher than I mean. He frowns.

"I asked Tracey for the night off. I thought I'd come so . . . you wouldn't be . . ." He can't hide the disappointment in his eyes when how I'm acting isn't what he wanted. "Moral support. But maybe it wasn't a good idea."

It's not a good idea. It's a nice one, but now he has to leave, so whatever's between us can stay nice. I skim the yellow shirts again, make sure more backs are to us than aren't.

"I'm just—" I take another step away and turn my face from his, so it doesn't look like I'm talking to him, exactly. "I wasn't expecting this."

"Okay," he says slowly. "But it's fine with you I'm here, right?"

Brock's voice blares over the megaphone again, makes me twitch.

"If you haven't signed in, please sign in. We need everyone accounted for."

Leon reaches out his hand. I can't hold his hand.

"Should we do that?"

"No," I say. One more step back. How many more can I take before he catches on? He lowers his hand, looking more and more confused. "I mean, let me do it for you. I'll write you in. The guy behind the table is a—he's an asshole, okay? I'll be right back. Wait here. Don't—"

Don't talk to anyone.

"Just wait here," I say.

Don't even look at them.

I leave him there. My heart is beating too fast and my palms sweat badly. I wipe them on my shirt. I reach the table, Brock. He takes me in and he's so hungry but the only thing he can do in front of all these people is look. It's enough, though. It's enough to be looked at by a boy like Brock like you're meat, like he'd take you to satisfy himself.

"Sign in," he says. "Or out."

I stare at the paper. I'm supposed to note my arrival time and there's a space to fill for when I leave. Next to the binder, there are bottles of water, a pile of whistles (TAKE ONE) and a card with a phone number on it that says POINT OF CONTACT—*if you get lost searching, call.* It's the sorriest possibility I never considered: someone going missing during a search.

"Forget your name?" Brock asks, after a minute. "Want me to write it down or are you afraid I'll get it mixed up with another four-letter word?"

I write my name, but not Leon's. I don't want Brock to have it.

I don't want anyone here to have it.

"How do we do this?" a girl asks beside me. I move down the table quickly, grabbing two bottles of water and whistles. Brock's attention drifts from the girl to someone behind me—

Leon, behind me.

Brock nods at him. "We're asking people to sign in—"

I can't handle it. I move because if the two of them are close, I want to be far, far from it. I'm almost halfway out—am I leaving? I should leave—when Leon catches up.

"Hey! Romy—" He said it, my name. Too loud, like he knows me. "Ro—"

I face him quickly, holding the water out. It keeps him from saying it again, keeps him from asking what's wrong with me, but I can tell he wants to. He takes the bottle.

"I told you that guy is an asshole," I say. "I told you I'd sign you in."

Leon glances back at Brock. "He seemed nice enough to me." It hurts, that he'd give Brock the benefit of the doubt, instead of trusting what I say. He looks around. "Are those Penny's parents?"

"Yeah."

"I could tell from the posters. She really looks like them," Leon says. "Who's the boy with them? She have a brother?"

"Boyfriend. He's the sheriff's son—" As soon as it's out of my mouth, it feels like too much information. I hold out a whistle. "Take one of these too."

He takes it and I pull my hand back too quickly, like our skin would burn if it touched. I look around. Brock is still at the table but—Tina. When did she get here? Tina's here and she's sidestepping people, making her way over to . . . me? My stomach clenches, imagining all the things she'll say if she sees me with a boy who likes me. I move away from Leon and she—passes us. Waves down Yumi. Leon bridges the distance I've created—it's too noticeable now—and touches my arm.

"Romy, what—"

It's like Brock senses it, Leon touching me, because he looks at us then. It turns Leon's closeness against me. My body revolts. I yank my arm away and it makes his eyes widen, makes him step back and I think—good.

The whine of the megaphone sounds again.

"If we could have your attention," a deputy, Cory Scott, says. His voice is all business and his expression is grim. Leanne Howard stands beside him, looking equally grave. "There's a few things need to be said before we break you into groups—"

"We shouldn't search together," I tell Leon quickly.

"Are you kidding me?" he asks.

The crowd begins filtering between us to get closer to the table.

"We can't search together," I say. "We'll just distract each other."

"First of all, thank you for coming," Cory says at the same time Leon opens his mouth to protest it, call me out, something. He closes it, though, because now's not the time to talk.

Thank God.

I keep my eyes straight ahead. The Youngs are just behind Cory, and Alek and Helen, just behind Leanne. Alek pulls at his fingertips, his eyes darting past faces, toward the opposite side of the lake. There's something in the way he holds himself that's—expectant.

"And thank you to Grebe Auto Supplies for funding this search."

Helen nods stiffly. I hear the soft click of the cameras, from the Ibis and Grebe reporters. They continue to take photos while the deputy speaks on behalf of the Youngs, who are too distraught to talk. Their faces belie everything that's coming out of Cory's mouth. He says they believe in us, that we'll be what brings Penny home, safe and sound, where others couldn't. Not the law, not some strangers she didn't know, not the helicopter last weekend. Just us. Here.

Today.

He breaks down how all this is going to happen and I forget Leon's eyes, still on me. First, we need to program the contact number into our phones. If we get separated or lost, too far out to be heard, this is how to touch base. Call the number and Helen Turner will pick up. The whistle should *only* be used in the event we find something relevant to Penny, or I guess, Penny herself. If you hear the whistle, we're to stay where we are and wait until we're given clearance to move. We should be vigilant in searching and don't forget to sign out when we leave, so everyone is accounted for. The more Cory talks, the more put-on this feels. It's a show. It's like . . . a funeral, something you only do for—the people left.

"Romy," Leon says softly, too close again. That's the price of paying attention to one thing; I lose track of something else. This is too much. Someone turns. Andy Martin. He stares at us, his forehead crinkling, trying to figure out how Leon and I fit. "Can you tell me what's happening here?"

"A search party."

"That's not what I mean."

"Nothing."

"Then why are you—"

"Why am I what?" Dare him to put it to words.

He shifts as the deputies start forming groups. I don't know how to keep Leon from being in my group but I know he can't be in anyone else's.

"Why didn't you put my name down?" he asks.

"I did," I lie.

"No. You didn't. And—" He steps closer and I step back and he does it again and I'm not sure why he's doing it until I realize he's proving a point. I hate him a little, for catching on. "You obviously don't want me here."

"It's not about you."

But it is. It's about keeping you.

"Then why are you being so—"

"Because this isn't a date."

"Jesus, I didn't come here thinking it was—"

His words start to blur because bodies are shifting, and I'm losing everyone's places.

"I don't want you here," I say and it must be the last thing he really expected me to say, even though he was the one who suggested it in the first place. And Brock, still watching. These worlds can't meet. They can't ever meet. "I don't want you here."

"Romy—" My name again. He reaches out and grabs my hand, holds it tight. It's the kind of contact I couldn't deny to anyone or pretend didn't happen. It makes my heart go terrible and it makes me do something terrible. I wrench my hand from his and say, too loud, "Don't *touch* me—"

The words taste and sound so bad out of my mouth. People stare and Leon backs away. One step back. Two. Three. A man I don't recognize, with salt-and-pepper hair and a stomach so big it precedes him, comes over. He puts himself between me and Leon, like he's my savior.

"You know this guy? He bothering you?" he asks. I open my mouth and nothing comes out because I don't know how to say *yes, I do, and no, he's not, but I need him to leave* and in that second's worth of silence where I should have said something, even if it was just stuttering over nothing, I memorize the hurt on Leon's face, what I caused, and I feel so sick.

"Maybe you ought to leave." The man steps closer to Leon. "Look, this is a search for a missing girl. This isn't the place to be making a scene . . ."

"Don't worry," Leon says, disgusted. "I'm gone."

He leaves. He doesn't look back at me once. He gets into his Pontiac and drives as slowly out as he did in, and when he's gone, the knowledge I've fucked things up badly is only second to the relief I feel that none of these people will have him. The girl he knows is still here and she can fix this. I know she can.

"Ms. Grey, we'll have you over here—"

Principal Diaz is at my side, ushering me into her group with Cat Kiley, a few freshmen, a woman who says she's friends with Penny's mom, and a deputy, Mitchell Lawrence.

The search begins.

We're told to walk in a line, side by side, and every time it goes ragged, if we get too far ahead or behind, Diaz yells for us to straighten out. We round the water and step into the brush and there's something unsettling about the way we weave ourselves into the trees. The lake is still, behind us. It's hard to imagine this place meant for anything but this. Not parties, not nice summer afternoons or family picnics. Just searching for the missing girl.

"What even gave you the idea anyone wants you here?" Cat asks, beside me.

I don't look at her. "Just trying to make up all the time everyone thinks I wasted."

Then, one of the freshmen, a boy, asks, "Are we looking for a body?"

I want to shove the question down his throat until he chokes on it.

"*No,*" Mitchell snaps, and the boy flinches.

"We're looking for a girl," Diaz tells him.

It's quiet after that. The farther into the woods we get, the darker it gets, and the air turns just so slightly cooler. Bugs hover curiously at our faces and we wave them away. Diaz holds herself like she's done this before, but there's no history of missing girls in Grebe that I know of.

"You can't," Cat says to me.

"What?"

We fall back a little. Enough to talk, but not enough to get yelled at for it.

"You can't make up that time." She steps over a large tree branch. "They probably would've found her if they'd started out with enough people looking for her."

I think of Cat collapsing on the track, think of her listless in Brock's arms. How jealous Tina was when Brock carried Cat off and what he said after Tina asked him if he got Cat to the nurse's office. *Eventually.* I wonder what Cat would think if she knew Brock said it and how when he did, people were deciding things about her, things she had no control over.

"I was on a *road.*" My voice cracks. "I had no idea where I was—"

"Then maybe you shouldn't have gotten so fucking drunk."

"I *wasn't* drunk—" And she rolls her eyes. "I think Brock slipped me GHB." The thing I didn't want to think about bubbles off my tongue, nothing I can stop. Cat's mouth drops open, and then she shakes her head over and over and I imagine her hands around my phone, aiming its lens at me. "Or maybe if I *was* that fucking drunk, someone should have taken me *home*—"

Diaz turns, furious. We've broken formation and we're too far behind.

"Ladies, *keep* up."

Cat hurries forward.

"So why didn't you take me home?" I call at her.

"*What* was that, Ms. Grey?" Diaz asks.

"Nothing."

The faint rumblings of another group breaking into the brush to our left reach my ears. I turn my attention back to the ground, waiting for something to catch my eye. Garbage all over. Tossed wrappers; dirty, broken red cups. I wonder how old it all is. If it's from the party and has been rotting away ever since, or if it's from some party years before.

How can we even be doing this?

We're combing through trash, looking for a girl.

I stare at a plastic bottle and try to decide if it's important. Twigs snap underfoot. Something moves above me. A crow flying from one tree to another.

A whistle sounds.

"stay here," deputy Mitchell says, and he goes.

I imagine Penny, her perfect body, bent and broken in these woods with no life left inside it. I imagine her hair matted with dirt. I imagine her pale face lighting up the ground and her eyes seeing nothing.

The whistle came from behind us, to the left. There's a flurry of voices. Other groups make themselves known. *What is it? Is it her? Did you find her?* The questions echo through the trees and after a long moment, a deputy, with the Youngs and Alek behind him, comes scrambling up the path.

A girl wails.

It's the kind of sound you run from, not to.

But I need to know.

Diaz calls me back, tells me to *stay* but I'm not a dog. I push through the brush until I find the girl and it's—not Penny. She's a small, pale thing, no more than ten, her knobby knees pointed toward each other, too tall for her age. She stands in front of us, shaking, her face red and tear-streaked. It's Lana Smith's sister, Emma.

And then the Youngs are there, and Alek, and another group, and another group, all of them wildly hopeful as they force themselves onto the scene and then—not.

When he realizes who it isn't, Alek stumbles back, turning in a dazed circle because no person in the world can go through that kind of having and taking away in such a short amount of time and still be okay after. He breathes hard, his face damp with sweat. And then he stiffens—clamps his hand over his mouth and staggers away. Brock runs after him, calling his name. Emma sobs through it all and Lana is suddenly there, like we're all suddenly here, pulling her little sister into her arms and she's apologizing to the Youngs for none of this being what they wanted except I don't know what anyone wants anymore.

"I got separated." Emma sobs. "I got scared—"

"It's okay," Lana says. "It's okay. She was scared. We're *so* sorry. Emma, tell them you're sorry—" and Emma bleats over her, *I'm sorry, I'm sorry, I'm sorry* . . .

Mrs. Young does something I don't think I could do if I was her. She doesn't lash out, doesn't yell or cry. She gathers Emma in her arms and tells her *it's okay, we understand, it's okay* . . . and then more people, more witnesses to this, all this nothing. It's nothing. Someone says something about taking a five-minute break and I hear a deputy mutter *waste of time* and that's when I decide I have to leave.

I make my way back through the woods and around the lake and the rotten, stagnant scent of the water makes me nauseous. I text Mom, begging a ride home and realize I didn't even let her know I arrived, like I said I would.

The point of contact comes into view. Helen Turner at the table, on her cell phone, getting the news that it's not Penny. As much distance as I can put between us is not enough. Being this close to her makes me want to bury myself. God, did my dad hate her. Hated her. I think part of him was always secretly happy she fired him because it proved it, didn't it, that she *was* the cunt. Helen is still on her phone when the New Yorker pulls up. Todd's in the driver's seat. I climb in and buckle up. I press my hands against the cold air vents until my fingers go numb. He drives us out.

"How'd it go?" he asks.

I think of Leon and how much he must hate me now, when I see a flash of blond hair, a girl on the road. I twist in my seat and it's—not her. Again. And I don't know what about it is worse than what happened at the lake, but it is. It is. I duck my head and wipe at my face. Todd reaches over, his hand against the back of my neck long enough for a reassuring squeeze, which makes it harder to stop crying.

"I didn't sign out from the search," I say.

"You need to go back?"

"I don't think anyone's going to worry about it."

i need leon to know I'm sorry.

I don't need his forgiveness. I don't believe in forgiveness. I think if you hurt someone, it becomes a part of you both. Each of you just has to live with it and the person you hurt gets to decide if they want to give you the chance to do it again. If they do and you're a good person, you won't make the same mistakes. Just whole new ones. I grab my phone from my nightstand. I could text it out, but that doesn't seem right. I hurt Leon to his face so the least I can do is apologize to it.

But first, there's school.

I get dressed. I stare at myself in the mirror, at my dry

and flaking lips. My nails are fine but this isn't. I pick off pieces of dead skin and then rub a toothbrush across my mouth until it's smooth. I wash my face and apply my lipstick one layer at a time and then I'm ready. I tie my hair back and wonder how Penny's mornings start now. They still start, don't they?

When I come downstairs, there's breakfast waiting for me. A piece of peanut butter and jam toast, cut into thin strips. It was all I ate, every morning, the entire summer I was nine and back then, I called the strips "fingers." Peanut butter and jam fingers. Comfort food.

"I wanted you to eat with us," Mom says.

I don't know who it's comforting.

I nibble at the toast while Todd flips through the paper in the seat across from mine and Mom fries them up bacon and eggs. He slaps the paper down and taps it.

"It's going to rain this week."

"I don't believe it," Mom says.

"It's right here in the *Grebe News,* though, so you gotta."

She sets his breakfast in front of him and then rests her hand on top of his head. Todd gets hold of it before she can move to fix her own plate. He brings her hand to his mouth.

"Love you, Alice," he murmurs, easy as that.

Mom catches my eye and there's something guilty on her face, like this is something I should have had in front of me all my life. Todd is different from my father. Dad was thirsty, not given to great displays of affection, like his father and his father's father before him. A long line of self-indulgent men who couldn't give love but lived to take it, which isn't the same as receiving it. They were all in so much pain and that's always the perfect excuse.

"Next week, they'll probably put in something about the search party," I say.

"Probably," Todd agrees.

Mom settles in with us. "Maybe you could take the night off and we could have some mother-daughter time. Go shopping, end the day at the Ibis McDonald's or something."

"What's Todd going to do?"

"Wither and die," he says dryly. He reaches across the table and scruffs up my hair. "Seriously? What the hell kind of question was that?"

"I just want to spend some time with you," Mom says.

"Maybe the weekend? I'm trying to prove to Tracey I'm reliable right now, after . . ." I trail off. "And I just took yesterday off for the search."

"Before the weekend would be better."

I study her. "What's going on?"

"Just do your mother a favor and humor her."

"Okay. Before the weekend," I say but I really have to go to Swan's tonight, to see Leon and try to untangle that mess. "It can't be today, though."

I take my time on the walk to school because I'm in no hurry for an aftermath. The air is as sweltering as it ever is. Hard to picture it raining. Hard to picture it any other season but this one, which isn't even the season it's supposed to be, really.

The street is quiet for the first half of the walk, but soon the hard, rhythmic sound of feet hitting pavement is at my back. I glance over my shoulder and Leanne Howard is jogging my way. She's wearing a black shirt and shorts, accented with bolts of neon to tell the world she's doing this for the exercise and not because she's being chased. I move off the sidewalk so she can pass, but she breaks when she reaches me, hunching over to catch her breath.

"Whew." She gasps, straightening, wiping the lower part

of her sweaty face on the collar of her shirt. "It's too hot for this, isn't it?"

"You're crazy," I say.

"Well, it's maintenance." She squints at me. "How are you, Romy?"

"I'm headed to school."

"Mind if I walk with you?"

"Free country."

But I don't like it. Leanne falls into step with me. I take her in. She's young, but she has the same kind of lines Coach Prewitt does, I think. I wouldn't fuck with her.

"Search party was something else," she says.

"I left after Emma Smith. What happened?"

"Alek had to be walked out. He was a wreck—"

"Really?"

"Yeah, and nobody had the heart to keep going after that. I think they'd probably do better searching the highways, honestly," Leanne says. "But I don't think they really wanted to find anything yesterday."

I remember the deputy muttering to himself after the false alarm.

Waste of time.

"Then why would they even bother with it?"

"Combat helplessness," she says simply. And then, just as simply, "Romy, you have to know they're looking for a body at this point."

It stops me. Stops my heart.

No, I want to tell her. *You're wrong.* Penny isn't dead. Penny made it through almost four years of high school beloved by all, except for me and even I was won for part of it—you don't make it through high school like that and not survive whatever it is she's gotten into.

"I've been thinking about what you asked, when you came

down to get your phone," Leanne says. "That maybe looking for you was the reason we didn't find Penny. And then I heard some of the kids talking about you at the lake." She looks at me, pities me. "They were saying it."

"That surprise you?"

"I don't know," she says.

I shrug in a *conversation's over* kind of way, hoping she'll let me continue on without her, but she doesn't. She's at my back and then she's at my side again. It's too early to start the day with this kind of headache.

"Look, whatever anyone feels about you, it's no small thing you got found." She puts her hand on my shoulder and then we're stopped again. "When I saw you on the road, I was so damned relieved. And it eats me up that we haven't found Penny yet, but when it comes to missing girls, you barely get that lucky once, let alone twice. Anyone trying to guilt you—that's bullshit."

I stare at the ground. I don't know what to say to the idea that finding me was worth anything to anyone beside my mother, and Todd. And Leon, who's probably sorry about it now.

"So it wouldn't have made that kind of difference?"

I want to hear her say it—that, exactly—if it didn't.

She bites her lip. "Even it did . . . it wouldn't have been your fault."

"What's that supposed to mean?"

She looks away from me. "Just what I said."

I pause. "How'd they rule out the connection between us, Leanne?"

"I can't tell you," she says. "But I promise you it wouldn't be your fault. I just wanted you to know, okay?"

I laugh a little. "Well, thanks a lot for that. I'll just keep that thought close when they're telling me over and over

I'm the girl no one wanted to find."

I start walking again, try to forget this whole waste of my time, but then she says, "I need my job, Romy."

I turn. "So?"

"So when Turner tells me I'm not supposed to say something, I don't," she says. "Sometimes I don't whether or not I think it's right. I still think I should've driven you to the hospital that day." She stops. "But I *need* my job for my family."

"I wouldn't say anything," I promise and the more torn she looks about it, the more my heart wants to know what she knows. "And no one would believe me if I did."

It deepens the lines on her face.

"It was Ben Ortiz's daughter," she finally says. "Tina."

Tina.

A name like a razor on my skin.

I know whatever Leanne tells me next is going to cut me open.

It does.

my palm rests against my chest. I knead my skin. I listen for my heart because it went quiet a while ago and I'm not sure it's there anymore.

Wait for it. I'm waiting. Waiting for the girls coming down the hall. Their voices arrive ahead of them, float sweetly under the crack in the door. I stare at the dirty floor tiles of the locker room and. Wait. For. It. Tina comes in. I stare at her feet as they walk to her locker. I watch her slip out of her shoes and when she starts undressing, let my eyes wander, up her legs, her hips, her soft belly and her breasts.

"Know why half the sheriff's department was wasting time

looking for me when they could've been looking for Penny?" I ask.

Tina's fingers pause behind her back, stop seeking the clasp of her bra. She doesn't say anything, just raises her chin in a way that dares me to go on. Dares me to say out loud how she was at the sheriff's department that Saturday night, telling them what she did to me so they'd start looking in all the right places for Penny. I stand, my legs trembling like a newborn colt's until I feel it, a soft *thud* in my chest—my heart, coming alive—and I get steadier.

"You put me on that road. You dragged me out to that road," I say. "You wrote *rape me* on my stomach and then you left me there."

She holds my gaze. This is what I want to happen: I want the girls to realize *she's* the thief who stole that time from Penny. I want them to round on her. I want them to eat her alive without once opening their mouths. I want this to be the end of Tina Ortiz, but the things I want to happen never do. No one makes her guilty. No one makes her pay. Even the sheriff wouldn't do that. Not to his good friend's daughter.

"Nice story," she says.

Thud, again, louder now and not so soft. Tina goes back to fumbling for her clasp. This is how little it matters to her, as little as it did the night she stood over me and wrote on my skin.

"Besides, anyone would have done it," she says quietly, so only I can hear it.

My heart pleads with me to do something about this, so I can breathe around it. Tina and that road.

She put me on that road and invited people to my body, anyone.

What happens next is something I don't remember deciding to do but knowing, after, that I would do it again and again, a thousand times.

I shove her into the lockers, drive her into that metal as hard as I can. The sound she makes is better than any song I've ever heard. I want it on repeat. I dig my nails into her arms, feel her softness give in to me. Her eyes widen and she shoves me back and then there's a space between us, enough to paralyze me with all of the things I could do to her next. I could raise my hand and hit her in the face or bring my knee into her stomach, take a fistful of her hair and rip it out of her skull. You don't get to do this when you're a girl, so when the opportunity for violence finally presents itself, I want all of it at once. That same stillness seems to come over her too, and for one second there is nothing—and then—

Inside me goes wild, turns all of me into a weapon. I was born to hurt and so was Tina. I strike her, break her skin, but she doesn't just stand there and let it happen. She comes back at me as hard and in the ways I want her to, in the ways only Tina would.

At first, the only thing I feel are the parts of her I'm trying to ruin. Then her elbow finds my center and steals my breath and everything is alive in me after that. *Everything.* Every blow she lands, I return however I can. It's messy. It's my foot on her bare toes and the sound she makes, it's her hand in my hair, it's those strands free of my scalp.

Girls are shouting, girls are too scared to pull us apart. Tina pushes me into a row of lockers, some of them open, and my forehead meets the edge of metal, and there's pain but what is pain even, really—this is release, nothing worth stopping for.

We are not going to stop.

Someone will have to stop us.

It isn't until Coach Prewitt comes in with Principal Diaz that I realize there's blood in my eyes. *She's bleeding,* a girl whispers. I'm bleeding. I bring my hand to my forehead and the tips of my fingers are soaked in myself.

I lower my hand and Tina is across the room from me and she looks like hell. There's a scratch on her shoulder and a bruise on her cheek. I did that. But . . . I stare at my hand again, the red. Her bared stomach. This can't be over.

I haven't written on her yet.

I lunge for Tina, but Diaz grabs my arm and shouts, "Hey, hey, *hey*! *Enough!*"

Tina stumbles into Prewitt, her eyes wide and terrified, like she was never fighting back because now is exactly the time to act that way. I should act that way, but I can't.

I want to hurt her until I feel finished.

"*What* is going on here?" Diaz demands, her voice echoing ferociously around the room but before anyone can say anything—and Tina's mouth is open enough to do it—she takes a look my face and changes tack. "Ortiz, get dressed and go to my office." She shakes her head. "*Disgraceful.* This is—" She casts around for another word, finds none. "Disgraceful. I expect better from all of my students, but you two—"

"Grey started it," Tina says. Did I?

"I said *get dressed*, Ortiz," Diaz snaps. "Grey, follow me."

She leads me out of the locker room, the sound of her heels clacking on the floor. I bring my hand to my head again. The cut is above my right eyebrow and the bleeding hasn't stopped yet. Diaz glances at me. "It's all over you."

I look down. She's right. My collar . . . everywhere.

"Where are we going?" I ask, a little thickly. Blood doesn't make me woozy at all but the adrenaline from the fight is fading and this is so strange.

It's strange, feeling it all come out of me like this.

"I'm taking you to the nurse's office to get that cleaned

up," Diaz says. "I don't know what possessed you. That was an awful display." *Awful,* I think, and then I laugh, just a little. Diaz rounds on me. "You think this is funny?"

I press my lips together and look away. I think it's hilarious. There's a girl out there everyone thinks is dead and maybe she is because you know all the ways there are to kill a girl? I do. But I'm supposed to worry about whatever trouble this stupid little fight at school is going to bring me beyond the satisfaction I felt while I was in it.

In the nurse's office, DeWitt looks me over. I wait for him to tell me I'm old enough to take care of myself, but instead he inspects my forehead with gentle hands and says it's beyond any of us.

the stitches seem so unnecessary once most of the blood is cleaned away and I can see the cut, but Dr. Aarons numbs my forehead and says *it's deep enough* and *hold still.*

I've never gotten stitches before and there's something about the odd pressure of the needle as it goes in and the pull of my skin as it's brought together. Mom can't handle the sight and waits for me in the waiting room. She's been having a hard time looking me in the eyes since she picked me up from school.

"Explain it to me," she says on the drive home. I lean back in my seat and close my eyes. "Romy, explain it to me. What was going through your mind that you would do something like that to another girl?"

"No," I say. "Nothing."

She pulls into the driveway. I'm out of the New Yorker before the engine is off.

"Romy, wait—"

I cut a straight line for my room because I figure I'll get sent there anyway, but Todd is in the way and he stops me at the steps. He stares at my forehead like he can't make the connection that what happened to me is something *I* made happen because if I made anything clear before I left school, it was that I was nobody's victim.

"Jesus, kid," he says softly.

He steps aside and I let myself into the house. By now, my head is starting to feel like it met the sharp edge of an open locker. I hear Mom throw her purse on the floor. I'm halfway up the stairs before she says, "Romy, you stop. Stop *right now.*"

I do, but I stay pointed in the direction of my bedroom until she tells me to turn around and look at her. I turn around and look at her, them. Because Todd is still there and for once, I wish he was as absent as the man he replaced.

"Explain it to me," Mom says again. "Because I don't want to hear about it for the first time in your principal's office tomorrow when we're finding out if you're still welcome at school. You will *not* do that to me."

She sounds like someone who's already lost the war, but just won't stop fighting in spite of it. And she's right; I won't do that to her. I wouldn't and couldn't do that to her. Every day, she's got to be my mother in this town. I don't need to make that harder than it already is.

"Tina ran her mouth, so I shoved her and the whole thing went from there."

"Really." Mom crosses her arms. "That's all?"

"Yeah."

"You're not telling me something. This isn't like you," she says. I think she's wrong. It has to be like me, if I did it, otherwise I wouldn't have. "What did she say to you?"

"Doesn't matter what she said."

"Yes, it does. If you don't tell me, how can I help you?"

"What could you do to help me?"

She looks like I've slapped her. The truth is, I don't really know if she could help me, but I know she really wants to believe she could and I know she wants me to come to her believing it too. My love should be knowing this about her and being able to pretend, but I can't. I go to my room. No one tells me to. I just go.

a week's suspension.

I thought there'd be more trouble than that, but since Tina's the one who left me on the road and the Ortizes know I know it, they don't demand answers from me, for what I did to their daughter. I wouldn't have said it anyway, not in front of my mom. I just stare at Tina's father and I hate him. I wonder if he's already told the sheriff about this, or if he's waiting for their next round of golf. Because Tina and I have never conducted ourselves in such an unladylike manner before, Diaz says we're getting off easier than we would have otherwise. I want to ask her what *unladylike* means.

We leave the office an awkward fivesome, just before the

bell goes. Our parents duck out as soon as it rings, opting to wait in their cars while Tina and I get our homework for the week. She's immediately flanked by girls who want to know the whole story. I catch Tina's beginning—*She's a fucking psycho, they won't do anything*—but I don't hang around for the end.

Teachers are cold to me when they hand me my assignments and I wonder if it's an honest reaction or one Diaz told them to have. When I reach Ms. Alcott's room for my English homework, Brock is at her desk. She hands him a pile of papcrs.

"Give Alek my best. Tell him I hope we see him back here soon."

"Yeah, I will . . ." Brock tenses when he sees me. "Thanks, Ms. A."

He leaves with her smiling sadly after him and the smile disappears when she turns her attention to me. "I have *your* homework right here . . ."

"What's wrong with Alek?" I ask.

She looks at me like I'm an idiot and in this moment, I get the feeling she truly doesn't like me.

"You can't imagine the kind of stress Alek is under right now, but I hope it gives you something to think about, Romy. There are people with actual, real troubles out there and—" She grabs a stack of worksheets, and hands them over. "There are people who make trouble for themselves."

Brock is waiting when I come out. I barely have time to register him before he's too close. Too, too close.

"You're telling people I slipped GHB into your drink at Wake Lake?" he asks, and he sounds almost amused, like he's been so bogged down by the weight of all this Penny stuff, he's okay with this funny little distraction. "Really?"

"Did you?"

"Why are you asking, if that's what you're *telling* people?"

As much as I want to run, I also want to corner him, want to turn this into a confrontation and scare a confession out of him somehow, but it would never happen, not with Brock. The safest thing my body can do is keep moving.

"I know you had it," I say. "I heard Sarah and Norah talking about it in the girls' room—"

"But can you prove that I gave you any?" Anger swells inside me, the kind that made me want to tear Tina apart. "I mean, are you *telling* me you remember a specific moment where I slipped GHB into your drink? Because if you can't, Grey, you better shut your fucking mouth."

"Did you?" I ask again because the only thing I can do is ask. People are looking at us, me and Brock, walking down the hall together. It's not right. None of it. He must sense it too. He breaks away, innocently holding up his hands.

"Did I?" he asks back.

When I get in the car with my loaded-down book bag, I'm shaking. I want to bite my fist. I try to keep it all off my face as Mom says, "You're going to call Tracey tonight and you're going to tell her you're not going to be at work until next week—"

"What?" I blink. "I can't—"

"I don't think suspension from that place," Mom says, nodding at the building, "is going to drive home the point that what you did, Romy, was wrong. You don't get to stay home all day and then go to work and see Leon. What about that is a punishment?"

Hearing his name is a painful reminder of what I still have to fix. I don't know how I'm going to do that because when I play the search over in my head, I don't know what I could have done differently.

"What am I going to tell Tracey when she asks why I can't come in for a *week*?"

"You'll have to figure it out."

"And if I lose my job?"

Mom sighs. "If I really thought you'd lose your job, do you think I'd make you do it? Last night, I told Tracey you got into some trouble at school, that you got hurt. She's waiting for your call."

"You tell her I started it?"

"Obviously not."

At home, I call Tracey from my bedroom and tell her I need time off and she makes her voice nice for me, loses that managerial edge that keeps everyone in line. Holly will cover my shifts. It's fine. It's totally fine. It takes me the afternoon to knock out my homework, penciling answers I have no confidence of being right but I'm confident I don't care if they're wrong. When Mom goes to her cleaning job, Todd puts dinner in my hands. He sits at the table, flipping through an old paperback while I chop up potatoes and onions and cut the skin off some chicken legs. It's sort of peaceful.

"You start a fight with Tina Ortiz because you're upset about something else?" he asks casually, turning a page.

Was sort of peaceful.

"What?"

He tilts his head back to look at me. "You heard me."

"Did I start a fight with a girl because I'm upset about something else?" I repeat and he nods. "That doesn't even make sense."

He cracks the spine of the book and sets it on the table. "You're telling me you never been mad or upset over one thing and took it out on another person?"

"I don't know what you're talking about."

"I think you do." He pauses. "You know, you can tell us what's going on. There's no one you have to keep it a secret from."

"I don't know what you mean," I say again. He sighs heavily. I wait until the oven beeps and then I put the chicken in and time it.

"Take that out when it's ready," I tell him. "I'm not hungry."

i wake up on my bed on top of the covers.

I feel like it should be morning, a new day, and I guess it is. When I check the time it's three a.m. I don't remember setting out to sleep, but it must have pulled me under.

I stare out the window. The street is so quiet. Lights off in every house I can see from here, all the people inside with their eyes shut. It's an hour before the first signs of life—a car headed down a road that's not this one—reach my ears. It's a few minutes more before there's another: a thin whine floating in through my open window, familiar but out of place this late. The screen door. I peer into the darkness, trying to figure out whether it's someone coming or going and then I hear a soft cough.

Mom.

I expect to see her move from the steps to the sidewalk, from the sidewalk to the New Yorker because maybe we're alike that way. Maybe sometimes she just has to get in a car and go too. She never materializes, though, and the telltale whine of the screen door never sounds again, so she's just out there, alone. I don't want to join her but I think I have to. It's kind of like stumbling upon the scene of an accident. Once you've looked, you're part of it.

Especially if you walk away.

I climb out of bed and tiptoe into the hall. Their bedroom door is open a crack. The sound of Todd's snoring drifts out. I creep down the stairs, to the open front door. I look out, past the porch, to where my mother is sitting on the steps, her head resting against her knees, and in that moment I'm struck by how young she is. I forget. Todd too. My father, even.

Sometimes, I feel like we all have so many lifetimes to go.

I step into the dry night air. Mom straightens, looks at me like she knew I was going to show. I sit beside her. She puts her arm around me.

"Dinner was good. I saved you a plate. Tried to wake you up but you were pretty out. You told me—" I hear the smile in her voice. "'Watch their feathers.' Thought I'd let you sleep."

I do that sometimes, when I'm really tired. I only let a small part of myself awake and talk nonsense until whoever wants me up leaves me alone. I could hold an entire conversation as long as it doesn't have to make any sense. Once I told her *this isn't ours.* Another time, *the glass won't break.* Mom revisits these moments sometimes, like they're such great memories. She runs her fingers along the outside of the bandage on my forehead and asks me how it feels. I shrug and tell her, *okay.* After a while, there's the sound of another car rushing the pavement. This one's headed our way.

"Blue Ford," she says. It makes me ache. It's a game we used to play, all of us. Her, me, my dad. Only on his good days. Guess the car and color by sound. Since my dad spent all his time around cars, he never seemed to miss the make—but color was anyone's game.

"Purple Honda," I say.

We're both wrong. A black Chevy goes by.

"I know why you started that fight."

It's slow going over me, what she's said. She knows. What does she think she knows? I stare at the walkway, those vines visible, even in this dark, imagining different possibilities. She knows about the photos? The words on my stomach? No—she can't know anything.

"That's because I told you why I started the fight."

"No, you didn't."

"Look, do we have to do this now? I—"

"*Yes,* we do. I don't push you to talk because I don't feel like I have a right after everything that happened—" She pauses. "I've been waiting for you to tell me why you started that fight with Tina but I know you won't. But I know why, Romy—I've known."

I close my eyes briefly. "Then why?"

"Kellan Turner's coming back."

All I feel is the shock of it and then the pain, and then all I can think is doesn't she know a name can be as good as a declaration of war? That I can say anything I want to her now, no matter how cruel it is to get myself—back.

Coming back.

"That's what happened," she says. "Isn't it? Tina said something about it to you."

Poison. It's traveling my veins, turning my blood into something too sick to name. It works its way through me, finds my heart and then—every vital part of me turns off.

"You knew." The words find their way off my dead tongue, slow and stupid, thick like syrup. I feel something new pulling me under now but nothing so merciful as sleep. I struggle against it, fight to stay here even though this is no longer any place I want to be either. "You knew?"

"Todd heard about it from Andrew Ryan on Monday. I wanted to tell you before the search, but it didn't seem like the time—and then I wanted to tell you on Tuesday, but—" *Maybe you could take the night off and we could have some mother-daughter time*. Oh. "I just couldn't figure out how to break it to you. But I knew there was one way I didn't want you to find out and you did." She exhales. "That's what Tina said, wasn't it?"

"Yes."

"Well, he's not back yet," she says and only the smallest part of me gives in to the relief of that, just the smallest part. "Monday—is what Todd heard. That was the soonest he could get time off from his job—" A job. A job. This little fact lights on me in a way I don't want it to. I don't want to know anything about him. "He's here for Alek, so I get the sense he'll be keeping a low profile, but . . . Romy, you don't have to be brave all the time, you know? You should talk to me."

I wait until another car moves down the road, its headlights in the distance. I let myself see them and nothing else.

"Black Chevy," I say because maybe it's come around again.

"Uh—no," Mom says. "No, no, I think it's a . . ."

Her voice breaks.

She never finishes.

Inside, in my room, I write my name on my lips over and over, but I don't feel right, I don't feel like myself. All those parts of me turned off. I don't want to be a dead girl. I don't want to be a dead girl. I need to come back. I pick up my phone and text Leon.

IT'S ME, I tell him but what I mean is *please*.

running seems more important now.

Running is the only thing I want to do. I leave in the morning and I run through Grebe until I can't anymore, until I almost have to crawl my way home. I want to learn how to pace myself in a way that means I'll never have to stop.

When I wake in the mornings, I'm so stiff I can barely move. I take showers hot enough to burn past skin to relax muscles. I eat breakfast because I don't want my body to cannibalize itself. I don't want to be weak. I don't want to be sick. I just want to be fast.

By the weekend, the air is changing. Today, I wake up

and the sky is a sick green-gray. It might actually rain, like the *Grebe News* said, or maybe it's just being a tease. I lace my running shoes, tell Mom I'll be home later. I walk until the house is out of sight and when it is, I start at a light jog, like this is my dirty little secret. I get the feel of myself before I circle the back streets and make my way out of town.

Coming back.

I interrupt that stray, unwelcome thought by focusing on putting Grebe behind me and by the time I'm at its edges, I feel the first tentative drops of rain.

The sky is darker now, promising a storm.

I reach the highway. I don't know where I'm headed. Ibis is closest, but there's nothing for me there. I keep to the shoulder and the rain falls with a little more certainty. I glance down the ditch, at all the overgrown grass and garbage in it, and think of my classmates searching for Penny and I think as long as no one finds her, she gets to be alive.

That's the thought that breaks the sky.

It's like the rain has been up there, accumulating for ages, getting heavier, too heavy, and now it's all coming down at once. It drenches me, plastering my hair to my face and my clothes to my skin. A semi goes speeding past and the sound of it makes my ears hurt. All of its wheels splash road water on me but I don't care. I push on until I reach Slab Road, a dirt road just off the highway. Mud road, now. My feet slop against the ground. Eventually, through a curtain of rain, I see a shape on the horizon. Something's not right. I squint, trying to make it out.

It's an accident.

An SUV in the ditch. All the way in. Tipped forward, its grille pressed against the earth. I double over and clutch my stomach with one arm, trying to pull air into my lungs while I reach for my phone with the other.

I stumble forward until it's clearer, what I'm looking at.

An Escalade EXT.

There's only one of those in Grebe.

I'm immediately set on going back the way I've come, leaving this here for someone else to find but—I stare at the wreck. I can't tell if it's the kind of accident that would hurt someone bad or just badly enough.

I don't have to help, just because I want to look.

My legs are numb, but I force them to take me to the car, to Alek. I get a good look at the wide gap between the back tires and the road and it's going to really take something to pull this out. My eyes drift down to where the vehicle's weight is pushing the front of it farther into the grass, the ground.

The driver's side door is flung wide open.

I inch down the embankment. My running shoes barely grip the grass. I fall into the car and my fingers slip over its wet exterior. I peer in the driver's side. Keys in the ignition, but the engine's off. Cell phone on the floor—his. I pick it up, check his call history, see if it's a tow truck or an ambulance or something. But his last call was last night, to his mother.

"Penny!"

I turn to the woods beyond the car.

How long has it been since I heard her name said like that?

Like it was being said to her.

Penny. If she's back, if she's in those woods, it can go back to how it was and no one needs to be here that doesn't need to be here. I move into the trees, where the rain comes lighter and I see a boy in the clearing. Alek, in the clearing. He's not looking at me, his right arm held tight to his chest. He's as broken as I've ever seen him but I don't care, wouldn't care, because I'm looking for her. Alek called her name. She has to be here. Has to. If she comes back, *he* doesn't.

Alek stumbles around when he hears my footsteps, his eyes wide. He loses his balance and hits the ground hard and then he's just sitting. He buries his head in his hands, his long, thin fingers creeping into his hair, and then he slumps onto his side, curls in on himself.

He's drunk.

He's drunk and she's not here. He didn't find her. I wonder if he was pretending he had. Drove himself off the road knowing she wasn't here, but wanting to feel the lie just for a second. He unfurls himself slowly, until he's on his back, staring at the sky, so resigned to this, me.

"I guess I'll call your dad," I say. I'll call his dad and nothing will come of it. I get pulled over sober, and Alek. He'll stagger away from this, untouched.

He closes his eyes for a minute and when he opens them again, says, "Gimme your phone. Gimme your phone, I want to show you something."

The sick understanding of what he's just given away washes over me.

He stares up at me, focuses enough to enjoy it.

"Oh, you saw them," he says.

"You—" I lower my phone. "You took the pictures."

He nods, the back of his head rubbing against the ground, a grin ghosting his mouth. This memory makes him smile, is the only thing that could make him smile right now. I close my eyes and I see Alek, I see my phone in his hands and I don't want to hold my phone if it's been in his hands. I don't want my skin, if he's seen so much of it.

"You let me," he says.

"No." I didn't. I wouldn't have.

"You did—" He starts to laugh and his eyes drift closed.

"I told Penny you let me and she didn't care. She told me to . . . she told me to stop. The last time I talk to her, we *fight*—" He stops laughing and opens his eyes. "About you."

I step away, but I can't untangle myself from this, what he's said. I can't . . .

"But you let me, you wanted it." He tries to sit up, but he can't, he can't, and Penny's in my head, and she's taking something from me, she's always taking something from me. A girl at a diner, a girl sitting across from me in a booth. She opens her mouth and she says—"Like you let him. Worthless fucking slit."

He looks so much like his brother these days. I want to bury him. The rain is on us both and I want to bury him. He flops uselessly against wet leaves and the mud, too drunk to stand and I walk over, the beat of my heart dulling until it stops and I plant my legs on either side of him. I grab him by the collar and pull him half up so I can push him in the dirt again because I want to be the worthless fucking slit that buries him. He desperately grabs at my arms until I'm on top of him, my knees in the ground on either side of him, he's underneath me and I'm pressed against him. He calls me that word again and the rain is on us both. I want to bury him. I want to burn a moment of helplessness into him so he can know a fraction of what I felt, what I feel, what's followed me every moment since, so I **You** cover **cover** his **her** mouth **mouth.**

i've been away but there's nowhere I've been.

I stumble out of the trees, use the wrecked car to climb up the bank. Alek is still on the ground in the woods and I feel like I'm crawling through time, a time, and my head is thick with it, my legs and hands numb with it. Something wants out of me, someone, some girl. No. Not her. Not. Her. I slip, come down hard on one knee. I get up slowly.

When I show up at Leon's, I'm not myself.

The rain follows me to Ibis, all the way to Heron Street, to his basement apartment. I walk until I see his Pontiac and then I round a little stone house until I find the door that must be his. I bring my fist to it. After a few minutes, Leon answers and when he sees it's me, he closes the door in my face.

"i shouldn't have done that," he says, backing his Pontiac out of the driveway.

I sit in the passenger side, picking at the seat belt. I keep my eyes painfully open because if I blink, tears will spill over. He's taking me home. I'm not sure I was even going to get that much out of him before he saw how drowned I was, before he took in the bandage on my forehead and my mud-streaked legs.

"You should have."

"No," he says firmly. "No, I shouldn't have. I don't treat people like that."

"But I do."

"Yeah, I guess you do."

"You didn't let me explain."

He turns off his street. "You sent me *one* text message."

"You didn't answer it."

"The more I thought about it, the more I didn't want to."

My chest aches. "Why?"

"You acted like you didn't know me. You acted ashamed."

"No—"

"Yeah, you did. And when I touched you, it was like—" He winces. "Like I was doing something wrong. You almost had me *forcibly removed* from a search party—"

"No," I say again. "No, you weren't—they wouldn't have—"

"You don't think that's how that was going to end?" he demands. "Jesus, Romy, I was the only black guy there and the way that asshole was with me when he thought I was bothering *you*—I know the kind of look he was giving me."

This—*this,* I am ashamed of. I can taste it, my shame, his hurt, and like that, the only thing I can say isn't good enough. But then, it never was.

I just didn't realize it until now.

"You're right," I say. "Leon, I am so sorry."

"You say that a lot." He comes to a stop sign and won't look me in the eyes. "I can't think of a reason you'd have for doing that to me that's good enough."

The reason is I need him. I need him to get this ghost off me because I still feel her. I still feel her and I want her to stay dead. The car starts moving again. I blink accidentally. Tears. I try to wipe them away before he sees, but I can tell he sees by the sigh he lets out, which makes me feel wrong, like it's some kind of manipulation. If I know anything it's that a girl never makes a case for herself by crying. It's just one more side of herself she's showed can't be trusted. He drives on for a little while longer, rain spattering the windshield as he gets us out of Ibis.

After a stretch of highway, he pulls into an abandoned parking lot where Fontaine's gas station used to be, before it burned down. He turns the car off.

"So tell me," he says.

The space between us only feels big enough for the truth. I try to quell my rising panic, the kind that makes it hard to breathe. I can't tell him the truth.

"Romy," he says.

But it doesn't have to be the truth, it just has to get close enough to sound like it.

That's how every lie about me turned itself into something honest.

"Grebe isn't a nice place," I say.

"So?"

"They don't think much of my family and I didn't want

you to have to deal with it." The way he's looking at me is suffocating. "That's all it was at the search party."

"You're saying knowing you would be a problem for me in Grebe."

"Yeah."

"You know how that sounds, right?"

"Grebe Auto Supplies—" I stop. "You've heard of it."

"Who hasn't?"

"That's Helen Turner's business, the whole thing—she's married to Sheriff Turner. Their youngest son is Penny Young's boyfriend. I pointed him out to you on Monday. Alek Turner."

"I remember."

"The Turners hate my family and once you get on their bad side, you get on everyone else's bad side too, so yes, it would've been a problem for you."

"And what the hell did you do to get on everyone's bad side?"

"My dad—"

"Your dad."

"He called Helen Turner a cunt—he worked for her—he drank . . . he's a drunk." I close my eyes briefly. "She fired him. It was bad."

He waits for me to say more and when I don't, he reaches for the keys. "If that's all you got for me, then I was right. It's not a good enough reason."

"Okay," I say.

"Doesn't help you don't even look like you're telling the truth."

It makes me—makes me want to get out of the car. How can he see that—how can he see that, if he can't see her? Does he see her? I can't—I turn my face from him so there's less of it to look at and then, before I can stop myself, "What do I look like?"

"Romy, come on." He sighs. "Something's not right here."

No. I'm wearing the red. I'm—I pull at the seat belt, my hands clumsily reaching to unbuckle it and he says, *what are you—what are you doing?* I taste metal in my mouth. If he can see it—he touches my arm, keeps me in place. I force myself to breathe, to not give anything away.

"It *started* with my dad," I say. "Imagine . . . you go missing the same night as a girl everyone loves—and you're the girl everyone hates, and you're the one who comes back." He doesn't say anything, but I don't know what it means. I don't know Leon's silences like I should. "You showed up at the search and—you think I'd hurt you like that on purpose? You're the good part—"

"They couldn't have done anything to me," he interrupts. "If I'd known why you didn't want me there, I'd have left to give you the peace of mind. All you had to do was tell me. But you didn't. You made it so much worse—"

"You're right," I say. "I fucked up."

I stare out the window at the sky, waiting for the sun to part the clouds. It's funny, to go all this time wanting for rain, but now it's too much.

"So I'm the good part," he says.

I exhale shakily. "Yeah. But how I treated you was ugly and something ugly happened to you because of it and there's no excuse for that. I'm sorry."

I turn to him. He's not looking at me. "I want you to be the good part too," he says. "And if you want to be the good part, then don't ever do something like that to me again, Romy."

"I won't."

He turns the keys, gets the car going. He reverses out of the lot. I listen to the hiss of tires as they skim the rain-coated road. Sheet lightning flashes across the sky when we reach the YOU ARE NOW ENTERING GREBE sign.

"So I'll see you at work," he says.

Our eyes meet. I see myself in his and something inside me locks into place. It's slower this time, but whatever he thought he saw before—is not there anymore. She's not there anymore. Impulsively, I reach out and touch his jaw, running my fingertips down that line, and he stops breathing. I lower my hand and get out of the car. I make my way up the walk and when I look back, Leon is still there, his fingers gently wondering over the places mine were.

i get my stitches out.

I sit in the doctor's office with my head tilted up and after it's over, he declares me *good as new.* Mom takes me to Ibis and we get milkshakes and sit in the New Yorker in a parking lot overlooking Egret River, watching the rain come down. I don't talk and she has no words to offer. She reaches over and squeezes my hand. On the way out of Ibis, she comes to a red light and Penny's MISSING poster is plastered to its pole. It's weatherworn. Curled at the edges and creased in the center. It feels like she's been gone forever.

"You girls," Mom says, staring at it. "Such fast friends."

The nostalgia in her voice forces memories I don't want.

Me, at the dinner table with my head ducked, texting frantically with Penny on my phone, and—when dinner was over—in my room talking with her until I could see her at school, and then school. Seeing her at school.

After Dad was fired for calling Helen Turner a cunt and Alek and I got paired for that English project, Alek wanted it difficult, wanted it as awful as it is now. He held me responsible for my father so it was only fair I hold Penny responsible for him. I don't know why it's the girls who always seem to have to take on that kind of burden. After my dad got fired, it was my mom who got the brunt of the town's pity and disgust, never him.

I must have impressed Penny, must have made a good case for myself because she talked to Alek and he got nicer. It was like I wasn't my father's daughter—I was one of them. We were fast friends, too fast . . . and both of those girls went missing and now neither of them exist.

The light turns green. When we get back to Grebe, it's different. Ugly. This place is always ugly, but in a way I could at least count on. I can't count on anything, now that he's back.

when todd drives me to work Tuesday, I ask him if he heard anything about Alek.

"Like what?" he asks.

Like if he was in a wreck because he was drunk driving. If he spent the night in the drunk tank. If they took his license away. But I just shrug and say, "Anything."

"Nope."

We pull up to Swan's, which is some kind of dingy picture, the rain bringing the outside of the building down a few shades in color. I climb out of the car and thank Todd for the ride.

"See you in a few hours," he says. I cross the parking lot

as quick as I can and when I step in through the back, to the kitchen, I'm only half-soaked.

"Hi," Leon says as I shake myself off.

"Hi."

He smiles, a very tentative smile. A smile that is still not sure it's what I deserve. A small gift. Tracey steps out of her office and smiles at me too. "I hope you're ready to work. The rain's been driving people in like you wouldn't believe."

"Hey there, stranger," Holly calls. I turn. She holds up a newspaper. "You've been gone so long, I almost forgot what you looked like 'til I saw this."

"What?"

I take the paper from her and my stomach sinks. The *Ibis Daily,* a week old, and there I am in black-and-white. It must have been before Leon arrived at the search because I don't see him—just me with my arms crossed, staring at a sea of people, all wearing the same shirt, all looking for one girl. But the girl that I'm looking at is undeniably, unmistakably me.

On the front page.

I tighten my grip so the paper doesn't shake and give me away because all I can think about is who might've seen this, about how they know what I look like now. No—just how I look in black-and-white. I live in color. There's no red in this photo, it's still mine. I could—I could cut my hair, if I wanted. I might have a scar now. I touch my forehead. If I don't, I could make one.

"Sorry the search didn't turn out," Holly says.

I crumple the paper and toss it in the recycling bin. I grab my apron and tie it and try to get my head back in the game. When I step into the diner, the fluorescent lights flicker and I hear someone from the kitchen groan before the door swings shut. Just be Tracey's luck to trade the AC trouble for power outages.

I scan my station and there's a man in a corner booth waiting on me and he looks familiar in a way I can't totally place. I don't like faces I can't place almost as much as I don't like the ones I can. I pull the pencil and pad from my pocket and walk over.

He nods at me, his brow furrowing.

"I know you?" he asks.

"No," I say but I take a closer look at him. There's something about him, something frustrating about him because I think I do know him. He's in a plaid shirt. One of his legs is half-stretched into the aisle. There's a hole in his jeans. He's young, early thirties, maybe. The kind of young that . . . that's been in the sun too long. The man in the parking lot, the one in the truck.

Not safe to be out this late around here. A girl's missing.

He seems to remember it the same time I do, snaps his fingers. "Well, damn. Didn't know you worked here. You're awfully young to be working here."

"Can I take your order?"

"How young are you?"

"I—" I shake my head a little. "The special today is the club sandwich and it comes with soup. The soup of the day is tomato."

"I'm just making friendly conversation," he says.

"I'm just trying to do my job."

"Well, what if I tip better when you talk?"

I press my lips together. He grins and leans back in his seat, turns to the window. The rain has eased up a little. "I'll have that special, with a cup of coffee. Black."

"Okay."

"Ain't you going to write it down?"

"I'll remember." But I write it down as I go, narrowly missing Claire on my way by. *Watch it, Romy,* she tells me.

By the time I've put the order in, I feel wrong. He just makes me feel wrong. Holly notices. She's getting ready to go out for a smoke.

"What's up?"

I take her over to the door and point him out. The guy is staring at the ceiling now, tapping his fingers along the table. "That guy there."

"What'd he do?" Holly asks sharply, because she's like that. Been here long enough to look out for us girls better than we look out for ourselves. I don't know what to say to her, though. That he makes me feel wrong isn't a good enough answer.

But I think it should be sometimes.

"I just don't like him."

"You want me to take the booth for you?"

Yes. "No."

She pats my shoulder and heads outside. I watch Leon work.

"Order's ready," he tells me.

I take it out. The man rubs his hands together eagerly while I set the food in front of him.

"Thanks a lot," he says. I wait for something gross to come out of his mouth, because that's what my gut tells me should happen—but it doesn't. I take another booth's order and head back to the kitchen feeling like I should have lightened up because he didn't meet the worst of my expectations, like somehow I'm the villain in his story.

"You okay?" Leon asks.

It's one of those rare, quiet moments when Tracey's in her office and most of the other girls are on the floor or on break and there's hardly anyone around.

"Break later?" I ask, because it feels like the easiest way I can be sure of his forgiveness.

He makes me wait a long minute before he wipes his hands

on his apron and crosses the room to give me a hug. It makes me want to cry. I forget everything and the forgetting is so nice.

"Sure," he says.

Leon reminds me of a time before the move across town. When Todd was over a lot, trying to convince my mom we all needed to live together. I came home from school and the house was quiet until a low moan drifted from upstairs and I followed it to her closed bedroom door. I couldn't keep myself from listening. I'd heard my mom and dad having sex a handful of times in my life. When he was drunk, when he was sober, when she was sad or so angry she couldn't talk to him, but she was still willing to kiss. It always sounded desperate, like the two of them were clinging to the last way they knew how to understand each other. The way my mom sounded with Todd—it wasn't like that. It seemed tender, beyond anything I'd ever experienced with someone else. This is tender. I press my fingers into Leon's shirt and try to memorize it but he pulls away. I want to forget myself in him again.

I get back to work instead. I send out another order and by then, the guy is finished with his. I get him his check. He palms it off the table and says, "Hey, you know you can be professional *and* friendly." Then he grabs a napkin and scribbles down some numbers on it, slides it over to me. "Give me a call, you want some advice."

I don't know why I take the napkin. It's something my body does without checking with my head first, like the obligation to be nice to him is greater than myself.

I go back to the kitchen, replaying that moment in my head, hating that I did it, hating that it's done and that I can't take it back. I slip into the bathroom and my lipstick is faded out. The rain? I don't know. All I know is it was mostly gone when that man forced his number on me. I fix it and step out of the bathroom and Leon's phone is blaring music from his back pocket. He steps away from the grill to answer it.

"What's up?" He listens for a moment. "What? How long? You—why didn't you call earlier? Really? Yeah, no—yeah, if I leave now I might—yeah. I can do that—okay, tell her I love her. I'll be there. I'll see you both soon." He hangs up in disbelief. "Uh . . . Caro's going to have her kid—like now."

"What?" I feel my expression mirroring his, that same weird shock. I don't know where it comes from. It's not like we didn't know she was pregnant.

"I know." He shakes his head and then strides over to Tracey's office, opens the door. "Tracey, you got to get someone to take the grill for me. I have to go. My sister's in labor. She's going to have her baby—"

"What!" Tracey hurries out and throws her arms around Leon. "Oh, congratulations! This is wonderful. How close is she?"

"They've been in there since this morning. Like . . . any minute now, the baby's going to be here, so I have to go . . ." He pulls away, laughing a little. "Wow. I have to go."

"Tell them I said congratulations," I say.

He smiles. "I'll let you know how it turns out."

I watch from the back door as he cuts through the rain in his Pontiac and makes his way out of the parking lot. I stick my hands into my pockets, my left closing over the balled-up paper napkin and that old thought comes, but stronger now.

Maybe it's a prayer.

I hope it's not a girl.

I hope it's not a girl, but later, after my shift, when I'm undressing for bed, Leon texts me to tell me it is.

the ground turns soft.

The lake fills to brimming and the river has more water than it knows what to do with. At times the rainfall is so light, it tricks us into believing it's stopped until we step outside and find it's misting. Other times, it seems angry, trapping walkers under store awnings, sending cars hydroplaning.

Most of all it's constant.

I ask Mom to drive me to school and to pick me up. It's amazing how easy it is to stay inside if it means not risking seeing a face you don't want to see, hearing a name you don't want to hear. Leon takes the week off work to help Caro and Adam adjust. I miss him.

On Saturday, he calls and tells me about Ava, his niece.

"She's amazing. Ugly-cute."

"Ugly-cute?"

"Yeah. She's all squished, looks like an old man," he says and I laugh. "What, don't you think babies are kind of tiny little ugly freaks until they're six months old or so? I do."

"I don't see enough babies to have an opinion. How are the new parents?"

"Blissed out on hormones, as predicted. Both of them. Nature at work."

"That's nice."

"It's weird. Caro would love to see you. Told me to invite you down." He pauses. "How about you come to Ibis tomorrow? Have lunch and meet Ava? I'll pick you up."

Oh. I'm glad he can't see my face because the idea repulses me in a way I don't know how to put to words. But that's probably a good thing because I have a feeling it wouldn't go over all that well if I could. I don't want to meet the baby.

"Sure."

"Great. You know, I can tell you one thing after all this—I definitely don't want to move in and babysit. I have gotten nothing done with the online stuff. I mean, I'll help them out when they need it but I feel too . . . not for this."

"I know what you mean."

"Yeah?"

"Yeah."

"Anyway, I've got to go. Caro and Adam are trying to catch some sleep and Ava's getting fussy. I'll pick you up in the morning though, around ten?"

"Sounds good," I lie. I hang up and stare at the phone and worry how it's going to end up, visiting Caro a second time. If I'll make a fool of myself again. I try to think of what I'll say when I see Ava. And I probably can't go empty-handed.

I go to the bathroom, and discover a rusty brown stain in my underwear, and on top of it, fresh blood. Not even a warning, this time. I don't know if it's a couple days early or late, but I don't want it, regardless. I put a tampon in and change my underwear and when I'm done, I head downstairs where Mom is curled up with Todd on the couch. They're watching television and the warm glow of the screen on their faces makes them look so settled. Mom asks me what I need.

"Can you drive me to the Barn? Leon invited me to see the baby tomorrow and I think I should probably bring something. Toys, I don't know."

Mom smiles. "That's sweet, honey, but I don't think you're going to find anything worth giving at the Barn."

I prickle a little, wonder if she's trying to tell me in so many words it's too cheap a place to buy something nice. She'd be right, but the last thing I want to do is buy anything in town. God knows what Dan Conway would get going if he saw me with baby stuff.

"Why not?"

"The baby's how old?"

"Like a week?"

"At this point, the baby probably has everything she needs," Mom says. "So think about Caro. What does Caro need?"

"I don't know."

Mom carefully unfolds herself from Todd. It's a slow process; he always seems reluctant to let her go and I think she likes to savor that as much as possible.

"Time. That's what she needs. Time and one less thing to worry about."

"Well, tell me where I can buy them and I'm set."

"Food," Mom says, giving me a look. "Take her some

freezable homemade meals. That's time Caro won't have to spend making dinner and it means it's one less thing she'll worry about. The first month after you were born, anytime anyone showed up with a casserole, I *cried,* I was so happy." She nudges me to the kitchen. "Come on. We've got work to do."

We figure out a menu that demands more food than we have in the fridge. I make a long grocery list and hand it and some money to Todd, who salutes us both on his way out.

"I get a dinner out of this too, right?" he asks.

"If you're good," Mom tells him. He leaves and she starts pulling what we do have out of the cupboards and fridge. She gives me a bag of carrots to chop, because we're starting with her famous carrot soup. We settle in at the kitchen counter, shoulder to shoulder.

"How are you?" she asks after a minute.

"They kept the sex a secret," I say, which isn't even an answer. "Caro and her husband. They didn't want to know what they were having until they had it."

Mom smashes some garlic with the side of her knife. "Your father and I did that."

"I didn't know that."

"As soon as we found out I was pregnant, I wanted to keep it a secret. Your father didn't, but since *I* was the one giving birth, that got to be my call."

"Did you want a girl?" I ask.

"I wanted a baby."

"Did Dad want a girl?"

I ask it before realizing it's nothing I really want to know. She pauses and answers too carefully.

"He was happy when you were born, Romy. It was different then."

"I didn't ask if he was sorry he had me. I wanted to know if he wanted a girl."

"Okay. Well . . . at first, he wanted a boy because he was nervous about having a girl. He was afraid he wouldn't be able to understand you or relate to you if you were a girl but when you were born—he cried harder than I did. He was thrilled."

It's too hard to picture, so I don't.

"How often do you talk to him?"

I don't know why that's the next question inside me.

"I don't," she says. It surprises me. I thought they were still in touch. I always imagined her hiding up in the bedroom, whispering furiously at him over the phone. That's what they did when I was really young. Stood behind closed doors and whispered, like I would never be able to tell things were bad if they were whispered.

"Even when I was missing?"

She hesitates. "Do you want me to—if there's ever an emergency—"

"No. I'm just—I just thought you would have."

"Maybe once," she says and I know we're both thinking of a time she made excuse after excuse for him until finally, there were none. "Your father loves you, Romy—"

"Mom, don't—"

Because I don't need her to tell me because—

"But it's not enough."

I know.

I knew it before she did.

"And you," she says. "You feel how you want to feel about your dad. It's not ever going to be wrong, you understand me?"

I don't know what to say. She continues to prep and I try to do the same but it's hard to focus. Todd comes home forty minutes later with all the groceries. I keep my eyes on my cutting board, don't realize there's anything worth looking up for until Mom asks, "What is it?"

I turn. Todd stands in the kitchen doorway, the handles of the plastic grocery bags twisting slowly in his grip. He looks paler than I've ever seen him, paler than he gets when he's in the worst kind of pain. He sets the groceries down and runs his hands over his mouth a couple of times before he finally speaks and when he does, he says—

He says, "They pulled Penny Young's body out of Gadwall River last night."

ARE YOU OKAY? he asks.

I CAN'T SEE YOU TOMORROW, I tell him.

He says, I UNDERSTAND.

He says, IF YOU NEED ANYTHING . . .

But what could I need?

What could I need, that she doesn't anymore?

MISSING GIRL FOUND

A headline terrible enough to stop hearts and a story to crush them. A story the *Ibis Daily* isn't supposed to have yet. They missed the weekend print edition, but put it on their Web site and that's what Todd shows us, the crumpled printout someone passed to him at the grocery store, like a note in class.

> A family friend, who does not want to be identified, says the body of 18-year-old Penny Young was recovered from the Gadwall River early Friday night. The Young family was notified of the discovery earlier this morning.

> The Grebe and Ibis Sheriff's Departments would not confirm this, but said they will hold a news conference Sunday at 1 p.m. to discuss the latest developments in the case.
>
> Young, who divided her time between her mother's residence in Ibis and her father's residence in Grebe, was last seen at a party in Grebe. She was reported missing by her mother when she did not arrive at her house the next morning.

I smooth the paper out on my desk and then I press my left hand flat against it. I reach for my nail polish. Before I tore the label off, this color was either called *Paradise* or *Hit and Run.* I wonder what it would be named if they had to call it what it really is. *The color of your insides. The stuff your heart beats. Nothing you can afford to lose.* I lift the brush and watch the red drip unhurriedly back into the bottle.

"Romy," Mom calls.

I run the brush against the edge of the bottle's opening, until the bristles are barely coated. I start at my pinkie finger and paint it carefully. My hands don't shake. Not even a little.

"Romy, it's starting soon."

The first coat is dry by the time I'm on the last nail of the first hand. I move onto the next one. And then the second coat. I don't go outside the lines. If you don't go outside the lines, not once, you're even more the person you're trying to be, maybe.

And then I'm ready.

"Romy, it's starting now."

I sit on the couch between Mom and Todd. The sides of my legs touch theirs. I lean forward, my fresh-painted fingernails against my fresh-painted lips.

There's a table of officials stretched across the length of the television screen, all of them somber. A man I don't recognize stands at a podium, too tall for its microphone. I want to reach through somehow and adjust it for him. He thanks an audience I can't see for attending and when he tells us what happened to her, his voice doesn't shake.

Not even a little.

He says the body of a girl was located in Gadwall River by two campers. He says they noticed something tangled in a tree's low-hanging branches in the water, upstream from their camping site. The postmortem indicated the body was likely held under by those branches, likely submerged until the rainfall made the river wild and moved what was left of her just enough to be seen. The postmortem indicated that the deceased died from suspicious, nonnatural causes, but no further information regarding that will be released at this time, so as not to jeopardize the ongoing investigation—into the death of Penny Young.

Mom puts her arm around me and holds tight like she wants to be sure it isn't a mistake, that they are definitely talking about some other girl that's not me.

I listen as the man runs through every little thing they did to try to make this ending happier. Interviewing every student at the party—which I guess is what they call it when Sheriff Turner sits across from you at a table and tells you that you're fine—the ground and air searches, following up on two hundred phone tips, volunteer searches. For all the good it did. When the world wants a girl gone, she's gone.

"Jesus," Todd says when the news conference ends. He turns the TV off. "Everything they did when the ground was dry and they couldn't find her. Now all that night is completely washed away. I don't know what they have to go on."

I feel Mom looking at me. She moves a strand of hair from my face.

"You okay?" she asks.

I stare at the blank TV screen and everything feels far away.

"If it's a suspicious death, what does that mean? Someone put her there? In the river?" My voice sounds stupid and my head feels that way too. Someone put her in the river after they—what? "I don't understand what that means."

Todd says, "It has to be bad if they don't want to tell us."

mom drives me to school.

We pass Leanne Howard, jogging in the rain, and I want a glimpse of her face, to see what all this looks like on her, but there's not enough light for that. The sky is dark gray and the clouds are hung so low, it doesn't even feel like it's day.

Mom pulls up as close to the building as she can get. I stare at the front entrance. The FIND PENNY display is gone. I know it couldn't stay, but it seems wrong there's nothing in its place. She's not here so she was never here.

I get out of the car, hurry through the rain. Inside, everything is so quiet, I have the fleeting thought it's just me in this space, but I climb the stairs until I reach the mourners crowding the halls. Everyone in clusters, close to their lockers, heads bent together, whispering, bodies humming with grief. It all feels familiar and unfamiliar at once. That moment we discovered she was gone is here again, more real than it was before, and we can't hope our way through our uselessness this time. She's never coming back.

I get my books out of my locker, go to homeroom. I'm the first one there and McClelland sits at his desk, sorting through papers. He's stone-faced, but his breathing gives him away: every breath a gasp, every gasp a failed attempt at regaining control. I sit at the back and try to make myself not hear it but it's all I can hear. I watch the door, watch students file in one by one. Some of them come in messy and tearful and some of them look like they've just managed to stop crying and others are determinedly dry-eyed, just like McClelland.

The bell rings.

McClelland turns the television on. After a brief delay, the screen fades in on Penny's photograph, nothing else, and now she's too here. It's the same photo they used on the MISSING posters, clearer on the monitor than it was on paper. Not blown-out black-and-white, but color and her eyes look—more alive than they did when I thought there was a chance she still might be.

McClelland stands, resting his hands against his desk.

"We have been advised to take a few moments this morning to talk with you about—" He runs his hand over his mouth, already overwhelmed. "About the death of Penny Young. Penny was—" He stops again. "A light . . . in the lives of all those who knew her. We were privileged to know her. This loss is unfathomable. This loss is cruel."

I stare at the two empty seats at the front. What if her empty seat was mine?

What would they say about me?

"There are guest books in the library and you are encouraged to leave your memories of Penny and your condolences in them. At the end of the week, they will be sent to Penny's family. A memorial assembly is being planned. We will keep you notified of when the funeral—" He can't deal with this word, presses his lips together for a long moment. "Reporters have begun to arrive but we ask you to please honor our friend and classmate and her loved ones by not speaking with them."

McClelland sits. Speech over. He stares at the clock. I follow his gaze and watch the second hand tremor forward until the bell rings. I tally the missing. Brock, Penny, Alek. But that seems to be it. Everyone else is here to share in the devastation. The bell rings again and again, and by the time it's Phys Ed, there's a little more life in the halls. The presence of the news vans outside have made this no less a tragedy, but—more of an event. It's what Cat Kiley is talking about in the locker room.

"Are you going to speak to them?" she asks Yumi.

"*No,*" Tina says before Yumi can answer. "And neither are you."

"Why not?" Cat asks. "Marie Sinclair went out there and said they only wanted a sound bite about how people were taking it—"

"Penny is *not* a fucking sound bite." Tina takes her shirt off. Cat makes a face and turns away. Tina throws her shirt at Cat. It nails her square in the back. Cat whirls around, furious. "Do you hear me? You say *anything,* Cat—"

"*Fine.*"

Cat picks up Tina's shirt and throws it back to her.

"That goes for the rest of you too." Tina's eyes skim over everyone before settling on me. "If I see you on TV tonight, you better hope to hell it's worth it tomorrow."

We size each other up from opposite sides of the room, looking for cracks. She's radiating anger, holding it to herself, keeping it close and not making room for anything else because anything else would be too much. She won't let anyone see her pain, but you'd have to be a fool to think it wasn't there.

"So what do you think happened to her?" Yumi asks quietly.

Tina finally tears her gaze from me. Throws her shirt onto the bench and goes into her locker for her gym clothes. "Doesn't matter what I think."

"Were you talking to Brock? Did he say . . . ?"

"What would Brock have to say about it?"

"I don't know. Maybe he talked to Alek. Maybe Alek heard it from his dad . . ."

"Sheriff Turner won't tell Alek anything now," Tina mutters.

Cat crosses her arms over her chest. "I've got a curfew, so does my sister. Eight o'clock. Just in case some creep had her and he's still out there. That's what my mom thinks. She thinks Penny got raped. She thinks that's what they're not saying because—"

"Shut your fucking mouth."

I'm expecting anyone's voice but my own, don't even realize I said it until it echoes back at me in my head. That was me. It was me. I stare at my open locker, my hands at the edge of my shirt. I forget what I was doing. I forget what I'm here for. There's a point to all of this but I don't know what it is anymore.

It's quiet, and then, "What did you say?"

I bite my lip so nothing else accidentally comes out.

"What did you say to Cat, Grey?" Tina asks.

I close my locker and face the room. They're all staring. Cat seems closer to Tina now. Tina may bite, but I'm the one that walks away from fights covered in blood.

"I told her to shut her fucking mouth."

"Why?"

"Because she doesn't know what she's talking about."

"And *you* do? Really?" Tina runs her tongue over her teeth and I'm so sorry I started this. I don't want to be the place she puts her anger. "Well, wait. You're good at playing pretend about this kind of stuff. So you think she was raped before she was in the water?"

Cold. I'm cold. I don't feel the floor under my feet, don't feel anything. I flex my fingers and I wouldn't know they were moving if I wasn't watching them do it. I blink and the girls are still staring and I want to ask them if they feel it, that cold, because it can't just be me.

"You—" Tina stops.

You.

If it had been me instead of Penny, no one would call me a light. No, they'd think of me the way they think of me now, think of it as some kind of natural conclusion to my story, sad, maybe, *deserved it,* well no, of course no one does, but. That girl. You can see it. It's written on her.

They wrote it on her.

"Come on, I want to hear it from you," Tina says. "What if she was?"

"Then she's better off dead."

in the girls' bathroom, I run the water hot and hold my hands under it until I feel

a reporter tries to flag me down in the parking lot, some Ibis news station. He wears a stiff-looking suit and tie, smells like a sickening combination of hair spray and cologne. *Would you be willing to say a few words about Penny Young?* I shake my head and make my way to the other side of the street, where Todd waits in the New Yorker. I glance over my shoulder, pausing briefly to watch the reporter try and fail again to get someone to say something about Penny, and then finally—a bite. A willing freshman who must like the idea of being on television more than he fears the consequences. I climb into the car. Todd waits for a few walkers to go by before pulling out. I rest my head against the window and watch the school get farther and farther away.

"It should settle down soon," I say.

"What's that?" Todd asks.

"Everything. After they bury her." I don't have to look at him to know I made him cringe. "And then everyone will go back—" Back to where they came from. Todd doesn't say anything, so I say it again. "Everyone will go. Right?"

"Likely, yeah," he finally says.

"You think we should worry if someone's out there? That did this to her?"

"Well, it's crossed our minds. Your mother's and mine."

"Yeah?"

"Yeah, we'll be driving you to work and picking you up. Should've been doing it sooner. I don't know what the hell we were thinking." He looks like he wants to say more about it, but he doesn't. A few drops of rain hit the windshield, and a few more. "I've got to stop at the hardware store and pick up a shelf kit for your mother. It'll just take a second."

We head up the main street and park in front of Baker's Hardware. At first, I think I'll stay in the New Yorker, but then I think about who might walk or drive by and see me. I follow Todd in. The manufactured scent of pine fills my nose. Manufactured pine and real dust.

"Howdy, Bartlett," a feeble voice says. I follow it to the cash register, where Art Baker sits. He's the kind of seventy-five that acts ninety. "Romy."

"How you doing there, Art?"

"This rain keeps up, it won't come down."

Todd chuckles politely. "That's for damn sure."

"Shame about the Young girl, huh?"

"Yes, very." Whatever trace of a smile was on Todd's

mouth disappears. "Really is. We were hoping for a better outcome."

"We all were."

I wander a little down the aisle to the fishing supplies, start picking through the lures. My dad tried to teach me how to fish once. Short-lived, failed experiment. I loved the lures, though. The flashers. They were too interesting for such a boring sport.

"Ken Davis near killed three kids out looking for her the other week," Art is telling Todd. "Searching the back roads in the dark, none of them wearing reflective anything. I put a sale on some reflective tape. Thought it would drum up some business. That was right before they found her."

"That's . . . how about that."

Missing girls. Good for business.

"How about you? You loving your domestication?"

"I got a family now, Art. What's not to love?"

Art laughs. "You got a breadwinner, is what you got and now you have even less to do." The ancient asshole. I glance at Todd and he just stares at Art, doesn't join in on the laugh at his expense until Art is uncomfortable he made the joke in the first place. "Anyway—I missed what you needed. What was it?"

"I didn't say. But a shelf kit. Those ones in the flyer?"

"Right. Yeah. Follow me." Art shuffles out from behind the counter and leads Todd through the store. He could just tell Todd where it is—this place is barely two rooms—but no doubt he wants the excuse to keep talking. He touches my arm as he passes. "You doing okay there, Romy?"

I don't look at him. "Yeah."

They disappear, but Art's voice carries. I tune it out and walk over to the front window. It's raining harder now. The main street can't even pretend it's something nice in this kind of weather. I turn away and a display at the cash register catches my eye.

POCKET KNIVES

MUST BE *18 OR OLDER* TO PURCHASE

The knives rest in a box, propped up by a plastic display stand. One knife is open across the top and I can see myself, a distorted mess, in the blade. I scan the colors and patterns laid out below. The knives on the left side are different from the ones on the right. They are steely grays, forest greens, browns, and solid reds. On the right, the colors seem softer. You wouldn't call them for what they are, but give them names like *blush, rose* . . . there's a pink camo pattern. I'm sure it's the perfect knife for some girl out there, but I wonder what, if any, kind of sincerity the manufacturer made it with. If they were thinking of that girl, or if they just thought it was a joke.

Maybe they don't know how easily a girl could make this knife serious.

I reach my hand out.

"Romy."

I step back. Todd and Art make their way toward me. Todd holds up his shelf kit.

"I'm ready. Are you?"

"Yeah."

I stare at the open knife while he pays.

I wonder if it would have made a difference.

leon's waiting outside for me when Mom drops me off at work. She honks the horn at him twice, and he waves. His eyes light on me, concerned, like when he first saw me after the road. I don't like being reminded of that. He asks me if I'm okay and I tell him I'm not the one they pulled out of the river. He frowns.

"They're not giving you a hard time about it, are they?"

"Leon, that's what they do."

"You can talk to me," he says. "If you need to."

"I know."

"I'm really sorry, Romy."

"It's okay."

We weren't even friends when she died.

He hugs me before I can do anything about it. I like when Leon touches me, but not like this. I don't want to feel anything about her in the way he's holding me. He pulls away and I give him a weak smile and we go inside. Holly tells me she's been having nightmares about Annie, terrible things happening to Annie.

"She won't listen to me," she says. "And I can't watch her all the time. She just wants to push me, she doesn't *think*. This thing with the Young girl—I can't convince her to be afraid of it. I don't know how to make her scared enough."

"She'll grow out of it," I say because I don't know what else to say.

Holly pulls a pack of cigarettes out of her apron pocket.

"Yeah," she mutters. "If she lives that long."

I work my station, try to lose myself in the repetition of walking the floor, waiting on the tables, taking orders, placing orders, but I can't. I feel uneasy, like something's not right beyond everything that's already wrong and that feeling gets worse the more the night goes on. It gets so bad I end up stopping in the middle of my shift, looking for its cause, so I can make it go away.

Penny's MISSING posters.

They have to come down. I can't believe no one here has done that already, that it wasn't the first thing they did. That not one customer has said anything about it yet.

But—they would have, if they'd seen her.

Penny stares at me. She stares at me until I rip the posters down.

They didn't see her and now it's too late.

when the weekend comes, Leon says maybe it would take my mind off things if we go to Ibis and see the baby and I say *yes* because there is no good way to say *no*. I paint my nails and my mouth and then I'm ready. I sit on the couch and watch TV until midafternoon, when Leon's Pontiac pulls up. I have a feeling there's no point in trying to beat Mom to the door, so I let her and Todd answer it while I fill a cooler with the week's worth of frozen food she and I made for Caro and Adam.

"Uncle Leon!" Mom opens the door for him and he laughs. "Congratulations."

"Yeah," Todd says. "Good to have good news these days."

I drag the cooler out. Leon stares, impressed. "You really didn't have to do that but they're going to be thrilled you did. Thank you."

"Anytime," Mom says. "Give them our best."

Leon and I leave. There's a break in the rain today, clear enough to run and I'm sorry I'm not doing that instead. He turns the radio on and I don't know what to talk about, so I let the music fill the silence until he can't seem to stand it anymore.

"Reporters finally clear out?" he asks awkwardly, when we're almost there.

"Yeah," I say. "I forgot to tell you. The last of them left Wednesday. I don't know what took them so long."

"Maybe they were waiting for the Turner kid to show. Hoping for something from the Grebe Auto Supplies heir. Makes it all a little more interesting."

"Because it's so boring, otherwise."

"Hey, that's not what I said. News loves a good tragedy, they love known quantities. You get the tragic, known quantity and you've got something."

"I don't think they'll be seeing Alek soon. I don't know if he'll even be able to handle the funeral on Tuesday."

"You going?"

"It's private," I say. "They're having an assembly at school on Monday and the visitation is Monday night."

When we reach Caro and Adam's place, I get out of the car more nervous than I was my first time here. If Leon notices, he doesn't say anything. He hauls the cooler out of the backseat and I follow him up the driveway. Caro opens the door before we even reach it.

"Excited to see us, huh?" Leon sets the cooler down and gives her a hug.

"Ava's sleeping. I wanted to beat you to the doorbell, so I

wouldn't have to beat you *at* the doorbell," she says. "She should be up soon, though."

She lets Leon go and turns to me and there's this brief moment where we look each other over. I want to see how motherhood wears on her. She wants to see how a dead girl wears on me. Caro's in a pretty blue tunic and black leggings and a pair of slippers. She looks tired, but her contentedness makes the tired look good. She takes me in and I don't think I work my look so well, because the corners of her mouth turn down.

"I'm so sorry about Penny," she says.

"It's okay." I don't know why I can't think of something better to say than that because it's such a bad answer. It's not okay.

"Leon told me it was complicated, between you and her," she says and he looks away from us. "But still. A shock. I hope you're all right."

"I'm fine. I'm . . ." I force the next words out. "I'm excited to meet Ava. Oh—and I brought you some food." I point to the cooler. "My mom and I made it. There's about a week's worth of meals in there for you guys, all freezable."

"Oh my God, thank you." She gives me a big hug and I let myself fall into it a little. "We just finished the last casserole a friend sent over. I get so intense about making sure the baby stays alive, by the time that's taken care of, I can barely muster an interest in keeping myself watered and fed. Thank your mom for me."

Leon takes the cooler inside and we follow after him. Caro assigns him the task of *quietly* filling the freezer while she asks me if I want anything to drink. I turn red, even though she doesn't mean it that way.

"Where's Adam?" Leon asks. "He around?"

"Milk run. He'll be back soon. He gets separation anxiety."

"That softie." Leon closes the fridge.

"So how was it?" I ask. "Having her?"

"Disgusting," Leon says.

"No one asked you and you weren't even in the room," Caro says, smiling at him before telling me, "Disgusting. But easy, I think. With an epidural. No complications. It was—gross, though. Childbirth is a messy business."

"I'm sorry I didn't come to see you last week," I say. "With Penny . . ."

"No, that's fine." Caro waves her hand. "I wanted to see you, but Leon wasn't thinking, bless him. We were a little too overwhelmed for visitors *that* soon."

"Bless *you,*" Leon returns. He glances at one of the casseroles. "Oh, lasagne. This looks great. Want me to pop it in the oven? I'm starved."

"Can't let my baby brother go hungry." She rolls her eyes. "Our parents were down and so were Adam's sisters, and that was enough. It's been a *huge* adjustment. It still is, but that first week, I felt like a walking train wreck. I kind of still do, actually."

"You don't look like one."

"I like Romy, Leon," Caro says. "Don't mess it up with her."

Leon doesn't say anything. Keeps his eyes off me.

"It'd be me, if it was anyone," I say. "He's too good."

He smiles a little, puts the lasagne in the oven, and helps himself to a bottle of water from the fridge. "So has the memory of pregnancy receded enough yet that you think you'll have another kid, Caro?"

"Shut up," she says pleasantly.

A car rumbles up the driveway.

"Adam," Leon says. "I'm going to give him a hand."

And then he's gone to do it. Caro watches them from the window.

"So how did you guys choose the name Ava?" I ask.

She returns her attention to me. "We both liked it. Simple. It was the *only* name we liked, actually. We don't fight that much, me and Adam, but I swear we had three world wars over names. Just vicious. And then we saw *Ava* and it just worked."

"You seem more—" I try to find the words. "I mean, since I saw you at Swan's . . ."

"Oh, right. That was a weird day. I don't know." She shrugs a little, embarrassed. "It's just . . . my pregnancy was so miserable and I felt so out of control for most of it. I like being in control."

"Me too," I say.

"So I thought, I just have to have her and everything is going to fall into place because I'll have myself back, that part will be where it should be again. But the car accident made me realize how out of my hands all of it is . . . I got really scared."

"Are you still scared?"

She nods. "But I have to deal with it because she's here now."

The front door opens. Leon and Adam come in carrying bag after bag of whatever it is you run out of in the weeks you bring a newborn home, which must be everything.

"What is that amazing smell?" Adam asks.

"Romy's lasagne," Caro says. "She brought us an entire week's worth of food."

"Wow. That's fantastic. Thank you."

"You're welcome and congratulations."

"Thanks for that too. She up yet?" Adam asks and as if on cue, these tiny, grainy cries sound through the baby monitor I didn't notice on the counter. Adam's face lights up. "See, she knows I'm home."

"You get the baby," Caro says.

Adam takes the stairs two at a time while Caro gets a bottle ready. My hands start to sweat. I rub them on my pant legs and try to look like, I don't know. I hope I don't look like I want to hold a baby. It's not long before Adam's come down with Ava bundled in soft blue blankets in his arms. She's still crying.

"There's my favorite niece," Leon says. He plants a kiss on her forehead.

"Okay, here we go," Adam says. Caro holds out the bottle to him. "Here we go . . ."

"Latching issues," Caro explains, like it's something she has to justify. Or maybe she was already forced to. "So . . ."

"I was bottle-fed from day one," I tell her. She gives me a small smile.

Adam watches Ava. I can only see a little of her from here, a bit of black hair, the side of her face. Caro turns to me and says, "Ava's kind of fussy about being held before she's fed, but after she's fed, she's fine."

"Oh." I swallow. "Okay."

The rich scent of tomato and cheese fills the air while Leon tells Caro and Adam about how he was contacted by a *New York Times* bestselling author who wants him to redesign his site. Big project, big payout. He's happy.

"Look at you," Caro says. "That's great."

"Yeah," I say. "It is."

But my eyes are on Adam and Ava, my stomach knotting, waiting for the moment they'll pass her to me. I don't know why I didn't just say it, *I don't want to hold her*.

Just before the lasagne is done, Caro takes Ava from Adam. She coos at her for a minute, stroking her cheek. "You want to meet Romy?" She grins at me. "You look terrified."

"I've never held a baby before," I say.

It doesn't deter her. Caro brings Ava to me, nestling her in my arms. "Not much to it at all. Just make sure you support her head—cradle her like—there you go. You've got it. Ava, this is Romy. Your Uncle Leon's sweet on her."

Leon laughs softly.

"Hi, Ava," I whisper.

Her weight is in my arms, my palm cradling the swath of blankets cushioning her head. She's got more hair than I thought a newborn would and her skin looks so smooth, so soft. She's sleepy and full, her eyes half-open and not tracking anything. She yawns and shifts a little, and I feel it through the blanket, her legs pushing out, and it startles me enough that I flinch.

It gets so quiet, them watching me, watching her. I should say something but I still can't find words, not the right ones. Because I can't stand this. Because Caro's right. She should be scared. Everything's out of her hands now. All the things coming Ava's way they won't be able to control, things she won't always ask for because she's a girl. She doesn't even know how hard it's going to be yet, but she will, because all girls find out. And I know it's going to be hard for Ava in ways I've never had to or will ever have to experience and I want to apologize to her now, before she finds out, like I wish someone had to me. Because maybe it would be better if we all got apologized to first. Maybe it would hurt less, expecting to be hurt.

"Okay." Caro gently takes Ava from my arms. "Oven's about to go. I'm going to put Ava down for a nap and then we're going to eat."

"Can I use your bathroom?" I ask.

"Sure. I'll show you where it is." She turns to the boys. "Set the table."

Caro leads me to the downstairs bathroom. I lock the door and rest against it a minute, waiting for whatever moment this is to pass, for my throat and chest to feel less tight, but all of it, it just gets worse.

You think she was raped before she was in the water?

I press my palms against my eyes.

Don't.

on the way home, Leon asks if I'm okay.

"She's so new," I say because I have to say it to someone because I think it will kill me, more, if I don't. "So new . . ."

"Yeah," he says.

I close my eyes, focusing on the sound of the road rushing beneath us, trying to convince myself there's nowhere we're going, or that where we're going isn't Grebe. After a while he asks, "You fall asleep on me?" But he keeps his voice quiet enough so he won't wake me, in case I have. I pretend I have.

i wonder if it feels like something, the dark.

I wonder if she was alive when she was in the river, her eyes open and hoping for the surface. I imagine the tiniest points of light, the stars through the water, but she can't reach them before she goes out.

A body in the water rots. Her body in the water, rotted. Those beautiful blond strands of hair would have separated from her, drifted away with the current, and all that tight skin would have come loose. All her healthy colors would have faded into a pallet of green and gray and wrong. Insides spilling themselves out, everything unable to hold itself together, a final coming apart. It's why they turned what was left to ashes.

I pull my nightshirt off and stare at myself in the mirror. My hair is matted and tangled, just skimming my sloped shoulders. My skin is pale, too easily marked. I drag my nails across my collarbone and watch red streaks appear there almost instantly. My chest, small and flat, is more a suggestion than anything else. I tilt the mirror down to my stomach, all soft, no definition, a tiny belly I inherited from my mother's side. On my grandmother, it came with child-bearing hips and the kind of breasts that cause back pain. On my mother, it fit nicely with the rest of her curves. I'd look at pictures of them both and stare at my stomach, thought maybe it hinted at my potential, but it only turned out to be fat I don't think I'll ever get rid of. There's more of my father in me than there isn't, and of course the way I wear him would only suggest what could have been. I take my underwear off and glance over my dark and wiry pubic hair, and then I study my hips. They're bony, remind me of how middle school dances made me so uncomfortable. Boy hands feeling my edges. It seemed more personal than a kiss.

It feels wrong to have all this.

It always feels wrong to have all this, but especially today.

I pick clothes that cover all the places of me that seem like an insult. I wear dark colors, ones to blend into the background with. Long sleeves and pants. Hair down. My nails are fine, no chips, so I only do my lips and then I'm ready. When I get downstairs, Mom is in the kitchen, staring out the window and sipping a coffee.

"Where's Todd?" I ask.

"Still in bed. You're up early."

"Then so are you. The assembly for Penny is today."

"You need to go this early for that?"

"Yeah."

I want to see the setup before anyone else. I want the shock of the display to be something I don't have to share.

"I should drive you—"

"Nothing's going to happen today."

It's not a promise I can really make, but she thinks it over and must decide it seems more unlikely than not, that anything bad would happen to me. "Okay. I'm going to send some flowers to the funeral home. Do you want me to put your name on the card?"

I swallow. "Sure."

"Come here."

She holds her arms out. I step into them. She pulls me so close, I can hear the beat of her heart and I wonder if she's thinking this is a day that could have just as easily been mine and hers. I could be dust. She could be waiting to put me into the ground. But I was the one that came back. And there's no *why* to it. I'm not here because I'm special, because I'm meant to be. It just worked out that way.

"I love you more than life," she says.

The sky is overcast. In the school parking lot, there are reporters. Again. Back for this. They don't ask me anything when I pass, so maybe they're just here for visuals. Get a shot of devastated faces to round out some segment.

The school is cold and empty. I don't see anyone, but I hear voices, noises coming from the auditorium. If I didn't know better, I could pretend it was setup for a dance, anything else. I follow the sounds. There's a picture mounted next to the auditorium door and it stops me because it's not the one they used on the MISSING poster. It's from last year's yearbook and Penny's shining in it because so much hadn't happened yet, when that photo was taken. I could look at my yearbook photo then and see myself like I see her now, still new.

I try to keep hold of that feeling long enough for it to fold itself into me because I will never be that new again and I want to remember. I want that memory but it's hard because I don't think it wants me.

Mr. Talbot comes out of the auditorium at the same time someone steps through the door behind me. I stay where I am, my eyes on her, while he says, "Oh—thank you for bringing these and thank your mom for donating them. They'll be beautiful next to her picture . . ."

The sickly sweet smell of roses is in the air.

"Yeah, they will."

A voice like a song you never want to hear again. A voice I want to shut my eyes to, but I'm afraid to shut my eyes to. A voice that makes me want to run and makes me forget how. I can't move. A wreath of red roses moves past me, and the boy who is carrying it comes to a stop when he notices me, his eyes lingering on my nails, first, and then my mouth before he opens his own and says—

"romy."

I can barely hear Leon over my heart, its erratic beat.

I watch his mouth move.

"Romy," he says again, but it's not enough. It's just a name, anyone can say it.

I need him to show me who it belongs to.

"I couldn't be there," I tell him, and he lets me in. "I didn't want to be there."

"Okay. All right." He walks me through his small apartment and I look around, but I can't process his place beyond its walls. He tries to get me to sit but I shake my head. I stand behind a chair at his tiny kitchen table instead.

"Did you walk?"

He's wearing an undershirt. Pajama pants hang off his hips. He wasn't expecting anyone, but now I'm here.

He asks again, "Romy, did you walk?"

"Does it matter?"

He opens a cupboard door, pulls out a glass. He fills it with water from the sink and sets it in front of me. I don't want it, but I take it, clumsily clacking it against my teeth. It tastes like nothing going down, but I drink it all and when I'm finished, I wipe my mouth and realize, too late, what that might have done to my lips. I check the back of my hand for red but there's none. Leon watches uncertainly.

"I wanted to be here," I say. "I wanted to be here with you."

He tries to parse the meaning behind the words because he knows there's more to them than that. This is what they mean, Leon: I need to see myself.

"Okay," he says.

I follow him into the living room and we sink into his couch. His eyes travel over the pieces of me in front of him, but he's not bringing them back together the way I need.

"Roses," I say.

"Roses?"

"They brought roses for the memorial. I had to leave . . ."

"It's okay," he says. He grabs my hand. "It's going to be okay."

No, no, it's not. Something is happening inside me and I need it to stop, I need to stop this feeling, the past trying to put itself on me because it's too heavy to wear.

"Leon, kiss me."

"What?"

I need to see myself.

"Please."

He hesitates and then he moves to me so slowly, maddeningly slowly. The first parts of us that touch are his legs against mine. He brings his hand to my face, palm open against my cheek. He runs his thumb over my lip, the red.

"Romy," he says. "I . . ."

"You're the good part," I tell him, so he won't say anything else.

He brings his other hand to the other side of my face and leans forward. He kisses me, presses his mouth softly against mine and then starts to pull away, like that could be enough but it's not enough. I wrap my fingers around his wrists, and keep his hands where they are. He exhales and then he brings himself to me again, kisses me again. His mouth opens against mine but I still feel his hesitance so I kiss him back, hard, because I want him against every part of me so I can feel every part of me. I want her back, that girl he stopped for.

Leon's hands move down and I inch back into the arm of the couch, my knees between us and he leans against them like they're in the way, finally kissing me the way I want him to. He kisses me until my mouth feels bruised, but it isn't enough. But now he's hungry.

I get myself under him and then he's on top of me, breathing heavily, and he is so against me I know where the blood goes. My hands on his back. His hand moving up and down my thigh, then his fingers drifting past my jeans and under my shirt, under my shirt. My red on his face, his lips. I hear another heart beat under my heartbeat and it's louder than all of this. His mouth against mine and all I can hear is the heartbeat of some other girl, no—I close my eyes.

"Hey," Leon says. "Hey, look at me."

he covers her mouth.

That's how you get a girl to stop crying; you cover her mouth until the sound dies against your palm.

He says, *okay? Okay.*

When he's sure she's going to be quiet, he lets her breathe again.

He tells her, *it's okay.*

He brings two of his fingers to his mouth and slides them inside it and it makes her want to be sick and maybe if she pukes, he'll stop. She wills it to happen, it doesn't happen. He takes his fingers out of his mouth and puts that hand between her legs, moving her underwear aside and then—a sharp, unwelcome pressure.

I want to make you wet, he whispers.

She makes the kind of noise she never thought she'd hear herself make, small and pleading whimpers. She closes her eyes, while his fingers stay inside her.

If she can't be sick, she'll just go away.

Look at me, look at me, hey, look at me.

At some point, he moved his hands from there and she comes to herself, her legs spread open. His pants are down. His weight is on her, heavy. She closes her eyes again. He makes her open them. *Wake up, wake up. Wake up* because *you want this, you've always wanted this.* But she didn't want this. She doesn't want this. He forces himself inside her. She's tight and she's dry.

It hurts.

Open your eyes.

But it hurts.

Open your eyes.

She's sick then, five-six-seven-eight-nine shots coming out of her. Her body doesn't make sense to her, can't move when she wants it to move, but this? She turns her head to the side and vomit spills out her mouth, pooling in the ridges of the truck bed and he swears, but he doesn't stop. It'll hurt him too much if he stops. They can clean up together, after. Like that's a promise, like she'd want it. Not that it matters, because he'll leave her there anyway, half-awake and raw, her mouth bitter. Her head is so heavy. Why isn't this over yet? She closes her eyes and he makes her open them again.

Look at me, look at me, hey—

"Romy—"

Wake up, wake up. Wake up from this, wake up from this. But it's never over and she can't stop making those sounds and he says—"Romy—" and I push at his shoulders and his eyes are on me, lingering on my mouth and my nails but he sees past them, he sees the dead girl and says "Romy" and brings her back.

"Don't look at me," I whisper.

leon sits beside me on the couch.

It has been—minutes. And I want to fade out. I want to fade out and be on my feet, past this, but every ugly moment is one I have to live and so I'm sitting beside Leon, on his couch, waiting for my heartbeat to decelerate and the ache between my legs to disappear. He's waiting for me to speak and if I can talk—if I can figure out how to do that—then I can figure out how to walk, I can leave.

"I have to go." My first words in this after.

"What?"

"I'm sorry, Leon."

I stand. My legs are stiff, trying to work around the ache,

my body's betrayal. I pass the couch and step into the kitchen. I see the door I came through.

"Wait, wait, wait," Leon says. "Talk to me, come on—"

"I have to go." My tongue feels as thick as my head, nine shots thick, and these are the only words I can get out. I reach the door and I say, "This was a bad idea. I'm sorry."

He puts his hand on my arm. "No. I don't know what just happened—"

I pull away slowly. I don't want to be touched because I feel too touched. I have to go home. There are miles ahead of me. I press my head against the door and Leon stands there, so helplessly, all this beyond anything I could or want to explain to him.

"I don't want to talk. I have to go home."

"I don't know what I—" He breaks off. "You don't look—"

Don't tell me what I look like. I fumble to open the door, don't coordinate enough at first, to get out of my own way. I squeeze my eyes shut and then I open them and I put all I can into making myself sound steady.

"It's okay," I say. "Don't follow me."

I step outside, closing the door behind me but he catches it, holds it open. I wish he wouldn't. He doesn't follow me, but I feel his eyes on my back, on the awkward, uncomfortable way I'm carrying myself, trying to move in spite of how sore my body wants to believe it is.

When I'm outside of Ibis, I get a text from him.

WE HAVE TO TALK ABOUT WHAT THAT WAS

And then I know what I need to do.

I head for Swan's. Tracey is shocked to see me and tells me I look awful. We sit in her office, where it's too hot and the fluorescent lights above us make my head hurt. I tell her I need to quit. I tell her there's too much school and missing girls. She tells me she understands but that it could've waited, that Swan's is the last place I need to be right now. She seems to want to say more, but doesn't.

"There's always going to be a place for you here," she says. She frowns. "There'll be some people pretty sad they missed their chance to say good-bye."

"I have their numbers," I say.

She gives me a hug and tells me to check my apron pockets before I leave. I find a few hair bands, a bracelet that must have slipped off my wrist at some point, and a crumpled napkin, with black markered numbers on it. I shove it all into my pockets.

It starts to rain on the way home. I'm drenched by the time I get there, cold, shivering, but not numb. I feel the prickling of my skin, the way it has me.

"Romy?"

Todd was in the recliner in the living room, but he's on his feet by the time I'm at the bottom of the stairs. He takes one look at me and gapes. I feel wet strands of hair stuck to my neck and face. My shirt clings to me.

"Where the hell did you come from?"

"Where's Mom?" I don't know if I want her close or the assurance she's far away.

"She wanted to take the flowers for Penny over to the funeral home herself." Todd peers at me. I'm dripping puddles onto the floor. "You okay? Whcre were you?"

"I'm fine."

I drag my feet upstairs and lock myself in the bathroom. I start a bath, running the water as hot as it will go because I want to stop shivering. I let the water get dangerously close to spilling over while I strip out of my clothes, avoiding the mirror. I turn the tap off and step into the bath without testing it first, letting it burn. This. This is what pain feels like when it's happening now and I beg my body to know this difference.

It won't listen to me.

I lower myself in, but that ache persists and I can't. I can't. I open my legs, resting the outside of my knees on either side of the tub. I put my hands in the space between, exploring with my fingers, pulling skin apart, half expecting it to feel the way it did then.

It doesn't.

This isn't then.

But I can still feel it.

I lean my head back and cover my face, let the water get cold around me. I wait until I'm shivering again before I pull myself out. By the time I've dried off and crawled into bed, I'm sweating. I lick my lips and they taste like dirt. I pull my sheet up over my head and cover my body. Her body. I wish I didn't have a body.

when i open my eyes, the house is quiet and I blearily wonder why Mom let me sleep past my alarm when I remember they're burying Penny today. Her ashes.

I get out of bed slowly and make my way downstairs. No sign of Mom or Todd, but there's a note.

Errands in Ibis, back before dinner. XO, Mom

Even though I just woke up, sleep is the only way I can think to turn myself off again, so I lay on the couch and between the inhalation of one breath and the exhalation of another, the sound of the car comes round but that almost seems too soon. But then I hear a knock.

"Anybody home?"

I open my eyes.

"Romy?"

I get off the couch and make my way into the hall, thinking I'll just check, I'll just peer through the front door and see if it's really him, and if it is, I'll walk away, but Mom and Todd left the door open, laid the view out for Leon through the screen, so I can't hide. He sees me. He looks so together, and I'm—not.

"We have to talk," he says.

"No."

"You just quit," he says. "You owe me an explanation . . ."

I don't say anything.

"Please."

I hear it, his need. It's hard to shut myself off to it, when I said that same word to him yesterday and he answered. I do owe him something: I need to end this, I think.

I hesitate and then I open the door. He steps inside. I keep my eyes on the wall just behind him because I'm afraid to look him directly in the eyes. This already hurts. Like every time my heart beats, it makes a bruise.

"Did I do something wrong?" he asks. He sounds so uncomfortable. "Because all I know is one second, you're there—*we're* there—and then you've got this look on your face and then you're pushing at me, like I'm—"

"You didn't do anything."

"Then why can't you look at me?"

The bitter urge to cry closes in on me.

"You didn't do anything, Leon."

"I think I triggered you."

"What?" I let out a breath, something that wants to be a laugh, something to make him reconsider what he said enough to take it back. But it's weak and it gives me away. I know what that word means, but he shouldn't. "What, you think you know something because—"

"Because what?" he asks. "Why can't I know something like that?"

"Because you don't know anything."

"Romy—"

"Stop. You don't know *anything.*"

And he says, "Romy, I'm sorry."

Anyone begins anything with *I'm sorry* after you've told them they didn't do anything wrong—whatever follows won't be good. I step back, instinctively distance myself from it.

"I—" He pauses. "I drove down here to see you last night. I was worried and I was . . . so tired of doing this runaround with you because I felt like we were just getting back to a good place after the search . . . I came here, but I didn't have the guts to talk to you and on my way back, I got gas at Grebe Auto. There were a couple kids there, talking about Penny Young and the funeral, and they brought up this 'wasted search' on Romy Grey. I told them to go fuck themselves and they told me—"

His voice. His voice is all over me. I want to rip it off my skin. And his face—the shame on Leon's face for what he's saying makes me want to rip it off his face and—

Stop.

"Romy, they told me."

They told him.

"I'm so sorry," he says.

He's so sorry.

I close my eyes.

"But I could see through it, I could see through all the bullshit. I don't know the details—I don't need to know them—but the way you were at the search, what you said about everyone here, your dad and how you fell out with Penny—everything just started to click into place . . ."

Click into place. This is how I make sense to him, when I'm a dead girl. He can't even believe I'm a liar, the only thing that makes it barely tolerable at school—that they think I'm a liar before they think I'm a dead girl.

"I didn't mean to find out that way," he says.

I open my eyes. "But you did."

"I'm so sorry that happened—"

"Don't." My heart thrums, more bruises. I look for exits, but this is my house and he's standing in front of the door. "Don't be. Just go."

"I'm sorry," he says again and he *is*. He sounds so sorry that he found out this way, so sorry that he had to tell me he did, sorry that I make more sense to him now. But it's not enough that he's sorry because now, when he looks at me—

I'll be her.

"You need to leave," I say.

"Romy—"

"I don't want you here if you know."

He steps back, puts space between us and I swear the space makes every part of me I'm trying to hide more visible. He's not going. I want him to go.

"Tell me what I can do."

"There's nothing you can do."

"There has to be—"

"Make me feel like I wasn't—" I falter and then my voice starts breaking all over the words and I can't stop it, any of it. "Like you did when you didn't know. Because I hate her, Leon, and when I was around you, I wasn't—her. You . . . stopped. That's why you were the good part. So if you want to help, pretend you don't know and we could—"

I can't finish. It's too impossible to finish. And I wait for him to speak, all of this washing over him slowly, too slowly.

"You're right," he finally says. "I can't help you if that's what you need from me. And if I'd known, this whole time, you were using me like that . . ."

I bring my hand to my forehead and dig my nails into the skin there, hard as I can, because I want to be able to choose what hurts me for once.

"How did you think you would help?" I ask faintly. "Tell me to accept it?"

"I wouldn't do that. You don't have to accept it." He pauscs. "But maybe you should hate the people responsible. Because it's not you."

"I don't want you here if you know," I say again.

He sighs and turns away, his footsteps leading him out and I close my eyes until I hear the screen door whine closed, until I hear the sound of him driving away and the only thing I feel after is her, this slit, this dead girl, trying to burn herself out of me—

"hello?"

I'm on the phone in the kitchen. The man's voice on the other end of the line is gruff and half-awake. The sound of it sends a surge of adrenaline through me, enough to make me light-headed. For a moment, I forget how to speak.

"Who is this?" He's more awake now, and still I can't speak. I pick at one of the phone buttons and accidentally push it in. The tone blares in my ear, in his, and I startle, pull my hand back.

"It's the girl from the diner," I manage.

"Who?"

"The one who doesn't like to talk."

The longest pause before he laughs. "This a joke?"

"You said you'd tell me how."

"I'll be damned. That doesn't usually work."

I stare at the phone cord, twirled nervously around my finger. My body tremors, a sick chill up and down my spine like a warning.

"Will you meet me?"

i scrawl a note under the note my mother left me. I keep it as simple as *I love you* because that's always there to say. I get my bike from the garage and wheel it over the vines on the walkway, before I throw my leg over its side and push off. The streets are quiet, the pall of Penny's funeral cast over everything. I feel more relief passing the YOU ARE NOW LEAVING GREBE sign than I ever have before.

The bike ride to Taraldson Road tests me. All the running I haven't done has made me soft where I should be stronger. I have to break halfway, my calves aching, my stomach churning.

The highway is some kind of nightmare, the way the cars

and trucks rush by me. The feel of them, the sound. It hurts. It makes my teeth ache. It starts to rain and I bike so far, I bike through it—I can see the point I've left that weather behind me.

It's forever before I make the turn off the highway onto the dirt road I'm looking for, my road. I drag my feet and come to a stop. I climb off my bike, letting it clatter to its side. I ease myself to the ground, on my back and I can't breathe, I can't breathe in this air and I wonder what it's like underwater, wonder again if she was dead before she hit the river or if that happened after. It's hard to think of what's left of her in any kind of dark.

I wait, listening.

I wait, tracing letters on my stomach.

I wait.

And then I hear it, the truck, ahead of me.

The truck slows, grinds to a halt and then it's just the sound of the engine idling. I dig my fingers into the dirt, I dig them there, anchoring myself to it, while the truck stays where it is, its driver inside. Maybe someone nice. Maybe someone finally come to finish what's been started. I don't care, as long as it's finished . . .

My heart beats frantically in my chest.

Her heart beats frantically in my chest.

The engine cuts.

And I—

I scramble to my feet, stumbling past my bike. I leave it there and move down the bank as fast as I can, trying for the trees before he gets out of his truck. The grass is slick from the rainfall and I lose my footing, end up sliding down on my thigh, turning one side of me grass-stained and mud-streaked.

I get my feet under me and look back once, glimpse the

truck parked and silent, and I imagine the man inside not understanding, trying to understand what he's supposed to do about this girl who was just there and isn't anymore. I fight through a cluster of trees so close together, I'm afraid I won't fit in their spaces but I do. The branches tear at my arms. I hear the truck door open and close and I stop, leaning against a dying birch.

"Hello?" the man yells. I don't even know his name, didn't ask for it, just like he didn't ask for mine and it didn't seem scary then, but now—"You there?"

I press my fingertips against bark. Silence. I wait for the sound of his driving away but it doesn't happen. I hear the crunch of his shoes on the ground instead.

"I saw you," he calls. "Your bike's out here."

I move back and my rustling interrupts the safe quiet I've carved out. I can't see the road from here. Maybe he can't see me. I listen for him, for his footsteps, ready myself to run, if I have to, and pray I'm fast enough.

Pray I'm fast enough.

"You think this is funny?" he demands. And then, "Think it'd be funny if I took your bike? How about I take your fucking bike?"

I hear it; my bike lifted from the road and tossed into his truck bed. The loud, ugly clatter of it makes me take another step back.

"I don't fucking believe this. I know you're there."

And then the—graceless sound of him coming down the bank, slipping the same way I did. His curses fill the air and he's furious and I don't care how noisy I am, I run.

I crash through a good half mile of woods before I see hints of light, the trees getting sparser. I break through them and there's a different bank, overgrown and wild. I can't tell if anything's behind me because all I hear is the struggle of my own lungs gasping for air, and when they've finally settled, I listen.

There's nothing.

And then I'm crying, I'm crying so hard and I can't stop. I just want it to stop. I turn and there's nothing there to turn to. I try to get a hold of myself as much as I can and I see—I see—

Pebbles skitter under my feet. I walk forward until I'm standing over a white Vespa, half-hidden in the trees, slopped onto its side, wearing weeks of neglect.

"you know that was there before? This whole time?"

"No," I say.

"What were you doing out on the road in the first place, if you didn't know?" Before I can answer, Sheriff Turner asks, "Was Penny with you that night? Were you lying to me?"

I'm in the backseat of his Explorer, behind the cage, and the space is getting smaller and smaller every mile. I try to think of anything but what I know. Penny's Vespa in the woods. I shiver. I'm freezing but my skin is damp, sweaty. My eyes are swollen and sore from crying.

"I don't feel well."

"Answer the question."

I don't know if it's right, that he's asking me the question in the first place. But it never matters if it's right, not in this town.

"I don't—I can't remember anything about that night, I told you . . ."

"Then what were you doing out there in the first place? How could you just *happen* to find Penny's Vespa like that, if you didn't know it was there the whole time?"

"I don't know."

"I don't believe you."

They came when I called them. I sat on the road, waiting until I saw the police and then I had to show them the Vespa, had to tell them if I touched it and where. Some of the questions, I didn't have answers for, couldn't think around the shock. Sheriff Turner shouldn't even be here, but when he heard it was about her, and that I was involved, he came. He's post-funeral; jumped out of one suit and into another. His whole face is pinched and ugly. Makes me afraid. I hate this man and I'm afraid of him.

"She was like a daughter to me."

"I know," I say.

"You best pray this don't come back around to you, Romy."

Mom and Todd pick me up at the sheriff's department and by the time they get there, I've thrown up and they only find out because Joe Conway tells them. Mom puts her hands to my face and says, soft and surprised, "You have a fever."

On the ride home, I struggle to keep my eyes open.

"Go upstairs, Romy," Mom tells me when we get there.

I do what she says.

I go to my room and I peel out of my clothes.

By the time I've found my way into bed, I hear my mother in the bathroom, the water running. I drift. She comes in a few minutes later. The mattress dips and she starts me awake, a little, when she presses a cold washcloth against my forehead.

"What are you thinking?" she asks quietly, like she always does. "What on earth were you thinking?"

"It was a funeral," I say because nothing feels like the wrong thing to say anymore. It's not long before I hear her crying and it breaks my heart. I break her heart. I grip her hand and tell her *it's okay* and *don't cry* and *you don't have to cry* but I can't make myself convincing enough.

time passes or it doesn't, but it must—because it has to.

When the fever breaks, I don't know what girl is left.

I don't know what I've done to myself.

on friday, i open my eyes to the late-afternoon sun and the sky is empty. No clouds, no blue, just white nothingness stretched across town.

I hear Mom's and Todd's voices drifting through the window, along with the crackly sound of music playing from Todd's old radio, some golden oldies station. I get out of bed and follow the song to the front porch. They stop talking when I come out.

"Why didn't you wake me?"

"You could use the extra rest," Mom says. "And now you should eat. Let me make you something up."

She slips past me, inside, and Todd says, "Come on, kid." I follow after her, to the kitchen, and he follows after me. I open the fridge and stare at the food inside. My stomach doesn't connect with any of it.

"I said let *me* make you something." Mom nudges me gently. The song on the radio changes. She points to the table. I sit beside Todd. "I'll make you toast, okay?"

"Okay," I say.

I think of Alek. I wonder what he's doing. If he's still in his bed, so leveled by grief he can't move, or if he has the kind of grief that doesn't settle, that pushes him from one moment to the next so fast, he never has to think about how much it hurts.

I wonder if he can make his own toast.

Mom sets a plate in front of me.

"Oh." She touches the top of one of my fingernails, a ruined canvas. All ragged edges and chips, red disappearing a coat at a time. The girl I was, or only tricked myself into thinking I was, quietly making her exit. "Do you want me to fix them?"

I want to ask her what the point of that would be, when the song on the radio cuts off abruptly for the DJ's voice.

"Breaking news this afternoon. A suspect is currently being held in custody in connection with the disappearance and death of seventeen-year-old Penny Young. The Grebe and Ibis Sheriff's Departments are releasing no further details at this time. Young was last seen in Grebe, at a party at Wake—"

"What?" Todd asks.

"Oh my God." Mom brings her hand to her chest.

Todd turns the radio up and the DJ says things we already know, like when Penny was last seen, and about how desperately hard we tried to find her, but something is gathering in the spaces between what's been said and what hasn't, gathering in me. The Vespa, the road.

You best pray this don't come back around to you, Romy.

But if it didn't come around to me, who did it come around to?

I go upstairs and grab my phone off my desk and dial the sheriff's department. Joe picks up. I ask for Leanne. She comes on the line and she sounds unhappy. When I tell her it's me, it only makes it worse.

"Why are you calling?" she asks.

"Who do you have in custody?"

"I'm not about to tell you."

"What about the Vespa?" I ask and the line goes silent. "Does where they found it have anything to do with this? The road I was on? What about Tina Ortiz?"

"I can't comment on this, Romy."

"Please—"

"I *can't,*" she snaps. She lowers her voice. "You promised you wouldn't repeat what I told you about Tina leaving you on the road and you did."

"But—"

"And I got *reprimanded.* I've been on desk duty ever since. I can't tell you who we have in custody, Romy. I wouldn't. I need to keep this line clear."

She hangs up on me.

Later, when Mom and Todd are in bed, I open my laptop and light my room with the cold glare of its screen. I search Penny's name, over and over, and keep the Grebe and Ibis

Sheriff's Departments' Web sites up for any further details. The only trickle of something new is that the suspect in custody is a minor. A stranger—or someone we knew? Maybe it was someone from a class below us or a senior just weeks or months away from their next birthday.

I can't picture a familiar face, not for this.

Everyone who knows her loves her.

Except people hurt the people they love all the time.

I try to tie so many of our classmates back to her death, but it's impossible. I can't even tie it to Alek, who loved her the most. If it was me, it would be different, I could draw those lines so clearly from myself to them, and all the pain they'd want to cause me.

My phone buzzes. I pick it up.

Texts from Leon.

I WANTED TO CALL, SEE HOW YOU WERE DOING.

I DIDN'T THINK YOU'D WANT THAT, THOUGH.

I delete them and stare out the window, at the stars scattered across the sky. I don't know why he still cares. What a stupid thing it is, to care about a girl.

but nothing can stay secret long in Grebe.

Word travels. It gets slurred in bars, murmured over fences between neighbors, muttered in the produce section of the grocery store and again at the checkout, because the cashier always has something to add. When Mom tells me Todd went out to run errands, I wait for him to return with a name. It takes forever for the sound of the car rolling back up the driveway, and I think I'm prepared for anything, but really, I'm not.

I'm afraid.

I don't move until I hear heavy and unfamiliar footsteps on the porch, until Mom wanders into the hall and says, "Oh." It's not Todd.

A wolf's at the door.

"Hello, Alice Jane."

He's wearing his uniform.

I hang back, my arms wrapped around myself while Mom lets Sheriff Turner in. My stomach turns as he paws through, his eyes skimming over the space, nose picking up scents. I don't like this and when he says, "I need a few words with your daughter," I like it even less.

He lays eyes on me like he's seeing me for the first time, like I somehow escaped his cursory glance. I shrink under the look. I don't want to think about why he'd want to talk to me because there's only one reason he'd want to.

"Why?" Mom asks.

"I need to go over some things concerning the developing situation with Penny Young."

There it is. And even though I expected it, hearing it is different. The shock of it turns everything in front of me to black spots for a second. I blink them away, and when they're gone, Mom, who I expect to crumble, doesn't. She straightens, looks from him to me. I open my mouth; nothing comes out.

Mom says, "Of course. Let's . . . sit and talk about this."

She gestures to the kitchen. Sheriff Turner looks like the last thing he wants to do is settle in, but she stares at him until his boots walk him there. The clomp of them on the floor is something I never want to hear again. The sound of him moving the chair, sitting in it. I stay where I am and Mom says, "Romy, come on." And then she makes a promise she can't keep, that no one could. "It's going to be okay."

She holds her hand out and I move forward tentatively, and then, behind her, through the door, I see the New Yorker pull up to the front of the house. Todd is forced to park on the curb because Turner's Explorer took the driveway. He gets out empty-handed, but I see bags in the backseat. He moves quickly up the walk and pushes through the door.

"What's going on?" he asks. "What's *he* doing here?"

"Levi wants to ask Romy some questions about Penny," Mom tells him. Todd stares into the kitchen and he looks like he wants to say something but he just shakes his head and goes in.

"Romy," Mom says. I step forward, facing the kitchen. Turner sits at the head of the table. Todd sits across from him. Mom positions herself beside Todd and I stay where I am, just in the doorway.

"Romy, sit down," Mom says.

"I'm fine here," I say, and I cross my arms. She doesn't push it, but Turner looks like he wishes he could, like he had no intention of having this conversation, whether it's about Penny or not, from a place where he had to look up at me to do it.

"It's just a few questions," he says. "Romy, you have no memory of Wake Lake and you have no memory of ending up on Taraldson Road afterward, am I correct?"

"Yes," I say.

"We have multiple accounts that this was owing to the fact you were extremely intoxicated, is this also correct?" I nod. "Is that a yes?"

"Yes," I say.

"That Saturday, when we first talked, you gave me the impression you must have blacked out and wandered to the road but that evening, Tina Ortiz called us. She told us she drove you out there and left you there as a joke—"

"What?" Mom looks at me, and then Turner, and I watch her become as furious as she was the day she told Dad to get out, something I thought I'd never see again. "You're telling

me that Tina Ortiz *endangered* my daughter and you didn't tell us—"

"Alice, come on," Todd says. "That's Ben Ortiz's kid. Think of the golf club."

"Your daughter knew," Turner says and Mom looks at me, a slow realization of what it means, if I knew all along. Her face falls and I can't stand seeing it. Turner eases into his seat a little, likes that he did that. He asks me, "You have no recollection of this?"

"No."

"And when I asked if you were injured in any way, you told me you were unharmed," he continues. "Is that correct?"

"Is this about the Garrett boy?" Todd asks, before I can say *yes,* even as I'm seeing myself in the dirt, with my bra undone and those words on my stomach.

At first I don't understand what Todd is saying, but the question does something to Turner. It makes his face red, a red that hints at the level of control it's taking to not give something away. Except it's too late.

The Garrett boy.

"Brock?" I ask.

"Yeah, that's who they have in custody," Todd says. "And you've got to charge him soon, don't you? If you haven't already."

Turner leans forward. "Where did you hear that?"

"It doesn't matter," Todd says.

"Like hell it doesn't. That's not officially released information yet. If you don't tell me where you heard it, Bartlett—"

I don't know how I have room for this, more of this. Every time I think I've been maxed out, there's something else. Brock Garrett, in custody for Penny's death, and every memory I have of him knifes through me. The fucked up things he did, things I believe he'd do—to me.

But her?

Penny?

"Why are you asking me questions, if he—" I bring my hand to my mouth. I see a road. I see a road and two girls on it. No . . . no, no, no . . . "Was I there when she died?"

Sheriff Turner doesn't answer. But he doesn't have to. Mom moves to me, wants to bring me back from this, but I shake my head, keep her where she is. There is no coming back from this. I was there when her light left her.

I've had that inside me.

"Bartlett, where did you hear it?"

"What's Romy got to do with it?" Todd asks.

"It. Doesn't. Matter," Turner says tightly. "I came here today to establish that she's not a viable witness and that's what I've done. You *tell me* where you heard—"

"You can't just come in here and do this to my family. What she's been through—" Todd nods to me. "I won't have it, Levi. You tell me what Romy has to do with this right now and I'll tell you where I heard about Brock. It's someone from your department. I promise you, you don't want to fuck around with this one."

Turner clenches his jaw, and the arrogance of him, that he can't think of a single name in his office who would betray him, not even one as easy to reach for as Joe's.

"If any of this goes *any* further than this room—"

"It won't," Mom says.

Turner's frayed, worn down to the bone. Something I've never seen in him before. He glances at me, and there's an anger I recognize. *Why her?* Why her, and not me. And because of that, he can't bring himself to tell me directly. He hates me that much. He tells it to Todd, to Mom, instead.

"It wasn't Tina who put Romy on that road. It was Brock."

I'm still, rewriting a night. The one thing I thought I knew—I didn't. I take Tina out of the picture, I put Brock in her place. He put me on that road. What does that mean? I was in his car? His arms? The idea of him, carrying me to his car—

"It was a practical joke," Turner says. "Romy was unconscious and unresponsive the entire time. When he came back to the party, he told Tina what he'd done and Tina told Penny. Brock eventually decided he'd go back to the road and bring Romy home."

"Bring me home," I say faintly, because Turner says it like it could be true, that Brock would grow a heart, come out to that road and bring me home. But he hasn't seen Brock look at me before, hasn't seen me on the track with him before . . .

"Penny had the same idea. She went out to bring Romy home and arrived at the road shortly after Brock did." Turner struggles to stay businesslike in tone. "The two had an altercation. Brock claims he can't remember exactly what transpired, but her death was accidental. He panicked and disposed of her body. The morning we found Romy, Brock asked Tina to cover for him to rule out any possible connection between the girls' disappearances. He wanted to make sure we looked elsewhere."

I step back. "Tina knew—"

"Tina did *not* know Penny was dead. Tina thought Penny disappeared on the way to her mother's house, just like everyone else," Turner says. "And when we recovered the Vespa, we brought her in for questioning. She told us the truth. And then we brought Brock in . . ."

The kitchen falls silent, weak light streaming through the window. I stare at it, I stare at it while this simple truth fills me. She came back.

She came back for me.

He killed her for it.

My breath escapes me. They look at me and I turn from them, seeing all the things they can't see. Things I haven't said, never said.

"Romy," Mom says.

Rape me. He put something in my drink. My lipstick on my stomach. My lipstick in his hand and his hand pressing it into my stomach. His hands. My shirt, still undone after the lake? Laid wide open for him. *Rape me.*

"He was going to rape me," I say.

"*What?*" Turner asks.

Mom and Todd are silent from the shock of it, I feel their shock, but Turner lets his fury come first, no listening, no processing—just a demand for more, from a place that doesn't believe what just came out of my mouth but she came back for me and she died for it. I turn back to them and I don't want to say it because I don't want it, I didn't ask for it—

But she died for this.

"I know—" My voice breaks. "When I woke up on the road, my shirt was unbuttoned and my bra . . . was undone and . . . *rape me* was written on my stomach in lipstick. Brock did that to me."

The sound my mother makes is one I'll spend the rest of my life trying to forget. *You know what the hardest part of being a parent is?* It was never supposed to be this.

"No." Turner shakes his head. "You didn't tell us this. Your shirt was open and you were written on? How come Leanne didn't report seeing any of that—"

"I did my shirt back up before she found me."

"Oh, really? And you think there's no chance this happened at the party? I wasn't going to bring it up in front of your mother, Romy, not at the time, but I have several accounts of you taking your shirt off there—"

"Levi, I'm *warning* you," Todd says.

"Brock brought GHB," I blurt out. "He drugged me."

Turner's mouth falls open. I know he doesn't believe me, I know this, but I'm desperate for him to understand what was taken from her, the *why* of her being dead. For her—for her, he has to understand.

"How do you know this?" he asks.

"He was handing it out at the party. He gave—he gave Norah Landers some. But I think that he drugged me—"

"You *think.*"

"I don't remember drinking. I don't remember drinking *once* that night." I close my eyes briefly. "He was planning to rape me—"

"Why would he *ever*—"

"Because he knew he'd get away with it, like . . ." This. This is why she's gone. "Like Kellan did."

Mom is crying, her hands over her mouth, and Todd, he's pale. But Turner—

Turner laughs.

"Oh," he says softly. "I see how it is."

Two girls on a road.

"She saved me."

"No," Turner says. "No—"

"She saved me—"

"*No,*" he says, and he stands and I step back. "Alice, you want to do something about your daughter. I have *never* seen anyone so desperate for attention in my life." He stares at me with such hatred and disgust and he tries to make me wear it. "You want to make Penny's death about your lies—" I step back again. "Your lies about my son. I will not let you do it—I won't—"

"I'm not—"

"You're *lying,* you—"

Todd slams his hand on the table. "*Don't* call her *liar*—"

"Romy," Mom says. "Romy—"

"Where does she think she's going?"

Going. I'm going. I push through the door and the screen door and step onto the walk and then they're following after me, and I hear my name at my back.

"Romy—"

And I run.

I run and I see Penny—

I see Penny, sitting in a booth across from me and I see her and she says—

No. I focus on my pulse. I breathe hard, forcing the air into me and I run and I see Penny, sitting in a booth across from me and she says—

I want to talk to you and then I'll leave.

No, no. I don't have to hear this because you've already left, Penny. You're gone. You traded your life for a girl who was already dead and I'm sorry you gave up everything for her, but I can't listen to you now.

Sweat coats my skin. My shirt clings to my back. I run and I see Penny, sitting in the booth across from me, and I don't know what I can give her for what's been taken away.

Please.

I know I can be faster than this, I know I can be faster than this. I can outrun the boy in the truck bed. I can outrun the boy in the truck bed and all the boys who made themselves in his likeness just because they could, just because no one said they couldn't . . .

Godwit . . . there was this girl . . . she told me it wasn't safe to be alone with him. She wouldn't say why, but the look on her face . . .

You can still report it.

And then the sick give of my body, the sound of it when I hit the ground. I push my palms to gravel, try to struggle to my feet, but I can't, so I sit in the road with my hands against my knees, pressing my fingernails into new wounds and when I pull them away, they're red.

They are so red.

AFTER

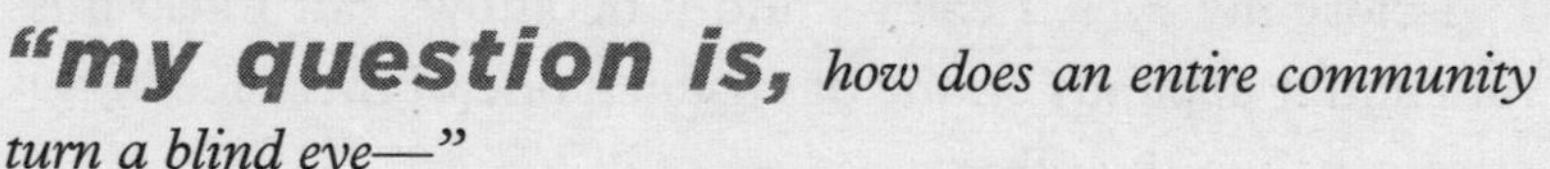

"my question is, *how does an entire community turn a blind eye—"*

It's cold out now. The air like metal in your mouth.

"—to a party where teens are unsupervised and known *to drink in excess? This isn't a party nobody knew about. It's a* tradition. *We're so eager to point fingers at this boy—and I wish people would stop calling him a young man, because he is a* boy*—but how much of the blame truly falls on him? It's sort of inevitable, isn't it? What happened?"*

I stand on the porch, staring at the street, trying to block out the voices on the radio in the kitchen, even though I was the one who turned it on.

"I don't think second-degree murder is an inevitability of a high school party—"

"Sorry to break in, but did he rape her? Have they—"

"His legal team has vehemently *denied that he raped her and the authorities have also confirmed no evidence has come to light suggesting that he did—"*

Because he wasn't there to do that to her. He wouldn't have done that to Penny.

Just me.

"*—well, now that we have that as fact, I hope people stop asking that question, but to go back to what you were saying—Laura, would you argue that teenagers and alcohol usually lead to very,* very *poor decision making?"*

"That's not what you were saying, Jean."

I stare at my phone. Yesterday, Leon sent me a text message. GOT THE HAT YOU LEFT AT SWAN'S FOR AVA. IT WAS SWEET. THANKS FROM ALL OF US.

This morning my fingers trembled a text back, YOU'RE WELCOME, and I've been staring at his reply ever since.

IT'S ALWAYS GOOD TO HEAR FROM YOU.

I close my eyes. I can't stand if he knows but I also miss him and it depends on the day, which one of these feelings is stronger than the other.

YOU TOO.

I turn my phone off and then I see her.

Tina. Coming up my side of the street. She reaches the house and hesitates when she sees my silhouette through the mesh. I raise my chin and she starts over the walkway. I open the door, stopping her at the steps because she's not coming in. She looks up at me, holding herself like she always does even though she doesn't look the same anymore. She's hollowed out a little, like maybe she's not sleeping as well as she needs or eating as much as she should. But that's me too. These days.

"Thanks for seeing me," she says.

She wouldn't stop calling. The first time her number lit up my phone, I didn't know who it was and when I answered, and heard her voice, heard her asking me to meet her, I hung up. She left messages, texted me. Every time I thought she'd finally given up, she'd start all over again. Yesterday, I finally told her to come and then to leave me alone. Now she's here, waiting for *me* to speak.

"I'm not going to stand out here forever, Tina." I say because I'll make this as easy for her as she would for me. "You're lucky I'm standing out here at all."

"Look—" She pauses. "Whatever you think of me, I didn't cover for Brock—for him."

"It wasn't for Penny."

"*Yes,* it was," she says shakily. "It was. He told me he took you to that road. That he knew Penny wasn't there and they'd just be wasting time if they searched it. He said he couldn't tell them what he'd done or he'd lose his place on the football team. I didn't want anyone to waste any time. I just wanted them to find her. I—miss her."

"You covered for him even though he wrote *rape me* on my stomach."

"I didn't know he did that to you before you said it in the locker room."

"But you knew Alek took the pictures of me. You were there for that, weren't you?" I ask and she doesn't even have the good grace to look ashamed, just keeps her eyes on me, like she's waiting for some kind of give. And it happens because I'm weak. "He said I let—" I stop. "Forget it. I don't need to know."

"I can tell you," she says and when I don't say anything—she does. "You said you were hot. Alek told you to take off your shirt and you said you wanted to go home and he said if you gave him your phone, he'd call your mom . . ."

I stare down the empty street. I was right. I didn't need to know.

"Brock brought GHB to the party," she says, like she's saying something new. "I think maybe he gave you some and that's how you got so messed up . . ."

"Oh. I thought that was just the best impersonation of my father you'd ever seen." I look back in time to see her wince. There's nothing satisfying about it. "Alek was going to send those pictures to the school. Penny stopped him. But you watched."

"Yeah," she says and she does, finally, look away at this. I stare at my nails, bare. She doesn't move. I don't know why, when this is so finished.

"I know Turner cut you out of this. My dad says I'm not allowed to talk about it."

"Then stop talking about it," I say. "And go home."

"No," she says. Then I'll stop talking about it. I turn away from her and she says, "Romy, wait."

I turn back. "Tina—"

"No, just listen. I don't think Brock would just leave you on that road and leave it at that. I don't think Penny died because she found you, I think she died because she stopped him—" Her voice breaks, and it breaks me, a little. "In the locker room, you said if she got raped, she'd be better off dead and you *meant* it. But you weren't talking about her. You were talking about what happened to you with Kellan."

His name winds itself tight around me.

"I'm so sorry," she says.

"You should have believed me."

It's been inside me so long, I can barely choke it out. I

carried it to the lake, when I thought I would say it to Penny, and I've buried those words since the lake with all the other things I'm never going to get to say to Penny. I bring a shaking hand to my eyes.

"I don't know why you didn't—" And then there are tears hot on my face before I can stop them. "*Why*—"

"Because it was easier."

She stares at me. Her hands are so empty.

"You're not better off dead," she says. "I'm so sorry. I can't . . . I know I can't make it right but I just wanted to say that to you because—I don't think anyone else here would—"

I can't stay for it anymore. I leave her there because I don't want *sorry*. It doesn't bring dead girls back. I go to the kitchen and brace myself against the table, listening to myself breathing. Those voices on the radio.

"—we need to talk about how this is a very promising boy who is now facing second-degree murder charges. His life is ruined and I barely have a sense of who he is. I want to know his story—"

I reach out and turn the radio off so fast it clatters back. *You're not better off dead.* It's suffocating, it's suffocating, hearing that when all this place has given me is the feeling that I should be, I would be, better off if I was one less girl . . .

You're not better off dead. I close my eyes, a fury building inside me, starting in the center of me, bleeding its way out because even now, *you're not better off dead* but *I can't make it right.* The same words Penny said to me in the diner. *I can't make it right.* But who could.

Where do you even start.

I open my eyes. I head back outside and Tina's halfway down the walk now, a slow leaving, like she hopes I'll call her back. I say, "Tina," and she turns. My heart is heavy with the weight of my body and my body is so heavy with the weight of my heart.

"You want to help me find a girl in Godwit?"

before I tore the labels off, one was called *Paradise* and the other, *Hit and Run.* It doesn't matter which is which. They're both blood red.

Proper application of nail polish is a process. You can't paint it on like it's nothing and expect it to last. First, prep. I start with a four-way buffer. It gets rid of the ridges and gives the polish a smooth surface to adhere to. Next, I use a nail dehydrator and cleanser because it's best to work with a nail plate that's dry and clean. Once it's evaporated, a thin layer of base coat goes on. The base coat protects the nails and prevents staining.

I like the first coat of polish to be thin enough to dry by

the time I've finished the last nail on the same hand. I keep my touch steady and light. I never drag the brush, I never go back into the bottle more than once per nail if I can help it. Over time and with practice, I've learned how to tell if what's on the brush will be enough.

Some people are lazy. They think if you're using a highly pigmented polish, a second coat is unnecessary, but that's not true. The second coat asserts the color and arms you against the everyday use of your hands, all the ways you can cause damage without thinking. When the second coat is dry, I take a Q-tip dipped in nail polish remover to clean up any polish that might have bled onto my skin. The final step is the top coat. The top coat is what seals in the color and protects the manicure.

The application of lipstick has similar demands. A smooth canvas is always best and dead skin must be removed. Sometimes that takes as little as a damp washcloth, but other times I scrub a toothbrush across my mouth just to be sure. When that's done, I add the tiniest amount of balm, so my lips don't dry out. It also gives the color something to hold on to.

I run the fine fibers of my lip brush across the slanted top of my lipstick until my lips are coated and work the brush from the center of my lips out. After the first layer, I blot on a tissue and add another layer, carefully following the line of my small mouth before smudging the color out so it looks a little fuller. Like with the nail polish, layering always helps it to last.

And then I'm ready.

look at me.

I want you to look at me.

acknowledgments

I would like to thank:

Amy Tipton, my agent, for all the doors she's opened for me. She was the first person who saw *All the Rage*, years ago, and she's read it a million times since. And she read it the millionth time with the same enthusiasm as she did the first. I can't imagine navigating publishing without her smarts, her humor, her support, or her perfectly timed *Apocalypse When* e-mail. It's an honor to have such a hardworking advocate.

Sara Goodman, for her sharp editorial eye and everything she's taught me about writing. It has been a privilege to explore many dark fictional roads with her as my guide. This one was longer than most, but that's what happens when you have an editor who never settles for less than what you're capable of. I'm grateful to have worked with and learned from someone so passionately dedicated to good books.

Everyone at St. Martin's who works tirelessly to bring my stories to readers. Special thanks to Lisa Marie Pompilio,

Talia Sherer, Anne Spieth, NaNá V. Stoelzle, Anna Gorovoy, Stephanie Davis, Jeanne-Marie Hudson, Michelle Cashman, Angela Craft, Vicki Lame, and Alicia Adkins-Clancy. Special thanks to Lauren Hougen for her incredible levels of patience.

Ellen Pepus at Signature Literary, for her hard work.

My family, of course. Immediate and extended. Always. All my love and gratitude to Susan and David, Megan and Jarrad, Marion and Ken, Lucy and Bob, and Damon. This is my foundation and it's a good one.

Emily Hainsworth and Tiffany Schmidt, for seeing this book—and me—through more than I could possibly fit into this space. I am so thankful for their amazing critiques and, even more than that, for their friendship. Amazing ladies.

Kelly Jensen, for her wonderful friendship and her listening and for talking the talk *and* walking the walk. "Awesome" is her default setting. Her tireless support, generosity, and enthusiasm cannot be overstated and I am so very grateful for her.

CK Kelly Martin and Nova Ren Suma, two amazing women who inspire me both personally and professionally. I'm so thankful for their friendship, kindness, and support, and I am in utter awe of their writing talents.

These diamonds: Whitney Crispell, Kim Hutt, Baz Ramos, and Samantha Seals, for years of an incredible friendship that I cherish so much. Shine bright.

Stefan Martorano, for his gracious help with the law enforcement–related details.

Thank you to all my friends, for their support. Special thanks and much appreciation to these terrific people: Bill Cameron, Brandy Colbert, Kate Hart for all the good work she does and goodwill she inspires, Will and Annika Klein,

Team Sparkle, Daisy Whitney, Brian Williams, and Briony Williamson.

My readers. The enthusiasm and support they have shown my work means more than I could ever say. I simply can't thank them enough.

Lori Thibert. Last but never least. And for more than I could ever list here. For her talent, humor, kindness, generosity, and for being an awe-inspiring, amazing human being, which inspires me. Her unwavering encouragement and belief in what is possible over the years has meant the world and made all the difference. It was one of my very first stepping stones to becoming an author. As far as best friends go, mine can't be beat.

Thank you.

If you have experienced any kind of sexual abuse or trauma and would like some advice or just have questions, here are some organizations that might be able to help.

Rape Crisis

A helpline run by Rape Crisis South London for female survivors of sexual violence. The helpline is run 365 days a year at the times listed below. It offers specialized, confidential support, information and referral details completely free of charge. The helpline is also available to provide an immediate source of support to friends and family of survivors, as well as other professionals, to help them understand how best to support female survivors of sexual violence.

Helpline: 0808 802 9999 (12 a.m.–2:30 p.m. and 7–9:30 p.m.)

http://rapecrisis.org.uk

Victim Support

A free, confidential service available to those who have been raped or sexually assaulted, no matter how long ago. Victim Support has volunteers available to meet with you (at home or elsewhere) and a freephone number if you need someone to talk to.

Supportline: 0808 168 9111 (Weeknights 8 p.m. to 8 a.m., weekends Saturday 5 p.m. to Monday 8 a.m.)

https://www.victimsupport.org.uk

The Rape and Abuse Line (RAL)

A registered charity that offers a freephone, confidential helpline to persons who have survived rape or abuse however long ago the experiences were.

Helpline: 0808 800 0123 (answered by women)

Pandora's Project

Support and resource for Lesbian, Gay, Bisexual, Transgender and Questioning Survivors of Rape & Sexual Abuse.

http://pandys.org

The Survivors Trust

The Survivors Trust (TST) is a UK-wide national umbrella agency for 141 specialist organizations for support for the impact of rape, sexual violence and childhood sexual abuse throughout the UK and Ireland.

Call The Survivors Trust on: 01788 550 554

http://www.thesurvivorstrust.org/

Rape, Abuse & Incest National Network (RAINN)

RAINN is the largest anti-sexual assault organization in the US. Its website has lots of useful advice and resources.

https://ohl.rainn.org/online/

about the author

Courtney Summers was born in Belleville, Ontario, in 1986 and currently resides in a small town not far from there. At age fourteen she dropped out of high school to pursue her education independently, and spent those years figuring out what she wanted to do with her life. At eighteen she knew she was meant to write.

When she is not writing, Courtney loves playing video games, watching horror movies and obsessing over the zombie apocalypse. Her favourite color is green and she's a total feminist.